THE PARISIAN'S RETURN

In the commune of Fogas in the French Pyrenees, Stephanie brains an intruder with a stale baguette, little realising that he's the new owner of the épicerie. Fabian's welcome gets worse when his attempts to modernise the shop are met with a resounding *non!* by the locals. Ready to admit defeat, he's suddenly hit by a *coup de foudre* and falls in love. Stephanie herself is too busy for *l'amour*. Working at *l'Auberge* and getting her garden centre off the ground are all-consuming. She doesn't even notice that her daughter Chloé has something on her mind. Troubled by a sinister stranger in the village, Chloé has no one to turn to. Her only hope is that someone hears her cries for help before it's too late.

Books by Julia Stagg
Published by The House of Ulverscroft:

L'AUBERGE

JULIA STAGG

THE PARISIAN'S RETURN

Complete and Unabridged

CHARNWOOD
Leicester

First published in Great Britain in 2012 by
Hodder & Stoughton
London

First Charnwood Edition
published 2013
by arrangement with
Hodder & Stoughton
An Hachette UK Company
London

A catalogue record for this book is available
from the British Library.

ISBN 978–1–4448–1522–1

Published by
F. A. Thorpe (Publishing)
Anstey, Leicestershire

Set by Words & Graphics Ltd.
Anstey, Leicestershire
Printed and bound in Great Britain by
T. J. International Ltd., Padstow, Cornwall

This book is printed on acid-free paper

For the Master Storyteller

You taught me all you know,
and still I know nothing . . .

Acknowledgements

As with its predecessor, this book has benefited greatly from the assistance of a variety of people. From wine expertise to first readings, from inheritance laws to local knowledge, I took all of the advice on board, but take the blame for what I chose to do with it! I owe the following a chunk of Rogallais and a bottle of Hypocras:

Ellen Mc, Edward, Craig, René, Matthew, Brenda, Claire, Ellen S, the amazing team at Hodder and of course, Mark.

1

Stephanie Morvan had never killed anyone before. Not that she knew of anyway. She'd called down a few curses in fits of temper but had never hung around long enough to ascertain the strength of her powers. But none of them should have been fatal. She normally inflicted only low-level irritations such as piles or bad breath. So as far as she was aware, she'd never been responsible for taking another life.

Until now.

She looked at the length of Lycra stretched across the cold floor of the bar, the body beneath the thin fabric all angles and bones.

Then she looked at the weapon in her left hand. Who'd have known that something so innocuous could be so lethal?

When they'd run short of bread and wine at the party at the Auberge des Deux Vallées, she'd volunteered to take the short walk up the road to fetch more supplies. Josette had handed over the keys and the deputy mayor, Christian Dupuy, had set out with her. But waylaid by a neighbour wanting to ask about the next meeting of the Conseil Municipal, Christian wasn't by her side when she reached the épicerie and realised something was wrong.

The building looked lopsided, its neat symmetry thrown out of kilter by one set of shutters, those on the side of the bar, being open

1

as normal, while the others on the shop window were firmly closed.

But there was something else not right.

The door. It was ajar. And unless Stephanie was mistaken, she could hear something, or someone, inside.

She slipped through the narrow gap between door and frame, not wanting to set off the new bell which Josette had recently had installed, and stood for a few seconds, her eyes useless in the gloomy interior.

Nothing. Only the smell of fresh bread and spicy saucisson mixed with the earthy scent of potatoes.

Stephanie was just convincing herself that Josette had simply forgotten to close the door properly when a creak of floorboards sent the nerves at the back of her neck tingling.

Someone was in the bar, the room adjacent to the shop. And as almost the entire village was down at the Auberge celebrating its reopening, this could only be bad news.

Without thinking, Stephanie had reached for something to defend herself with. Her hands had touched the cold surface of the fridge, gliding over the eggs in the basket on top and stretching towards the upright knife cabinet that stood near the centre of the room. Blindly, silently, her fingers brushed over the glass with a hope she knew was futile as Josette always kept it locked. There was no point in trying the one by the till either.

She inched to her right instead where she felt the mesh of a wicker basket.

The sound from the bar came again, this time louder. A metallic click-clack, click-clack. Coming towards her.

Panic blossomed in her chest in a way she hadn't felt in years. Not since she'd fled Finistère with her infant daughter, Chloé.

Frantic now, she dug into the basket, her long fingers probing, testing, trying to find the right one. There. At least three days old. She grasped it and moved across to the door separating the shop from the bar. The door that was slowly opening.

She positioned herself as weak rays of winter sunlight began to seep through the growing aperture, eroding the edges of the darkness in which she was hiding and outlining a creature of utmost hideousness.

Tall even by her standards, its misshapen head barely cleared the doorframe, the black, shaggy face turning slowly to reveal eyes deep-set in white circles. It stepped across the threshold, spidery legs ending in cloven hooves that rang on the slate tiles of the shop floor. Then, as she raised her arm to strike, it reached out with lobster-like claws, a bright red light flashing on what she could only presume was its tail.

Before it could get any closer, Stephanie empowered her left arm with all her redhead's temper and, screaming like a banshee, swung her improvised truncheon into the monster's face. She felt the soft resistance of flesh and cartilage before the beast lost its footing and toppled backwards into the bar, its head impacting heavily on the floorboards.

In the silence that followed when she realised her mistake, she could have sworn she heard laughter coming from the empty inglenook.

★ ★ ★

No matter how many times his teachers had said it to him, Christian Dupuy had never thought of himself as a born leader. He'd always believed their comments were simply to do with his size, as he dwarfed his fellow students and soon, even the staff, his huge frame outgrowing the confines of the small mountain school long before his brain did. So he'd never set out to be an authority figure and had been quite reluctant to stand for the Conseil Municipal, the governing body that ran the commune of Fogas which consisted of the three villages of Fogas, Picarets and La Rivière. But once voted on to the local council, he did his utmost to help his neighbours in any way he could.

Therefore it was no surprise, apart from to himself that is, that the shy farmer had been chosen as deputy mayor in the last mayoral elections. Nor was it surprising to his neighbours and friends that the mayor, Serge Papon, had announced that very afternoon that Christian was to deputise for him while he took an extended leave of absence following the death of his wife.

As he stood next to the bridge in La Rivière, talking to Philippe Galy about the latest developments in the politics of Fogas, the mantle of power was resting lightly on Christian's shoulders. It wasn't something that preoccupied him unduly, although he was slightly apprehensive about how the other deputy mayor, Pascal Souquet, would react when he heard the news, knowing how ambitious the man was. And even more so his wife.

But when Stephanie's scream tore through the afternoon air like a cold wind howling off Mont Valier, Christian instinctively displayed the traits that his teachers had been quick to see in him. Before her assailant had even hit the floor, he was shouting at Philippe to get help from the Auberge while he started lumbering towards the épicerie. He crossed the bridge in heavy strides, the vibrations dislodging soil from the cracks in the stones which fell into the stream beneath and then got swept into the roaring river that ran parallel to the road.

Christian thundered on, driven by the knowledge that Stephanie wasn't the screaming type. In all the years he'd known her, he'd only seen his friend cry once. He was aware however, that she had a fierce temper, so he was not unprepared when he crashed into the shop and saw Stephanie standing over a prostrate form, bent baguette in her hand.

'What on earth . . . ?'

Stephanie's eyes snapped on to his, and Christian took a step back at her wild expression.

'He came at me . . . out of nowhere . . . Christ! Have I killed him?'

She ran a shaky hand through her hair as Christian knelt down and slipped his fingers

5

under the strap of the helmet on the prone figure. He was relieved to feel a faint pulse.

'He's fine. Just unconscious. I think the helmet saved him. Do you know who he is?'

'Not a clue. I thought he was a monster . . . ' She faltered, realising how silly that sounded now it was clear what he was.

But Christian could see it had been an easy mistake to make. The man on the floor was very tall and extremely thin, his skeletal physique accentuated by tight-fitting Lycra. Under his helmet a woolly balaclava covered all but his eyes, and his hands were enclosed in claw-shaped mittens. His black leggings ended in bulky shoe-covers, each fitting snugly over the special shoes he was wearing, a cleat visible in the middle of the sole. And from underneath him came the dull glow of a red light.

'Why would anyone try to break into a bar wearing cycling gear?'

Before Stephanie could answer, excited voices filled the room as the people from the party at the Auberge crowded in.

'What's going on?' asked Josette Servat, as she pushed her way to the front, slightly out of breath from having rushed up the road.

'Stephanie apprehended an intruder. Felled him with one of your baguettes!'

'Bloody hell!' René the plumber gestured at the loaf of bread in Stephanie's hand. 'And it's not even broken! Think you need to rotate your stock a bit more, Josette,' he quipped to general laughter.

'But who is he?' Josette pushed her glasses up

her nose and leaned in to get a better look. 'We need to get his balaclava off.'

With slow movements, Christian undid the helmet and laid it aside. Then he gently peeled the balaclava up the man's face revealing a pointed chin, thin lips and pale cheeks stretched over high cheekbones. As the fabric came away from the man's head, his fine black hair was left standing on end with static, the only part of him revealing any sign of life, and Josette gasped.

'What is it?' Christian asked as René put an arm out to catch Josette as she reeled back. 'Do you know him?'

She nodded, the colour gone from her face. 'Oh yes. I know him. It's Fabian Servat. Jacques' nephew.'

She glanced at the inglenook where no one but she could see the ghost of her dead husband, silently laughing his head off, and felt a flash of annoyance. Didn't he understand how serious this was?

'Fabian? God, I wouldn't have recognised him.' Christian tried to reconcile the wan features with the boy he'd known years ago. 'Were you expecting him?'

Josette shook her head. But it wasn't entirely true.

The only child of Jacques' brother, Fabian had been a big part of their lives when he was young, spending the long summer holidays in La Rivière, and Jacques had adored him. But adulthood had changed him from a curious toddler who loved helping out in the shop to an arrogant man with only one thing on his

7

mind: making money. His visits had become more and more unbearable until, on the death of his father many years before, he'd simply stopped coming to the small épicerie in the Ariège-Pyrénées, preferring instead to spend his holidays on the Côte d'Azur. Jacques had breathed a sigh of relief as he'd come to despise his nephew who had immersed himself in the world of finance, working in investment banking and adopting all the attitudes that went with it.

The last Josette had heard from him had been when Jacques died last summer. Fabian had sent a sympathy card with a perfunctory message but since then, nothing. Not a word. Perversely, she'd been glad, given what she knew. What he must know.

But now he was here. Lying sprawled at her feet, telltale signs of life beginning to streak across his face and flicker under his eyelids.

And Josette, not normally given to violence, wished Stephanie had hit him a bit harder. Terminally harder.

There could be only one reason why he had darkened their floor after all this time and she had been dreading this moment since Jacques had died. As the months had passed with no contact, she'd dared to believe that her future might be safe. She'd worked in the épicerie day and night her entire adult life. It was all she knew. It was home. And now . . . ? Now everything might be about to change.

'I think he's coming round,' Christian said as a low moan issued from the spread-eagled form.

8

'Stand back a bit. Let him have some air!'

The villagers reluctantly retreated, necks straining to get the best view as the stranger started to twitch, his groans getting louder. His limbs jerked a couple of times and then his eyes flashed open, their dark brown gaze happening to rest on Stephanie just as consciousness returned.

'*Shit!*' Fabian screeched, scrambling backwards on his arse, long limbs propelling him crab-like away from the flame-haired beauty standing over him, weapon in hand. But there was nowhere to go as the robust legs of the long table that dominated the bar were in the way.

He tried desperately to get to his feet but the cleats on his shoes kept slipping until René thrust out a strong arm and hauled him upright. He stood there, swaying slightly as his head adjusted to the sudden change in altitude, and then, face etched in terror, he pointed a mitten in Stephanie's direction.

'She tried to kill me!'

'I tried to kill *you*? You were the one sneaking around in the dark. What was I supposed to think?'

He flinched as she took a step forward, unintentionally brandishing the baguette as she did so, a death-rattle of bracelets snaking down her arm.

'Keep away from me you vixen!' The stick-like arms he raised before his face made him more praying mantis than Karate Kid.

'For heaven's sake, Fabian! Calm down.' Josette placed a restraining hand on him and his gaze shifted on to the petite figure of his aunt with relief.

'Tante Josette. Thank goodness you're here. This mad woman tried to kill me.'

'You clearrrly don't know Stephanie, son,' barked Annie Estaque from the circle of onlookers. 'If she'd been trrrying, you'd be dead!'

Peals of laughter greeted Annie's interjection but her broad Ariégeois accent was impenetrable to Fabian's soft Parisian ears.

'I'm sorry? What did you say?'

'Huh! You still can't underrrstand me afterrr all these yearrrs. Not even with new teeth!'

More laughter.

Fabian squirmed with frustration. Plus the distinct odour of cows emanating from the old lady was making him feel queasy. He remembered her well from the countless summers he'd spent in these mountains. And he remembered the smell. Seemed like things were slow to change in the country.

As the banter continued around him, he ran a hand over the back of his head, which was pulsating with a dull pain, and traced the contours of a growing lump.

It wasn't the welcome he'd imagined, he thought ruefully. To be greeted by a hellcat wielding what felt like an iron bar. And then to be ridiculed. It was like being a child all over again.

Sensing his torment, Josette experienced a pang of sympathy. He was Jacques' nephew after all and perhaps the years had mellowed him.

'So, Fabian,' she continued kindly, her voice quelling the laughter. 'What brings you back to Fogas?'

Fabian blinked. 'You didn't get the letter? From my solicitor?'

'No.' Cold fingers of fear touched Josette.

'Well, that's a bit unfortunate. It explained everything. All the legalese. I'm willing to be reasonable. Pay market rates. Of course, you're welcome to stay. As long as you like really. I'm sure we'll get on fine. Just fine.'

He smiled to underline his point but Josette wasn't looking. She was staring at the fireplace with an expression of dread. And Jacques was staring back at her in horror, his white hair on end and his face as pale as a ghost's can be.

'Sorry, Josette. What does he mean? Are you leaving us?' asked Christian, as the tables turned and now the villagers struggled to understand.

'No, I'm not going anywhere,' she replied, the tremor in her voice undermining the confidence of her words.

'But then what — '

Josette cut across him, her sharp tone in stark contrast to her earlier warmth. 'Why don't you explain, Fabian?'

Fabian coughed, twitching slightly at the unwanted attention as all eyes focused on him.

'It's quite simple. Nothing much to explain. Needed a break you see. New life and all that. Thought this was ideal . . . '

Annie snorted. 'Forrr goodness sake. Stop pontificating like a Parrrisian and spit it out, man!'

11

'What he's trying to say,' Josette said, her hands gripping the table for support, 'is that he's come to take over the épicerie. Isn't that right, Fabian?'

Fabian nodded and in the silence that greeted this news, he wondered how long it would take to win over the locals.

2

'So he's come to stake his claim on the shop? Josette has no say in the matter?'

'Zat is what it looks like.'

Lorna Webster stopped wiping tables and looked across the restaurant at Stephanie who'd just returned from the épicerie with the shocking news.

'But surely there must be something she can do? Some law that protects her?'

Stephanie shook her head and gathered up dirty glasses from the top of the bar. The party already seemed a lifetime ago.

'Jacques, ze 'usband of Josette, 'e leaves 'alf of ze épicerie to 'is nephew. Zat is ze law in France.'

'What? You have to leave half of everything to your nephews?' queried Paul, back from taking several bags of rubbish to the bin.

'No stupid! Not to your nephews but to your family.'

'But . . . surely Josette *is* his family?'

'Not in French law.'

'I don't understand.' Lorna's face was suitably puzzled. 'Are you saying that if I died tomorrow, Paul wouldn't inherit my half of the Auberge? Even though he's my husband?'

'Yes, 'e would. But only 'alf of your 'alf. The other 'alf of your 'alf would to go to your family. And as you 'ave no children, zat means your parents.'

13

'WHAT?' Paul's voice rose to a shriek. 'Lorna's parents? But they hate me!'

Stephanie simply raised an eyebrow and grinned as he spun round to face his wife.

'I didn't know any of this, did you?'

'Why? Would it have put you off buying the place?'

'Maybe!' He ducked as Lorna threw a well-aimed dishcloth at his head.

'But I still don't understand,' Lorna continued, ignoring her husband who was pretending to be mortally wounded. 'How can this Fabian bloke throw his weight around if Josette owns the majority of the épicerie?'

'Zat is exactly ze problem. She does not own ze majority of ze épicerie.'

'But you just said . . . '

Stephanie held up a hand to silence Paul and gave an exasperated sigh. Her Anglo-Saxon friends were slow on the uptake today. It wasn't as if this was complicated. They simply weren't equipped to cope with the intricacies of French law.

'She does not own ze majority of ze épicerie because it belonged to ze family of Jacques. 'E was given it by 'is father. Before zey got married. By law, 'alf of it must to go back to 'is family.' She gave a fatalistic shrug. 'So, Josette is in ze *merde*.'

'Christ! Seems a bit harsh. Is she going to contest it?'

'What is ze point? It is ze law.'

'Still, it just seems . . . I don't know . . . '

'Unfair?' Lorna suggested.

14

'It is not fair or unfair. It is ze law!' Stephanie picked up the remaining glasses and walked through to the kitchen, leaving Lorna and Paul to discuss Josette's misfortune. She didn't have the energy to talk about it any more. The incident in the bar had brought back a flood of bad memories which had left her feeling drained.

It had been a while since she'd panicked like that. She didn't know why she hadn't simply run out of the shop and shouted for Christian. That was the bit that frightened her most. It seemed, despite the steep learning curve of the early years of her marriage, she hadn't yet learnt to walk away from fear. She still felt the need to confront it head on.

And that worried her.

She started loading the dishwasher, forcing herself to concentrate on something else. But it hadn't been the best of days and even Josette's predicament seemed to have impacted negatively on her.

She felt like a selfish cow for even thinking about it. But the second Fabian Servat had revealed that he co-owned the épicerie, she'd only had one thought. Had he inherited a share of the land across from it too? If so, then hitting him in the face with a stale baguette might not have been her brightest idea to date.

'Damn it!' Stephanie felt the sharp slice of pain before she was even aware that she'd snapped the stem on one of the wine glasses, a shard of glass piercing her palm. She ran her hand under the cold tap, welcoming the stinging

15

sensation as the near glacial water slipped over her flesh.

'Damn it,' she muttered again, turning off the tap. She was back to square one. Just when her dreams of opening an organic garden centre had been within touching distance.

Although the storm that had hit the commune over New Year had destroyed her polytunnel and killed most of the young plants she'd been growing there, she'd got to work and replanted them and with spring still a while off, she'd been confident she could overcome the setback. Then the Auberge had finally reopened despite the attempts by some in the community to scupper it, and this afternoon at the party Paul and Lorna had offered her a waitressing job. With that money she could support herself and Chloé while the gardening business got off the ground.

She'd even earmarked the ideal spot for her enterprise. Bordering the river and adjacent to the municipal car park, it was the field opposite the épicerie which was owned by Josette. Or so she'd thought.

If it was the case that Jacques' nephew had inherited half of it, then she was going to have to put her plans on hold. There was no way he'd rent it to her after she'd committed assault and battery with a loaf.

If only Fabian Servat had stayed in Paris.

She closed the dishwasher and switched it on. Her first day as a waitress had certainly been eventful, and if Fabian did indeed have a say over that plot, she was going to be relying on this job for a lot longer than she'd anticipated. So she slapped a smile on her face and went back out to the restaurant, berating herself for being so self-centred. After all, unlike Josette, whose future hung in the balance, she still had a roof over her head.

★   ★   ★

As is the case in January in the steep valleys of the Pyrenees, the sky had already started to darken by late afternoon when people began to wind their way back from St Girons up the road to Massat and the Col de Port. But as they took the familiar bend in La Rivière, following the river which turned sharp left, they were all struck by how much darker the road was than normal, making them switch their headlights on to cope with the growing gloom.

Some were driving too fast to spare a thought as to why this might be, having ignored the fifty kilometres per hour speed limit on entering the village. Others though, not in such a rush to get home, had time to ponder the cause as they negotiated the further twists that took them beyond the houses and back into the forest-lined gorge. But those that pulled off at the bend hoping to grab a baguette for their evening meal or a packet of cigarettes and a bottle of wine to help pass the long winter night, didn't have to think at all. The answer was obvious.

For the first time in living memory, the épicerie and the bar were closed during business hours, the windows and doors shuttered, cutting off the supply of light that normally flooded on to the road throughout the winter from the early morning and into the night.

Inside, a small group sat around the table in the bar, the dancing firelight shadowing furrows of concern on all their faces.

'Do you think he'll go through with it?' asked the woman at the end as she shifted to ease the weight on her right leg which was encased in plaster and propped on a chair.

Josette nodded.

'It's a rrright old mess!' Annie Estaque muttered. 'And to think he was such a nice lad when he was a nipperrr. Who'd have thought he was capable of this?'

'If I'd known,' said Christian, 'I'd have left him at the bottom of the old quarry that time he fell in. Remember that, Véronique?'

The woman with the broken leg laughed. 'Goodness yes! You made me run to get help.'

'Yeah and the whole time you were gone he didn't stop crying about the rip in his trousers. Said his mother was going to kill him. Poor kid. I scrambled down to him myself in the end because I couldn't bear to see him so upset.'

'So when I got back with Serge Papon, he had to pull both of you out with a rope!'

'I didn't know about that,' Annie said, her voice sharp at the mention of the mayor's name.

Véronique smiled. 'That's because I didn't tell you, Maman! Serge drove us back to his house and Thérèse gave us pain au chocolat and Orangina while she mended Fabian's trousers.'

'Poorrr buggerrr,' murmured Annie ambiguously, causing Christian to wonder whether her sympathies were with the young boy in the past or the recently bereaved mayor.

'Poor Josette more like!' Véronique retorted. 'There must be something we can do?'

'Not much.' Josette sounded weary. 'I consulted a solicitor a few months ago and basically I have two options. I can offer to buy Fabian out, which I can't afford and he's unlikely to accept anyway. Or I can try to run the place with him.'

'There is a third option,' Véronique suggested tentatively. 'You could sell him your share.'

Josette stared at the younger woman, her eyes wide behind her glasses.

'No!'

'You wouldn't even consider . . . '

'No! I'm not going anywhere.' Josette fell silent and Véronique was struck by how fragile she looked, the folds of her cardigan hanging from her thin shoulders, hands clasped on the table as her fingers nervously twisted her wedding ring.

Christian placed a huge arm around her, making her seem even frailer by comparison. 'We'll sort something out, Josette, don't worry. And who knows, he might hate it here and go home. It takes some getting used to after Paris!'

Josette tried to raise a smile but failed.

'And in the meantime, I'll move in with Maman and give the two of you some space,' Véronique said, aware that her occupation of Josette's spare room might cause a problem, now that Fabian was asserting his rights to the building.

Left homeless and jobless by the fire which had burnt down the post office during the storm on New Year's Eve, Véronique had been grateful for Josette's offer of a bed at the time. Nearly a month on, she was more adept at getting around on crutches and with Maman's farmhouse almost back to normal after the damage inflicted by the same hurricane-force winds, she'd made plans to move up there for the interim. It wasn't ideal, given that they didn't really get on. But perhaps moving back in with Maman would give her the kick up the backside she needed to sort out the mess over her apartment. The commune was really dragging its heels when it came to providing her with somewhere to live.

'That's very thoughtful of you,' Josette acknowledged. 'Fabian's asked if he can stay here tonight but beyond that, I don't know what his plans are. I rather imagine he'll be keen to get his feet under the table!'

'Huh! Cheeky blighterrr. What a nerrrve.'

'Well, if you two want a lift home, I'm about to head off.' Christian addressed the Estaque women as he stood up. 'Time I got back to rescue whatever meal Maman is planning on cremating tonight.'

'And it's time I fed the dogs,' said Annie, her joints creaking as she rose. 'Have you got all yourrr things, Vérrronique?'

Véronique gave a twisted smile and pointed to a small case in the corner. 'I don't have much these days!'

'God, what a mess,' muttered Christian. 'You lose everything in a fire and now Josette looks set to lose her home. It's like Fogas has been cursed or something.'

'Yes. Currrsed with bloody idiots like Fabian Serrrvat!'

'Talking of which,' Christian continued as he opened the door on to the encroaching dark, 'where is the masked man? Shouldn't he be back from his bike ride by now?'

'With any luck he's fallen into the quarry again, and this time I won't be running for help,' said Véronique as she hobbled past him.

As Annie helped her daughter get settled in the back of the car, Christian turned to Josette.

'Will you be all right? Tonight, I mean.'

Josette nodded, drawing herself up and giving him a brave smile. 'I'll be fine,' she said. 'I'm sure we'll come to some arrangement. He's not a bad person after all.'

Christian gave her a last embrace before folding his tall body into the small hatchback. With a spluttering cough, the Panda 4x4 drove off into the dusk.

Josette waited until its lights had disappeared up the road to Picarets and then she slowly closed the door and collapsed against it.

It was her entire universe, these two rooms where she'd spent most of her adult life. Through the connecting doorway she could see the shelves on the back wall of the shop. How many times had she stacked them? Jars of local honey, bars of chocolate, tins of cassoulet, cartons of milk. And the lengths of saucisson which hung over the counter. How many had she strung up over the years? How many kilograms

21

of cheese had she cut to order from the big rounds of Rogallais or Bethmale? And as for the hours spent polishing those blasted knife cabinets!

Her gaze drifted into the bar, taking in the bottles of Ricard and Cassis, the glasses that she had washed countless times in the small sink out the back, the table where the business of the commune was really conducted, the mayor preferring to hold court here rather than in the more austere town hall up the mountain in Fogas. And what parties they'd had! Her lips curved at the memories.

Could she really leave all this behind?

On the surface, Véronique's suggestion didn't seem unreasonable. After all, she had money put aside and with what she would get for her share of the épicerie, she should be able to buy a small property nearby. Take it easy. Put her feet up. It was even possible that retirement might suit her.

Only then did she allow herself to look at the fireplace and the reason for her torment.

What about Jacques?

When he'd first appeared, his ghostly presence had unnerved her. She'd walked into the bar, still in her black suit, the toll of the church bells reverberating around the hills, and there he was, sitting next to the fire as if he'd never left. As if his heart hadn't suddenly stopped and robbed her life of meaning.

She'd opened her mouth to scream but no sound emerged, only the rasp of the asthma that plagued her in the summer when the pollen

22

count was high. Or when she was in shock.

She'd turned on her heel and fled into the shop, her hands trembling as she leaned on the cabinet next to the counter trying to catch her breath while her thoughts skittered around like ball bearings off the flippers in a pinball machine. She'd tried to calm herself by concentrating on the knives beneath the glass: the stout blade of the Kenavo embedded in water-resistant wood, a fisherman's favourite in Brittany; the sensuous curve of the handle of the Couteau du Pèlerin, made for pilgrims following the route of St Jacques de Compostelle; and Jacques' pride and joy, a Laguiole with a Damascus blade covered in watermark patterns and a handle made of stag's horn.

When she became conscious that her fingers were leaving marks on the pristine surface, she knew she was back in control. And ready to face the bar again.

Of course she'd imagined it, she told herself. Such things didn't happen. But as she stepped towards the doorway, a large part of her was willing it to be true.

He'd glanced up as she entered, a bemused look on his face as though he too was confused as to how he'd got there. His thick shock of white hair had become even more prominent in death, almost glowing against the soot-stained stones of the inglenook. Beneath it, his face was paler and the outline of his wiry body almost blurred. But as his eyes latched on to hers she'd felt that familiar jolt of recognition which she'd had the very first day they met. And then her

23

knees gave way and she'd fallen to the floor in a faint.

She'd come round to him stroking her hair and they'd taken it from there. He moved only between the bar and the épicerie and never spoke a word. But the comfort she derived from his presence was immense. Her silent shadow.

Which was why this whole business with Fabian was tearing her heart asunder.

'You're not going to be able to move with me, are you my love?'

He gazed back at her with the same look of bewilderment that had greeted her six months ago. Then he shook his head and covered his face with his hands.

She knew what he was thinking.

'It's not your fault. You weren't to know.'

They were both to blame as far as she was concerned. They should have sought advice years ago. But they'd not seen the need. The law was the law, simple as that.

Of course, it turned out that there was something they could have done. After Jacques' death, the solicitor had told her that new laws had been passed, some quite recently, and they could have made sure Josette was better protected. But it was too late now.

She pulled a chair up close to Jacques and laid her hand on his, the heat of the fire doing nothing to stop the cold terror clawing at her soul.

She couldn't contemplate leaving the épicerie and abandoning her husband.

But the thought of running it with her nephew

24

was equally abhorrent.

So she was just going to have to make sure that Fabian Servat changed his mind.

* * *

At that very moment, Fabian was beginning to think he'd made a big mistake.

He'd been confident he knew the roads around La Rivière like the back of his hand. Clearly he hadn't done much hand-gazing lately, though, as he was lost.

Lost!

How could that be? The commune of Fogas only had two roads, each one branching out from La Rivière, which, as its name suggested, lay down by the river, to climb opposite sides of the valley up to the villages of Fogas and Picarets. There was no road between them and both ended in obscure hamlets in the mountains.

So when he'd stormed out of the shop after a heated debate with Josette and some of the villagers, he'd climbed on his bike and started up the road to Picarets, simply wanting to clear his mind in the only way he knew how.

He'd pedalled furiously, the steepness of the route helping to vent some of the frustration as he focused on the small screen attached to his handlebars: heart rate 180 bpm; power output 350W. Automatically he started calculating his fitness, the mere act of computation helping to relax him.

He'd been a kid when he'd first taken refuge in his freakish ability with numbers. Born into a marriage which strained towards divorce before the ink was dry on the certificate, he became adept at seeking out quiet spaces away from the incessant arguments and raised voices, where he found solace in the simplicity of addition or multiplication. When he was bullied at school for his skinny physique, his love of maths helped him to endure the endless baiting in the playground. And in his final year at university, with the blank slate of his future lying dauntingly ahead, it had seemed too good to be true when his mathematical talents had attracted the attention of a headhunter for an investment bank.

He'd known nothing about banking. Had never even considered it as a profession. But the fact that someone had sought him out won him over. After years of being excluded somebody actually wanted him on their team.

He had embarked on this unexpected career presuming that at last he would be amongst others like him, people who found more excitement in solving a difficult equation than hanging out in bars.

But it hadn't worked out like that. He'd been surrounded by young men who wanted to get ahead. Who would stop at nothing to close a deal. They weren't interested in maths or the flawless beauty of numbers. And they were hell-bent on making the skinny new recruit's life unbearable.

If he'd been normal, he would have left.

That was just it though. He wasn't normal. He was weird. He'd been told so often, there must be some truth in it.

Which was why, despite the constant harassment, he continued to turn up at the bank day after day. And when he secured his first major trade, which netted the company a good profit, his colleagues had begun to reassess him. When success kept coming, the abuse abated. Some had approached him to find out how he did it but he couldn't explain and they'd taken his reticence for arrogance. But how could he explain when he didn't understand it himself? All he knew was that he could see beyond the market data, see patterns and shapes that jumped off the page to create something almost tangible. And that was what he based his business on.

He'd lived like this for years, allowing numbers to dominate his life while he cloaked himself in the persona of an investment banker, pretending that the pursuit of money was his primary goal. Somehow he'd got away with it. Grown rich in the process.

Then, in 2007, everything had gone wrong.

He had failed to see the crash coming.

Of course, he wasn't the only one. While his personal finances had escaped relatively unscathed, Fabian never having invested his own money, his colleagues all suffered, some of them close to suicide at the losses they'd incurred, for the company and for themselves.

But none of them felt like he did.

His one source of comfort in life, the one thing he'd always been able to rely on, had turned out to be as false as everything else.

The numbers had betrayed him.

He'd struggled on for another year, trying to regain his confidence but it hadn't happened. Each time he'd tried to assess the markets he'd been left staring at squiggles on a page like a gypsy looking into a cup and seeing only the dregs of tea.

The magic had disappeared.

And that's when it came to him. The idea to return to Fogas, the only place he'd ever really felt at home.

Parcelled off to the Pyrenees for two months every summer by parents only too eager to be rid of the child who had failed to fix their broken relationship, he'd found a freedom there that he came to treasure. Living with two adults who enjoyed each other's company had been a revelation and the young Fabian was allowed to join Oncle Jacques and Tante Josette at mealtimes, encouraged to have an opinion on anything they were talking about, and expected to kiss them goodnight before going to bed.

Beyond that, the rules were simple. Don't be out past dark and don't touch the knife cabinet by the till.

No amount of pestering over the years had persuaded Oncle Jacques to let him hold the beautiful Laguiole or the robust Kenavo. He wouldn't even open the glass box to allow Fabian to breathe on them in wonder, gruffly telling him that they were too dangerous for young boys and too valuable. The knives weren't for sale and even Tante Josette didn't have a key for that cabinet! Instead Oncle Jacques would unlock the display case near the door and let him handle the Opinels.

Then one year he'd run up to his bedroom on the first day of his holiday and found a box on the pillow. An Opinel. For him. He'd spent the entire summer whittling wood and sharpening the blade. When it came time to return to Paris, his usual upset at leaving had been compounded by Oncle Jacques taking the knife from him 'to keep it safe', knowing that Fabian's mother wouldn't approve. Bad enough that the lad was sent home after his mountain sojourn with a broad Ariegeois accent, pronouncing the final consonants in words like Fogas and Massat much to his mother's chagrin, without him turning up with what she would consider a lethal weapon. But every July thereafter, the Opinel would be back in its box, on the pillow, greeting Fabian on his return.

It was little wonder then that when his life had imploded, he'd been filled with nostalgia for the halcyon days of summer holidays in Fogas and he'd convinced himself that life in the small commune was exactly what he needed after thirteen years caught up in the fast pace of Paris. Plus, he'd been offered the ideal opportunity. Part-ownership of the épicerie.

But after his reception this afternoon, assault and battery followed by open hostility, Fabian was afraid that he was going to meet with rejection yet again.

And so, as he'd cycled up the road to Picarets rather than face the angry questions from Josette's friends, he'd concentrated on the numbers dancing before his eyes on his cycle computer, trying not to think about what the future might hold. He hadn't noticed the dimming light, which faded far faster in the valleys of the Pyrenees than on the pavements of Paris, until he'd had to stop to fix a puncture. That was when he realised that he had no idea where he was.

Which was crazy.

He'd ridden up as far as the quarry and then backtracked but must have taken a side road, probably a new road put in since he'd last visited many years ago.

He was lost.

The puncture now mended, he glanced around but there were no signs of life, only trees growing on the steep slopes that rose above and fell below. Looked like there was no option but to turn around and try to rectify his mistake.

In the growing dusk, he mounted his bike once more and started back up the hill that he'd just descended, his city-strength headlight not really cutting through the gloom.

It didn't take him long to realise where he'd gone wrong. After a few minutes of climbing, the main road reappeared, Christian Dupuy's farm just visible off to the right, a stout, well-kept farmhouse surrounded by barns with chickens running around the yard. Down to his left was Picarets.

With renewed confidence, he freewheeled towards the outskirts of the village, taking in the changes that had occurred in his long absence. He noticed, for example, that the old cottage where Christian's grandmother had lived had been nicely renovated, the shutters brightly painted with vibrant yellow suns on each one. It looked lived in. But as he rode on, he saw it was the exception.

Apart from a few houses where light streamed out into the lengthening shadows, the place was deserted. Maybe everyone was still at work? But it didn't feel like that. He got the impression it was a ghost town.

He came to a halt in the closest thing the village had to a square, a handful of homes huddled haphazardly around a thickset lime tree. Planted to demarcate the centre of Picarets way before the age of the car and having been offset to one side as a sapling, the tree had since grown into maturity and its size pulled everything aslant, making the road bisect unevenly around it.

Fabian cast his mind back, trying to recall the names of the families that had lived here when he was a child. There'd been brothers in the property nearest to him, real rugby fans. The Rogalle brothers, that was it. One of them had gone on to play for Toulouse if he remembered rightly. He hadn't known them well as they'd been that bit older. And rougher. Judging by the two kids' bikes thrown in the front yard and the deflated rugby balls visible under the hedge, there was another generation in residence.

Next door was a different story. Once occupied by a rake-thin widow who took pride in her clean windows, now broken shutters hung listlessly over rotting frames, the ground covered

31

in shards of the very glass she'd once polished so diligently, and even with an untrained eye, Fabian could see that the roof was sagging where ancient beams could no longer bear the weight of the slates. It wouldn't be long before it collapsed.

Directly opposite, tucked into the hillside, were two other houses, well kept enough but with the neglected air of occasional use, last summer's late blooms all withered and brown and the garden chairs still strewn across the patio from the latest winter storm. They'd stay like that until the owners returned for their next holiday, probably when the weather changed in the spring.

But at least the Dubonnet house looked cared for, the gable-covering advertisement with its classic *Dubo, Dubon, Dubonnet* slogan vivid despite the faded blue background. It had been the residence of old Monsieur Papon, father of the present mayor, a gruff pensioner whose gnarled hands had always been quick to swat a troublemaker but whose wife used to give out sweets behind his back. Being a staunch Ricard drinker, he'd never got over the shock of coming home to a painted gable, the money his wife made from the transaction no compensation for the fact that he had to live in a property adorned with the name of what he considered a drink for ladies. And the kids, knowing this, would taunt him from a safe distance after a strong hand had made contact with a troublesome ear, chanting the slogan that defiled his walls over and over until he retreated inside in a temper.

It seemed unlikely now, in the silence that draped the square like the low-hanging smoke from early-lit fires, that these hills had ever rung to the sound of children's voices and the hum of conversation from the adults gathered under the lime tree. Where had they all gone?

Perhaps, like him, the kids he'd played with had grown up and left and been too busy to come back.

Although that wasn't entirely true in his case. He'd tried to come back a few times once he began his job in the bank. But it was too difficult. The persona he'd constructed around himself didn't suit the tranquillity of La Rivière or the slow pace of the mountains. And he'd been afraid that Oncle Jacques would see right through it. So it had been easier to accompany some of his less obnoxious colleagues on beach holidays in Cannes and skiing trips to Megève. He'd told himself that he'd outgrown the company of his country relatives and the simple pleasure of his Opinel knife.

As he stood there, watching the last rays of the sun streak the sky pink above the flat top of Mont Valier, he wondered how he'd managed to live that lie for so long.

Shivering slightly, he started off again, knowing that the valley below would already be in the dark. He left the village behind, heading into the forest that separated Picarets from the Estaque farmlands, and was plunged into premature night by the thick layering of bare branches above him. His headlight struggled to keep the shadows at bay and Fabian was torn between pushing on and risking an accident, or taking it slowly and giving himself time to negotiate the bends.

He was grateful when he emerged above the plateau dominated by the Estaque farmhouse, a place he knew well. Véronique Estaque had been his companion during the long summers he'd spent in Fogas. The same age, they'd been naturally thrown together, but had formed a friendship based on something more fundamental that they had in common; they'd both been bullied at school.

Born to an unmarried mother who refused to talk about Véronique's father, Véronique had suffered the stigma of being illegitimate. The local kids had preferred to use the word 'bastard'.

So they'd hung out in the woods above the quarry, building dens and forming clubs with passwords and secret rites of which they were the only initiates.

They would spend their days roaming the paths and trails that crisscrossed the mountains until it was time for him to go back to the épicerie, leaving Véronique to return reluctantly to the farm. She didn't have a curfew and her mother seemed to pay her no heed as she toiled away, refusing help and abrupt with all and sundry.

Fabian had been terrified of Madame Estaque who barked at him in a language he couldn't understand, the consonants slurred and the tone gruff. By the end of the holidays his ears would finally tune in to her Ariégeois accent but by

34

then it was too late. His fear had blocked any capacity his brain had found for comprehension.

It had been like that in the shop this afternoon. Madame Estaque had grunted at him and he'd frozen, able to see her lips working but incapable of making any sense of the sounds that emerged. Given how angry she seemed about his proposal to take over the épicerie, perhaps it was just as well.

He'd really been caught off guard by the negative reaction of the villagers.

He'd thought Josette would be glad of the chance to retire, relieved to be able to sell her share to a family member. He'd presumed the commune would be pleased to have someone take over the shop which was a lifeline to people like Madame Estaque, who didn't drive.

Perhaps he could win them round with time. Especially when they saw his plans for the place!

On that positive note, he entered the last stretch of forest which led down to the main road, his headlight useless and the lack of streetlights making the road almost impossible to see.

He slowed to walking pace, concentrating on the narrow strip of tarmac just about visible in front of his wheel, hoping he was right in thinking he wasn't far from the valley floor. Behind him he heard the roar of a car engine and white beams split the night, a dark shape hurtling past, swerving to the opposite side of the road at the last minute to avoid him as it veered round a bend and left him blinking and disorientated while his retinas struggled to cope.

Stephanie was running late. By the time she'd finished at the Auberge and picked up Chloé from school, the night was setting in as she began the ascent up to Picarets, her mind preoccupied by her financial concerns.

'So, can we, Maman?'

'Sorry, love?' Stephanie dragged her attention back to her daughter.

'Can we have pizza for tea?' Chloé repeated with exaggerated patience.

Stephanie shook her head. 'No, not tonight. Maybe at the weekend, all right?'

Chloé turned to stare out of the window and Stephanie felt mean. She was such a good kid. She never gave her any hassle, unless you counted her obsession with becoming a trapeze artist which Stephanie, for reasons she wouldn't disclose, refused to condone. And as any mother knew, the fact that Chloé was forbidden to do somersaults probably meant that she just did them out of sight.

But there were tough times ahead and the cost of a pizza from the van in Seix suddenly seemed like a luxury they couldn't afford. Probably not even at the weekend.

Stephanie sighed. At this rate, she was going to have to go back to teaching yoga up in Toulouse, making the long drive up the motorway just for a forty-minute class.

Why couldn't things go smoothly for once? If Fabian Servat hadn't shown up, she would have been a lot more certain of the future. But now she was back to fretting about how she was going to support Chloé through university.

Or circus school!

A wry smile formed as she changed down a gear, the old police van shuddering with effort as the engine whined about the incline. She was just coming to the last bend before the Estaque farmhouse when it came out of nowhere.

A car.

On the right-hand side of the road.

Her side of the road.

The lights dazzled her as she instinctively swung the van into the left towards the mountainside, knowing that the alternative was a steep drop into the river and certain death, her arm flying out to protect Chloé even though she was wearing a seat belt. She heard a tear of metal as the car clipped her rear end but she had no time to react, struggling to regain control as she reached the apex of the bend. And it was at that moment that she saw a faint glimmer of light in front of her.

There was a bang as she slammed on the brakes and the van came to a halt.

'You okay?' she asked as Chloé turned worried eyes towards her.

'I think we hit something.'

'I *know* we hit something. I just don't know what,' muttered Stephanie as she flung open her door and jumped out.

She hurried towards the pool of yellow spilling from her headlights and as she took in the lifeless form that lay in a crumpled heap before her, wheels and legs intertwined, she knew the gods must be laughing.

'Who's that, Maman?' Chloé had appeared at her side.

'That,' said Stephanie, 'is Fabian Servat. And for the second time today, I think I may have killed him.'

3

'You're not allowed in the shop? Not even across the threshold?'

'No. 'E 'as really taken zis seriously.' Stephanie grimaced as she placed two cups of coffee on the table and sat down opposite Lorna, glad of the chance to get off her feet.

The restaurant was finally empty after a frantic Friday lunch hour which had had them scurrying in and out of the kitchen. It hadn't helped that they were short-staffed with Paul away at an obligatory food hygiene course in Foix, the departmental capital. But the number of customers had been welcome, if unexpected as they were still in their first week of business. Clearly the advertisements on the local radio were having an effect.

That and the fact that Lorna's cooking was sublime and word was getting around. Today's menu had been duck breast accompanied by a sauce made from Hypocras, a spiced wine produced locally, and it had proved a great success. Not that Stephanie had tried it, being vegetarian, but she'd had extra helpings of Lorna's home-made rhubarb crumble which was exquisite. Better than anything the previous owner, Madame Loubet, had ever served and none of it out of a tin!

Some of the customers had even called Stephanie over and asked in a whisper if Lorna really was English. When Stephanie had disappointed them by asserting that she was, they'd insisted that she must have French parents. How else could one explain her talents with French cuisine?

Now though, the madness of lunchtime was over and the two of them had time to discuss the big news of the day.

'Is there anything you can do? Can you appeal?'

Stephanie shook her head, bouncing the red curls that framed her face.

'I think it is better if I do nothing. After all, I did almost kill 'im.' She grinned mischievously. 'Twice!'

'But you weren't to blame! Even he's acknowledged that there was another car involved.'

'Yes, zat is true. But it was me who runs 'im over. So 'e 'as got the . . . 'ow you say . . . *une injonction d'éloignement*.'

'A restraining order.'

Stephanie concentrated on the small espresso cup in her hand for a moment. Somehow hearing the words in English made it seem more serious. And even more upsetting.

When she'd seen Fabian Servat lying in a heap in front of her van on Monday evening, Stephanie had feared the worst. But she'd quickly established that he was still breathing and Christian, who'd pulled up behind her minutes later with Véronique and Annie in his Panda 4×4, had helped lift the unconscious Parisian into the back of the van. She'd been

40

surprised at how light he was, as though he were made of hollow bones and very little flesh. And as she'd closed the doors on his wan face, she'd felt a surge of sympathy for the poor man who'd met with nothing but disaster, all at her hands, since he'd arrived in the commune of Fogas.

That spark of compassion, however, had been snuffed out by this latest development.

It turned out that, luckily for him, Fabian had been riding extremely slowly and so had been almost stationary when she'd clipped him. But even though he'd emerged from the collision with nothing worse than a few scratches and a couple of bruises, he'd marched straight down to the courts and slapped a restraining order on her.

She wasn't allowed into the shop or the bar and was forbidden to approach him outside of those areas.

Sure, the inconvenience this caused could be reduced by asking Annie to pick up her bread and odd bits and pieces from the épicerie while she waited outside, like a dog tethered to a fence. And any gossip gleaned at the counter could always be relayed.

But it just felt horrible. To be excluded from the place that was the heart of the community and through no real fault of her own.

Of course, there was another consequence of the injunction. How on earth was she ever going to ask Fabian about renting the land across from the épicerie if she wasn't allowed near him?

Not that it was likely he'd permit her to use it anyway. He hated her.

41

When he'd come round in the shop to see her standing over him he'd writhed in terror for the second time that day. And when he'd realised that she'd been driving the vehicle that had hit him, he'd gone berserk.

Then he'd seen his bike.

Which was another thing. How was she going to pay for the repairs?

As the damage hadn't seemed much, just the scrunched up front wheel which had taken the brunt of the impact, she'd agreed right away to cover it. But yesterday, using Chloé as an intermediary, Fabian had presented her with a spreadsheet breaking down the repair costs and she'd nearly choked.

She couldn't just nip down to Decathlon and pick up a new wheel. Oh no. Mr Fancy Paris Pants just had to have the latest thing.

A thousand euros. For a wheel!

She'd thought at first he'd made a mistake so she'd sent a note via Annie asking him to verify the amount and he'd sent back a terse reply explaining that the wheels were made from carbon.

Should be made from gold at that price!

And another seven hundred euros for the stupid computer thing he'd had on his handlebars which hadn't survived its collision with a Pyrenean mountainside.

She tried to fight the rising sense of panic.

Where was she going to get that kind of money? It was so unfair. The reckless driver who'd caused the accident had fled the scene, leaving behind nothing but a dent above her rear wheel and a trace of dark green paint. She hadn't been able to see what kind of car it was, it had all happened so quickly, although Fabian thought it was a small van, but not very modern. Like that narrowed it down around here!

It wasn't even worth claiming on her insurance. For a start, she'd left it a bit late for sending in a declaration, thinking that she was looking at a hundred euros max. But also, she'd opted for a larger excess on her policy to reduce her monthly payments and by the time that was taken into consideration along with the loss of her no-claims bonus, it didn't make sense to ask the insurance company to cough up.

Lorna reached across and put her hand on Stephanie's arm.

'Maybe it's a good thing that you have to stay away from him,' she suggested. 'You two do seem bad for each other! And I can give you an advance on your wages to help you with the damages.'

'Zat is very kind. But I will cope.'

'Do you know how long the restraining order is for?'

Stephanie shrugged. ''Ow long is a piece of rope?'

She stared down at the remains of her coffee and wondered who or what had sent the idiot that was Fabian Servat into her life. And for what purpose.

* * *

'She's a liability. The woman is determined to kill me!' Fabian teetered on the rickety wooden

43

stepladder wobbling beneath him, none of its legs the same length thanks to generations of rats out in the shed gnawing on them over the years. Josette caught herself wishing they'd gnawed a bit more when Fabian regained his balance and descended safely to the shop floor.

'I think that's a bit of an exaggeration. It's just a coincidence and you know it.'

'Coincidence?' Fabian's voice rose several octaves and he dumped the bottles of wine he'd gathered off the top shelf on to the glass display case next to the till, making Josette wince. 'I'm sorry Tante Josette, I don't see that I had any other option but to take legal action against her.'

Josette turned away so he wouldn't see the wave of annoyance that rippled across her normally cheerful features. The past five days had taken a toll on her reserves of patience.

Once he'd got over the shock of being knocked off his bike, they'd agreed on his first night that he would stay for a trial period of two months. She'd made it clear that she had no intention of retiring just yet and had been surprised at how accommodating he'd been, how eager he'd seemed to work alongside her. Then he'd gone on to outline his plans!

A complete makeover for the bar and shop, new shelving, modern lighting, a proper bread rack . . . He'd had pages and pages of what he called spreadsheets already prepared, figures and statistics showing her the cost of the work set against the expected increase in turnover.

She'd listened to him with one eye on her dinosaur of a husband who was pulling faces of

44

dismay at the proposed changes and when Fabian had got to the bit about knocking down the back wall to extend the épicerie into the store-room, Jacques had started banging his head against the stones of the inglenook in despair. Silently of course.

What was she to do?

Part of her was thrilled by Fabian's ideas, changes she'd yearned for but had never dared to effect, tradition being Jacques' mantra. 'Modernisation'. It came close to 'capitalism' in Jacques' dictionary of rude words.

But the other part of her, the much larger part, felt treacherous when she saw how much Jacques was suffering. So she'd resolved to find a course between the two of them, just for the next eight weeks, and then, with any luck, Fabian would become bored with the whole project and flee back to Paris, his search for a country idyll having come to nothing.

She'd seen it so many times before. People who came from the cities saying they wanted to escape the rat race, get away from it all. She never really knew what they meant. Like the countryside existed in some vacuum or something. Clearly they'd never visited St Girons market in the summer when it was impossible to get round the stalls with the number of tourists. Or faced a winter stuck in some isolated hamlet with the wind tearing at the slates and snow, too thick to see through, falling all around and the oil-depot on the phone explaining that it was too dangerous to deliver oil to you this week. You'd just have to

45

make do with the wood-burner for now.

More than anything, she found the attitude insulting to all those who lived and worked here, with its implication that city living was oh so much harder. They soon found out though. Try driving up and down the mountain roads to St Girons or Foix to work every day, or making a living out of the stubborn land, and you soon realised. And that's when most of them simply packed up and headed off, for some other pasture where the grass was sweeter and greener and blessed by a hotter sun.

Not that this applied to all the newcomers. Stephanie had settled in, and it looked like the British couple at the Auberge were going to make a go of it too. But those who eventually called this place home arrived with their eyes wide open and not a rose-tinted lens in sight. They appreciated the distinct seasons which made the mountains so beautiful to live in but sometimes so hard to live with. They understood the vagaries of the weather and the curses and blessings they bestowed. And they didn't fight the pace of life, where there was no such thing as a quick hello, only a slow goodbye.

Somehow, Josette didn't think this was the case with Fabian. And she hoped to God she was right as two more months of biting her tongue was more than she could bear. But bite her tongue she must. And the reason why was sitting on the fridge watching the pair of them with a frown, his arms folded and his hair sticking on end.

She hadn't seen Jacques snooze in days. Where

he would normally pass the time sitting in the inglenook with his head dropped on his chest, his snores making the fire dance, since Fabian's arrival he'd spent the daytime hours following his nephew around the shop, a permanent glower on his face. She didn't dare think what he got up to at night. Perhaps it was just as well he didn't have any telekinetic powers. Especially given all the knives in the place!

'Oh, that's interesting!'

Fabian was wiping a great quantity of dust off one of the bottles and peering intently at the label.

'My God! It can't be . . . ' He leant even closer until his nose was almost touching the glass. 'It is! It's a 1959 Château La . . . TCHOOOOO!'

The violent sneeze rocked Fabian back on his heels and the bottle spun out of his hands and up into the air. It twirled once, twice, and then dropped towards the ground. But Fabian was quick. He lunged sideways, his bony fingers stretching out beneath the bottle as his long legs caught the wooden stepladder, tipping it off balance and sending it crashing against the wall, tearing the faded map of the knife-producing regions of France that had graced the épicerie for many years.

'That was close!' he exclaimed as he lay on the floor, cradling the wine with a grin on his face.

But Josette wasn't smiling. She was looking at Jacques who had jumped up off the fridge and rushed over to his precious map, and was now staring at Fabian in outrage.

'Do you know how much this could be worth?'

Fabian continued, unaware of the daggers Jacques was shooting at him as he got to his feet. 'A colleague once boasted that he paid three grand for a bottle of Bordeaux like this. Do you think there might be more in the cellar?'

'I'm sure there are. Why don't you go and have a look?' she offered, just wanting him out of her space and away from Jacques who was still looking murderous. 'Take your time.'

He walked towards the bar clutching the wine but in the doorway he turned to Josette, rubbing a hand on the back of his neck.

'You know, this might sound daft but I feel as though I'm being watched all the time,' he declared.

'You're right. It does sound daft,' Josette reassured him as she righted the stepladder and resolutely ignored Jacques who had glided silently up behind his nephew and was breathing heavily on his collar.

Aware of a sudden chill, Fabian zipped up his cardigan and hurried off towards the cellar.

Josette slumped on to the bottom rungs of the stepladder and hung her head in her hands.

How on earth was she going to bear it? It would be so much easier to just leave. But with Jacques, that wasn't an option. So she was stuck here, trying to mediate between the two of them, one of them oblivious to the other. It was impossible.

'Going well I see!' Annie Estaque gave a gruff laugh as she entered the shop, setting off a furious tweeting of birds from the chime on the back wall.

48

Josette rolled her eyes and managed a weak smile.

'Not got rrrid of him yet then?'

'No. More's the pity.'

'Well, you'll just have to make the most of him being herrre.'

'How exactly?'

'Get him to change that bloody doorrrbell forrr a starrrt!'

Josette laughed. Annie was right. The new chime that Paul had installed a couple of weeks ago had been driving her mad with its stupid bird sound but she had no idea how to change it. Perhaps Fabian could have his uses after all.

'Tante Josette, Tante Josette!'

Footsteps clattered up the cellar stairs then Fabian burst into the bar, his black hair dusted in grey cobwebs and his face streaked with dirt, looking just like the boy she remembered from long ago.

'There are eleven more bottles down there. A whole case in total!' he exclaimed, his dark eyes alight with excitement. 'It could make us a . . . oh!' He pulled up short, instantly wary, as he spotted Annie standing inside the shop. 'Bonjour, Madame Estaque.'

'Think you'rrre old enough to be calling me Annie by now,' she replied as she dipped her head in welcome.

Fabian shot a puzzled glance at Josette.

'She says to call her Annie.'

'Oh, right. Annie.'

'You were saying about the wine?'

'Yes, the wine. We should try to sell it at

49

auction. I know just the person to handle it. What do you reckon?'

'You really think it might be worth something?'

'I'm not sure. I'll have to look it up in the Hachette guide and do a bit of research on the internet. But it won't hurt to find out.'

Josette shrugged, not having any great attachment to the wine. Jacques had bought it at a fair in Foix years ago, just before they got married. He'd stuck a bottle on the top shelf and then forgotten all about it in the excitement of their new lives and it had stayed there ever since. If it could make them a bit of money, then she was all for it. She just didn't want to seem too keen. Which she knew was churlish but she couldn't help it.

'I suppose.'

'That's sorted then.' Fabian turned a smile on Annie, and Josette could see he was trying hard to impress which made her feel even worse for being so off-hand. 'Now, how about I get you both a coffee? You look like you could do with a rest, Tante Josette.'

And just like that, the tug of affection she'd momentarily felt was replaced with a surge of irritation at his casual assumption of the role of host. Plus his implication that she was old.

'That'd be grrreat.' Annie put a knowing hand under her friend's arm and steered her towards the table while Fabian started fiddling with the big red machine which stood on the shelf behind the bar.

'What's that?' Annie asked, in the nearest she

could come to a whisper.

Josette rolled her eyes. 'A new coffee machine. He brought it with him from Paris.'

A jet of steam screeched out of the silver wand sticking out of the side making Annie jump. Then the grinder roared into life.

'Crrrikey!' she muttered. 'Does it milk the cows too? Seems like a lot of palaverrr just forrr a bloody coffee!'

'Café crème Madame Est . . . er, Annie?'

She raised an eyebrow. 'Café crrrème eh? Verrry posh!'

With a bit more clattering than seemed necessary, Fabian eventually emerged from the other side of the counter with two cups.

'Sorry,' he said, flustered as he put them down, creamy coffee sloshing around the saucers. 'I'm not a very good waiter!'

He reached across for his own, clearly intending to join them, and it was only as he turned back towards the table that Josette realised the danger.

He was going to sit opposite her. With his back to the fire. And Jacques was sitting in the inglenook, a wicked grin on his face as he breathed on the flames.

'No!' Josette sprang to her feet, causing Fabian to spill his coffee. 'No, don't sit there, love. Sit over here. And you can tell Annie all about your plans for the place.'

Annie was staring at her intently but never said a word, while Fabian merely obeyed with an alarmed look as he took her seat.

But unlike her, neither of them knew what

51

Jacques could do with fire. She'd seen it first hand not long before and she wasn't willing to risk it again. The sight of a burnt backside was not one she wished to repeat. No matter how much she wanted Fabian gone.

Over at the hearth, Jacques was now sulking openly, his bottom lip almost below his chin and his eyes accusing her of betrayal. She picked up the poker, busying herself with the fire while Fabian started telling Annie his grand ideas.

'Not like that,' Josette whispered to her husband. 'Not through violence.'

Jacques writhed in frustration.

'We'll sort it out. I promise.'

She replaced the poker and sat down just as Fabian got to the bit about knocking through the back wall at which point Jacques started rocking in his seat, covering his ears in anguish.

Josette took a drink.

And she had to admit the coffee was very good. Very good indeed.

* * *

Annie had stayed longer than she'd intended in the shop. She'd only gone in for a few bits and pieces, mostly stuff for Stephanie thanks to the blasted injunction.

She shook her head at her perception of a world gone mad.

Who'd ever heard of such a thing! Calling in the lawyers to keep someone away from you. Why not tell them to their face, sort things out properly? Or buy a vicious dog? Ridiculous, that's what it was.

She'd been meaning to say that to Fabian today. But somehow it had slipped her mind as he'd rattled on about his grand schemes for the épicerie. And then there was the coffee. She'd never tasted anything like it. The minute the bitter-smooth nectar hit her taste buds she was hooked. She'd accepted another eagerly and would have had a third but for the fact that her brain was already cartwheeling on the caffeine.

Noticing her appreciation, Fabian had started waffling on about the blend, something about it being grown at altitude in Yemen under fair-trade conditions, but she hadn't been listening. Like a true addict, she didn't care about all that. She'd been staring at the bottom of her cup and wondering how long she could last before another hit.

So she'd completely forgotten to berate him about the restraining order.

She was still muttering in annoyance when she reached the door of the Auberge and let herself in.

'Bonjourrr!'

Stephanie looked up from laying out cutlery and glasses and broke into a smile.

'Bonjour, Annie.' She laid two kisses on the wrinkled cheeks of her friend as Lorna popped her head out from the kitchen.

'Bonjour, Annie! Sorry, I can't stopping,' she explained, holding up her arms which were covered in flour as she embraced the older

53

woman carefully. 'I must to prepare for tonight.'

'You carrrrrry on, love. It's Stephanie I came to see.'

Lorna retreated into the kitchen and soon the steady thump of her rolling pin could be heard as Annie placed a small bag of shopping on the bar.

'Oh, thanks for that. It's such a nuisance not being able to get bread and milk. Can I get you a coffee in return?'

'No! No morrre. Not today.'

Stephanie raised an eyebrow and Annie, never one for shying from the truth, ended up confessing where she'd just spent the last hour. And whose coffee she'd been drinking.

'I feel like a trrraitorrr!' she concluded. 'But it's bloody good stuff!'

'Well as punishment you can help me set these tables,' Stephanie said with a laugh. 'Paul's going to be late back so I've offered to work this evening which means I need to get up to the school to pick Chloé up. She'll just have to amuse herself here tonight.'

'I could take herrr home with me,' Annie suggested, glad of the chance to spend time with the young girl.

'Are you sure?'

Annie nodded.

'You're a godsend!' Stephanie planted another kiss on Annie's face.

Since she'd arrived in Fogas seven years ago, Stephanie had made no better friend than Annie Estaque. Not put off for an instant by her abrupt way of speaking or her brusque manner,

Stephanie had divined a heart of gold beneath the crusty exterior and more importantly, a genuine affection for Chloé.

Stephanie had also liked the fact that Annie didn't ask questions. Unlike some in the commune who were openly curious about Chloé's father. But then, Annie was fairly close-mouthed herself and the identity of Véronique's dad remained a mystery.

'I've told you beforrre, you can leave Chloé with me any time,' Annie said as she started folding napkins, her callused hands scratching on the paper as she made the creases. 'She's a good kid. Neverrr any botherrr.'

'Only because you let her do somersaults on the pasture by the barn!'

Annie concentrated on folding and smoothing the paper triangles, but her eyes were twinkling.

'Anyway, you two can sit and discuss your new hero all night.'

'Herrro?'

'Fabian Servat! Chloé has a crush on him. Says he looks just like her idol Jules Leotard, the father of trapeze. She keeps pestering me to ask him for dinner as she's convinced he must be an acrobat.' Stephanie snorted at the thought. 'Clown more like!'

'It's good forrr herrr,' Annie said softly as she put the last napkin in its place. 'Having a man to look up to.'

'I know,' sighed Stephanie as she untied her apron strings. 'It's just . . . '

'Why him?'

'Yes. Of all the people around here, why him?'

'Could be worrrse. Could be Berrrnarrrd Mirrrouze!'

Stephanie broke into peals of laughter at the thought of the fat *cantonnier*, who had plagued the commune with his deadly skills behind the wheel of the snowplough all winter, being an object of admiration for Chloé.

'He might not be all bad,' added Annie more seriously. 'Fabian, I mean.'

Stephanie pushed her red curls behind her ears and took a deep breath.

'Look, I haven't told anyone this,' she began, 'but I was planning on opening an organic gardening centre.'

'What a grrreat idea! But why did you keep it to yourrrself?'

'I wasn't sure I could do it. And now it seems I was right. Thanks to Fabian.'

'Fabian? What's he got to do with anything?'

'Absolutely everything. He owns the land I want to build it on. And with our recent history — '

'The Serrrvat land up in Fogas?' Annie interrupted. 'But that's no good. It's too steep and no one will go all the way up therrre just to buy plants.'

'No, not there. The small field by the river, across from the épicerie. It's the only viable place in the area.'

'Well, you'd best get potting up cuttings then, girrrl!'

'What's the point? He'll never agree to me renting it.'

'No,' said Annie, a broad grin on her face. 'But

56

Josette will. That's herrr land. Been in the Rrrumeau family forrr generrrations. Herrr grrrandfatherrr grrrew vegetables on it when I was a girrrl.'

But Annie was talking to thin air. The front door of the Auberge had slammed shut and through the window she could just make out the tall figure of Stephanie flying up the road towards the épicerie, her red hair streaming behind her.

'Everything is okay?' A worried Lorna had appeared at the kitchen door.

'Yes, fine,' Annie replied, waiting until Lorna had gone back to work before muttering a proviso. 'As long as she stays away frrrom the baguettes it will be!'

4

Three weeks. Three whole weeks. That's all it had been but to Josette it was more like three years.

She rubbed the small of her back which had already begun to ache. Soon the discomfort would spread to her right hip and into her thigh and she would be glad to get her feet up at the end of the day.

If she made it to the end of the day! It was only nine o'clock in the morning but already she was tired.

Had she felt like this before his arrival she wondered, as she watched him wiping down the coffee machine. He never seemed to stop, buzzing around the place like a fly trying to get out of a closed window. Perhaps she should try swatting him with a rolled up newspaper. Not that she'd be able to catch him.

Where did he get his energy? She'd been determined to be the first up every morning, wanting to be the one to fling open the shutters, to unlatch the door, to steal a few moments when the épicerie was still totally hers. Well, hers and Jacques'. But it was getting harder and harder as he rose early and went to bed late. Sometimes she would open the front door to him coming back from a bike ride, his face flushed, the cold air wafting off him as he passed her.

It made her feel so old. She was convinced that was why her back had started playing up. It had always been a bit temperamental but nothing like this. Now it only took a glimpse of Fabian striding around and her muscles would twinge in envy of his robust youth.

'I'm just going out to get wood, Tante Josette.'

She waited for the back door to slam and then scuttled across the shop to the wicker basket. She prodded the top loaf, her fingers meeting crust resistance.

She knew it! He'd done it again.

She dug through the basket to the baguettes below, the ones too hard for her fingers to leave an imprint on. Yesterday's loaves. No point leaving them at the bottom. There was no way they'd sell down there.

She muttered to herself as she fished them out and rearranged them.

No matter how many times she told him, he just ignored her. Plonked the fresh bread on top of the old. He'd actually suggested that she threw out any left from the day before. What a waste!

Same with the cheese. He'd bring a new round in from the store before the old one had gone. Who in their right mind would want a heel end when it was sitting next to an immaculate golden circle of Moulis or Bethmale?

She heard his footsteps, heavy under his burden, and resumed her position at the till just as he entered the bar. He dropped the wood on the hearth with a clatter, jerking a snoozing Jacques out of his slumber, and then proceeded

59

to prod and poke the flames while Jacques stared at him with indignation.

Josette turned to face the window. Could she really bear living with him for another five weeks? It might have been better all round if she'd let Jacques flambé him!

Her gaze drifted to the Auberge, just visible at the end of the village, where Paul was busy up a stepladder, stringing up heart-shaped bunting.

Valentine's Day! Of course. Véronique had stopped by a few days ago on her way back from hospital and told her that the Auberge was fully booked for the first time. All the rooms occupied and thirty people for the themed meal that evening. Josette was proud of the young British couple who seemed to be making a go of things, despite the difficulties they'd faced from some people in the commune who hadn't wanted them there.

Perhaps she was doing the same to Fabian, she mused. Putting up obstacles, legitimising her annoyances when really, she just didn't want an outsider coming into her space.

But there was more to it than a battle over stale baguettes and hard cheese.

She missed the way things had been before he marched into her life and gave it a good shake. His new coffee machine had proved a hit and they were busy every morning now with people dropping in for a shot of caffeine before work. People she didn't know. Never got the chance to know as he served them with brusque efficiency.

Same with the customers in the shop. No time

for a chat, arms folded on the counter, hearing how Christian had got on at the cattle auction or how run off her feet Monique Sentenac was at the hair salon. With Fabian in charge it was here's your bag, thanks for the money and au revoir.

Everything was rush, rush, rush. And all he ever seemed to think of was the bottom line and profit margins, constantly producing those blasted spreadsheets and prattling on about releasing equity and reducing overheads. Most of it went straight over her head. The other day he'd said they should think about amortising the renovations and she'd asked would it help keep out the damp. He'd started laughing, as had Jacques, and she'd stomped upstairs to find her dictionary.

She'd underestimated how difficult it would be. By comparison, sharing the place with Véronique had been easy. She'd virtually lived in the shop, before the fire anyway, coming over most afternoons when the post office closed, eager to help and catch up on any gossip. Now Josette hardly saw her and she missed the young woman's company. She had a wicked sense of humour and hid a good heart under a caustic tongue. Just like her mother really.

A crash from the bar pulled her out of her daydreams and she poked her head around the door to see Fabian picking up bits of glass off the floor.

And that was another thing. The breakages . . . He had to be the clumsiest person she'd ever known.

With a suppressed grumble, she went to get the broom.

★ ★ ★

Fabian couldn't do a thing right. He'd been trying to arrange the glasses on the rickety shelf behind the bar in the exact fashion that Tante Josette liked when his sleeve had caught on the wand of the coffee machine, sending the glass he was holding tumbling to the floor.

He saw the flash of irritation on his aunt's face as she bustled off, muttering under her breath. Knowing she'd insist on cleaning up, he wandered into the shop.

He seemed to be permanently under her feet. No matter what he went to do, she was there, working away in that slow methodical manner of hers that was beginning to drive him mad. There was no sense of urgency. Every task filled all the available time and quite often ran over. And every customer was expected to engage in a lengthy conversation. Even if they'd only popped in for a box of matches.

The slow swish of the broom commenced and Fabian shook his head in despair. At least half an hour it would take her. And that's if no one came in meanwhile. Then she would probably go over to the hearth and spend another thirty minutes there. What was with her and that fire? She was forever prodding and poking it, mumbling away. She was obsessed with the thing.

Feeling goose pimples on the back of his neck, Fabian turned up his collar and moved further

62

into the épicerie. He was always cold down here. Upstairs or in the cellar, he didn't seem to suffer. But there was a chill wind that blew through the shop and the bar and targeted him in particular. He'd already asked the builders to fit draught proofing on the windows and doors when they started the renovations.

He couldn't wait for them to begin. The place was so dark, he didn't know how Tante Josette had stood it all these years, peering out from behind the lengths of saucisson that hung over the counter. The walls, what bits could be seen behind the clutter, were mottled and stained, and so overloaded that they gave the appearance of looming in at the top like a cave.

As for the shelves . . .

Since he'd cleaned off their thick coating of dust, the rough wooden planks had looked less bowed but still they strained under the weight of items better suited to a museum: zips from manufacturers that had gone bust forty years ago, rusty tins of polish, hairnets and a faded map of Toulouse which didn't even show the metro. The one good find had been the wine. He'd yet to hear back from his contact about a possible auction but although he'd miscounted and there were only eleven bottles, one short of a case, he was hopeful it might happen.

He mooched over to the front door and his mood grew darker. She'd swapped the loaves around. Put the hardest, stalest baguettes on top, the ones only unsuspecting fools would buy. She didn't seem to understand that all the locals simply delved into the basket to get the freshest bread. It was only new customers who fell for her tactics and walked out of the door with an inedible loaf. And then, most likely, never came back.

But no matter what he said, she insisted on war-time frugality.

So he'd suggested they change the bread, bought something that wouldn't go stale so quickly. He'd even cycled halfway up Col de Port to the bakery which supplied them and talked to the baker who'd proposed an organic loaf. It was more expensive than the traditional baguette but it lasted longer, so they could sell it the next day with a clear conscience and have happy customers. He'd returned with a sample and she'd been impressed. But once she heard the price she refused to contemplate it.

Too expensive, she'd said.

It was the same with the croissants.

An abiding memory of the summers he'd spent here had been the ritual of soft, fresh, flaky croissants for breakfast which Oncle Jacques taught him to dip into his drink, the resulting combination of buttery pastry and hot chocolate being the closest to heaven a kid of that age could imagine.

He'd been looking forward to indulging in the same rite as an adult but had been bitterly disappointed. Now, if Tante Josette had them at all, she stocked the supermarket mass-produced rubbish that bounced under the teeth and would require a chisel to produce the light layers that so typified those of his youth.

But Tante Josette wouldn't entertain selling

bakery-fresh croissants once again.

No one would buy them, she'd said. We'd end up throwing them away.

He hadn't liked to point out that he'd already thrown away countless bags of the soggy, inferior imitations.

Tante Josette simply couldn't grasp that they would have less waste and so make more profit even with a lower margin.

And that was the real cause of his frustration.

The numbers meant nothing to her.

One look at the accounts and it was clear that the business wasn't making any money, running at break-even at best. There were so many things she could do to make it better but she wouldn't budge. Wouldn't use the till, despite his repeated requests, instead jotted down sales on scraps of paper and stuck the money in a drawer. Refused to keep official records. Paid cash for the famous saucisson and never got a receipt. And the price of every product in the shop was stuck in the 1990s.

He cast a furtive glance into the bar where the stooped figure of his aunt was still brushing glass into a dustpan. He had time.

Long fingers moving rapidly, he hauled the new loaves up from the depths of the basket and arranged them on top of the old.

He'd only just finished when the chime sounded and René Piquemal wandered in.

'Bonjour,' Fabian said over his shoulder as he hurried to get behind the counter, aware that Tante Josette was already in the doorway.

' 'jour,' René replied, his outstretched hand left

dangling in mid-air by Fabian's rapid retreat. René shrugged and crossed the room to kiss Josette instead.

'What can I get you?' she asked, edging behind the glass display case and hemming Fabian in next to the till.

'A packet of cigarettes and I'll take a baguette as well.' René reached over to the basket, his hand automatically rooting through to grasp one at the bottom. But it was rock hard. Puzzled, he prodded the top loaf. Fresh. But the crusty surface was all pockmarked.

'Didn't we get any Gauloises with the last delivery, Fabian?' Josette asked crisply.

'I didn't order them.'

'It's fine, I'll take — '

'You didn't order them?'

'No. I didn't think anyone smoked them any more.'

'René does!'

'Well, I bought Marlboro Lights instead. Perhaps he could try them. He might live longer.'

'It's fine,' René repeated, hesitant to get between them. 'I'll — '

'Maybe you should take over all the ordering then?'

'Maybe I should. Then we might make a profit.'

'Is that all you can think of — '

'*Please!*' René raised his hands in surrender. 'Just the loaf and a packet of . . . Marlboro Lights.'

He handed over ten euros and Josette

pointedly slipped it in a drawer with a sly glance at Fabian who chose to ignore her as he passed René his cigarettes.

'And I think you need to have a word with your baker,' René said gruffly when Josette had counted out his change.

'Sorry?' Josette said.

'Tell him to stop fiddling with the loaves so much.' He brandished the baguette. 'Got more finger holes than a bloody flute!'

And with that he departed, leaving Josette and Fabian contrite behind him.

★   ★   ★

Only when Stephanie had seen the back wheel of Chloé's bike disappear at the far end of Picarets did she close the front door and turn towards the table.

The computer was there, waiting for her, the sun streaming in the front window, spotlighting it like an invitation and a guilty thrill fluttered her stomach.

She should really be out in the polytunnel. Or down in La Rivière clearing brambles and dead nettles.

It was two weeks on from her mad dash to the épicerie, when luckily Fabian had been in the cellar as she'd burst through the door of the shop, disregarding his stupid restraining order. Josette had been overjoyed at Stephanie's request, glad to think that the overgrown field might be put to good use, and Stephanie had struggled to persuade her to accept any rent.

When they'd finally agreed on a ludicrously small amount, to be supplemented by fresh vegetables in season, Josette had insisted on showing her new tenant around. And they'd uncovered a real bonus. At the edge of the land was a rusty old tap Josette's grandfather had installed to water his tomatoes, running the water down from the village tap across the road.

Knowing that she'd never find a better location, or a better price, Stephanie had started work immediately, contacting the authorities in Foix and getting the basics on setting up a business. But the red tape was endless and after a few days of fruitless phone calls and dead-ends, she'd been tearing her hair.

Then Christian had offered her the use of his old laptop.

The Internet had given her instant access to information she'd have struggled to find on her own. And the forums were incredible! People she'd never met were willing to answer her questions and she'd been showered with advice, much of which would save her a fortune as one false move in the minefield that was the bureaucracy of business registration could be costly. Something she could ill afford.

Buoyed by the ease with which she'd learnt to negotiate the Internet, she turned her attention to other topics and it wasn't long before she found an excellent website, full of useful tips for the professional organic gardener. It also had a forum and Stephanie, in a matter of weeks, had become a regular contributor.

Which was one of the reasons she felt guilty.

She knew that she'd been neglecting Chloé recently but between waitressing and trying to get the garden centre off the ground, there wasn't much time left for her daughter. When Stephanie had apologised and explained that it was only for a little while, Chloé hadn't complained. Instead she'd offered to help by doing some weeding and had gone off on her bike this morning quite willingly. Her only demand, a pizza for tea tonight. As it was Saturday, Stephanie had agreed. She just about had time to fetch one from Seix before dropping Chloé off at Annie's on her way to work at the Auberge.

She switched on the laptop and made herself a coffee.

What first, she wondered? Finish the final form for the *Chambre de Métiers* and drop it over to Foix on Monday? That would mean she was fully registered and could concentrate on the neglected plot so that it looked less like a jungle when she opened at the beginning of May. Plus she needed to get started on the process of gaining her organic certification. It could take up to two years for accreditation, although she had her fingers crossed that as the land had been uncultivated for so long, a soil analysis would curtail the waiting period.

But where she was going to get the money to pay for all this, she didn't know. She'd called the yoga centre in Toulouse but they'd only been able to offer her week-long courses which she couldn't agree to because of her commitments at the Auberge. And anyway, she needed the best part of a thousand euros to cover the fees for one of the organic accreditation bodies who would oversee the inspections. A few yoga classes was hardly going to provide that. Plus she'd yet to pay blasted Fabian Servat for the damage to his bike.

Perhaps she ought to apply for a bank loan? At least go and speak to someone and see if they would consider it and not laugh her out of the place.

She struggled with the idea though. It went against everything she'd striven to create for herself and Chloé, making her financially dependent on someone else which she'd vowed she'd never be again. It also left a paper-trail which was something Stephanie didn't want. Bad enough that she was having to put her name to all the documents for the business registration. She only hoped none of it would come back to haunt her.

Mug in hand, she stared out of the back window, the plastic cover of the polytunnel rippling in the breeze and the snowdrops clustered beneath the large oak dipping their heads in unison. But even a sight which normally afforded her pleasure, today only added to her stress. She hadn't been out in the garden for ages. The young plants she was bringing on were surviving by accident rather than design and the oak tree was in desperate need of a good pruning. Several branches were encroaching on the house and if she didn't get the ladder out soon and start clipping, Chloé would be sharing her bedroom with squirrels.

While she agonised over the best course of action for the day, a ping from the laptop alerted her to a new email.

It was from him.

She'd thought he might contact her which was why she'd been glad when Chloé had said she was going down to La Rivière. While the small house suited them perfectly, its open-plan design made it impossible for Stephanie to do anything without Chloé noticing. And this was something she didn't want her daughter knowing about. Not just yet.

Which was the other reason for her guilt.

There wasn't much she kept from her daughter. But she hadn't told her about this latest development because she didn't want the well-meaning pressure that Chloé seemed to apply to any potential relationship. Not that there had been many in the seven years since she'd left Finistère. Her friendship with Christian Dupuy was just that, a friendship and nothing more, despite the wishes of his parents who were eager to see him settle down. Admittedly, there'd been a time when she'd wondered. Dreamed even. But she'd come to the realisation that he wasn't for her.

Beyond that, nothing. Perhaps that was how it was meant to be. Despite the prediction from her mother all those years ago.

Stephanie had come home upset from a disastrous date with a boy from school. Disastrous because he'd tried to force her into going further than she'd wanted, pushing her up against the harbour wall in the dark, fingers

71

groping beneath her top.

She'd asked him to stop but he'd ignored her. And her temper had flared.

She'd reached up over their heads to the rough wall where a lump of seaweed hung from the last tide and she'd pulled it down, right on to his head. His hands had snapped out from under her T-shirt the minute the wet tentacles slid across his face, and when a grumpy crab had emerged from the green slime and pinched him on the ear, he'd let out a roar. But by then Stephanie was at the far end of the beach, her long legs flying over the damp sand as she raced for home.

Her mother had been at the kitchen table as usual. She never slept when Papa was out on the boat. Even as a child, Stephanie had known to find her there whenever she woke in the dark, heart pounding after a nightmare. Lately though, thanks to ever stricter regulations and declining stocks of langoustines, Maman's night-time vigils were getting fewer and fewer as Papa spent more time at home, the boat pulled high on to the beach, out of water as much as the men who sailed in her. While they kicked their heels around the town, waiting for the next chance to fish, Maman's fears for Papa's safety were fast being replaced by concerns for her family's financial future.

So when Stephanie slipped in through the back door, she tried to make her way as quietly as possible across the kitchen floor without disturbing the woman who was sitting at the table, head resting on her hand. But it was useless. Without even opening her eyes, Maman knew. Just as she always knew.

'What's happened?'

'Nothing, Maman. Everything's fine.'

Maman had lifted her head, her swathe of black hair falling back from her face.

'You're trying to lie to me? Your gypsy mother?'

She'd opened her arms and Stephanie had run into them, her adolescent independence willingly abandoned for a few more moments of childhood. And she'd told her mother what had happened, how she hated boys and knew she would never find the right one.

Maman hadn't laughed. She'd simply taken Stephanie's palm and turned it towards the fire, her rough fingers tracing over the young skin in the flickering light.

'You will love, my child,' she'd murmured, her brown eyes focused on a fate Stephanie couldn't see. 'But you are stubborn! The man of your dreams will have to fall for you three times before you accept.'

Then she'd closed Stephanie's hand, as if sealing in her destiny, and kissed her fiercely on the forehead.

'Now go to bed before your father gets in and I have two crazy redheads to deal with!'

Stephanie had pleaded with her to reveal more but Maman had refused, saying her talents were a gift not a plaything. And she had never mentioned it again.

Five years on, neither of Stephanie's parents had been alive to witness her walk down the aisle, Papa drowned in a storm at sea and Maman dead from a grief-stricken heart which had never mended. It had made things easier three years later when Stephanie had to run from her home town, taking only her two-year-old daughter and a car full of gardening tools, to make a new life in the Pyrenees, far from the windswept coast of Finistère and her husband's brutal fists.

In the years that followed, Stephanie had simply got on with life, grateful for the fresh start that she'd been handed. She didn't dwell on romance, was quite content to be a single parent. But sometimes she did wonder what Maman had seen in her palm all those years ago.

Now she'd be hard pushed to see anything past the ingrained soil and the calluses, Stephanie thought wryly, as she dragged her attention back to the present.

She clicked on the email and her computer screen filled with a bouquet of Pyrenean meadow flowers. He'd known better than to pick them. Instead the posy was a collage of photos pasted together in a riot of colours which made her yearn for the spring when the pastures would begin to bloom. She could see some of her favourites like the multi-purpose bear's garlic, the regal Pyrenean iris, the snow gentian, the bright yellow head of an Arnica montana and she could almost smell the sweet scent of the rock jasmine. But the one that stood out the most, right in the middle of the bunch, was the bee orchid.

Three delicate lilac sepals fanned out above a

yellow and brown lip which looked just like a bee. It was what he used to sign his posts online.

The text beneath was short and to the point.

Dear Stephanie,
Happy Valentine's Day,
Pierre

She'd been conscious of the date because Lorna and Paul had begged her to work that evening as their Valentine's night promotion was proving incredibly popular. But she hadn't been expecting anything. They weren't at that stage. As an organic beekeeper who'd set up his own business a few years ago, he'd sent her a message in response to one of her questions on the forum. Gradually, their contact had become more personal and more frequent and now their exchange of emails was a highlight of her day.

Smiling inanely, Stephanie started typing a reply. Then, she promised herself, she'd get down to work. And maybe even call the bank. After all, it had been seven years. It was time to start living normally again.

5

Despite her offer to help, Chloé wasn't on the patch of land by the bridge, pulling up dead nettles and clipping brambles. Nor was she in the small wooden shed which Maman had brought down as an interim store for their tools in order to stop Chloé, who had taught herself how to ride without hands on the handlebars, cycling down the road with a hoe underneath her arm. Her bike lay discarded on the ground next to a trowel and a pile of weeds.

But of the girl there was no sign.

To be fair it wasn't her fault.

She'd fully intended to spend all her time working, knowing that Maman was busy. But the invitation had been too good to refuse.

A chance to be near Fabian Servat.

She'd only caught a glimpse of him that night on the road as Maman and Christian lifted his lifeless body into the van. But it had been enough. He was the spitting image of Jules Léotard on the poster she had on her bedroom wall, the one where the trapeze artist was leaning against a wooden balustrade, his profile all cheekbones and sharp nose, a lock of black hair falling across his eyes. Admittedly Fabian was a bit on the skinny side, his legs lacking the solid muscle of Chloé's hero. But she was willing to overlook that. And she'd become intrigued by this newcomer who had taken such

76

a dislike to Maman that he'd banned her from the shop.

Of course, it would be a betrayal of Maman to talk to him. So she'd toiled in the field, one eye on the épicerie in the vain hope that he would come over and chat to her, perhaps bring her an Orangina. Maman couldn't say anything about that.

She'd worked for what felt like an age to a nine-year-old girl, the hoe slipping in her cold hands, the brambles taller than her in places. But there had been no movement from the building opposite, no tall figure had come dashing across to rescue her from her self-induced gardening hell.

Instead, relief, when it came, was from an unexpected source.

★   ★   ★

Three days. She'd gone three days without setting foot inside the bar. But Annie Estaque could go no longer.

Bedevilled by desire, she'd pulled on her coat, mumbled an excuse to Véronique, and made her way down the road to the valley floor, her stomach twisting with anticipation while she berated herself the whole time.

It was ridiculous. At her age!

But still, her feet carried her forward.

Before she reached the T-junction at the Auberge, she turned right on to a narrow path which ran parallel to it, hidden in the trees and known only to locals. It wasn't one she normally used, especially at this time of year when the ground was covered in dead leaves which turned into greasy mulch underfoot, making things treacherous. But she was keen not to be observed so she picked her way carefully along, stepping over rocks and holding on to branches to keep her balance. When the trees thinned and the trail began to drop down to meet the Fogas road which wound round the back of the village, she stopped, still sheltered from view, and planned her attack.

She couldn't just go in there again. It was becoming awkward and Josette was sure to comment. No, she needed a diversion.

From her vantage point on the hill, she let her gaze drift across La Rivière, taking in the old school building, the burnt out carcass of the post office, the Romanesque church, the Auberge, the épicerie and the scattering of houses.

It was quiet, most of the villagers having made their weekly pilgrimage to St Girons for the market. There wasn't a soul around. Unless you counted the two weeping Marys who kept vigil at the bottom of the cross in the grotto next to the church. And well they might weep, for Jesus had abandoned his post a long time ago, the victim of an errant football many years before. A hefty strike had cleaved his head clean off and he'd been taken away to be repaired and never been seen again. His unfortunate accident had coincided with the disappearance of the curate which Annie had always found amusing.

She cast one last look across the village and

then she saw it. A flash of red, a twirl of black, coming from the land next to the broad ribbon of river.

Excellent! Her excuse.

She made her way, as quickly as a woman of advanced years could, down the slippery slope to the safety of the tarmac, her pace increasing as the tantalising aroma began to arouse her taste buds.

* * *

'Ah! That's good!' Annie sat back in her chair, savouring the bitter aftertaste of coffee.

'Mmmmm,' agreed Chloé as she licked a moustache of hot chocolate off her top lip.

'Everything okay Madame . . . er, Annie?' Fabian's dark head popped through the door.

'Fine. Just fine. Thought Chloé would welcome the brrreak.'

'Annie thought I needed a break,' Chloé piped up before Fabian's face could cloud with incomprehension.

'And did you?' demanded Josette as she entered the bar, her arms piled high with wood which she dumped by the fire.

'Oh yes. Most definitely! Weeding is thirsty work.' Chloé looked longingly into the empty mug, making the adults laugh.

'Would you like another?'

'Yes!' Annie rasped before Chloé could even get the words out. 'We both would.'

'If I didn't know you better, Annie,' Josette said with a smile as she gathered up their cups,

'I'd think you'd used our young friend here as an excuse!'

'I didn't use no one. We both have ourrr own rrreasons forrr coming in. Don't we, Chloé!' She winked at the girl who was now transfixed by the tall figure of Fabian, standing in the doorway in almost the exact same pose as her hero.

'Two more for our addicts, Fabian please.'

'I'd best get some more coffee out of the store then.'

He disappeared into the back room while Annie followed Josette into the shop to pick up the groceries that would shield her from Véronique's perceptive questions when she got home.

Alone in the bar at last, Chloé turned to the silent form that sat behind her in the inglenook.

'Bonjour, Jacques,' she whispered and the old man nodded in reply.

Chloé didn't question the fact that he was there. Or not there. Without knowing it, she was from a long line of mystics and had inherited her grandmother's abilities which at this age she simply accepted as totally natural. She was still able to see Jacques Servat, even though he'd died last summer. It didn't seem weird. Especially as Josette could see him too. It was their secret.

'What's the matter?' she asked, noticing his frown and the folded arms.

He put his hands to his neck and rolled his eyes, pretending to choke himself. Chloé giggled.

'You can't kill yourself. You're already dead!'

He grinned back at her and then Fabian

crossed the room and his grin faded, his eyes not leaving his nephew until footsteps could be heard going down the cellar. Chloé knew then.

'It's Fabian? You don't like him either?'

Jacques shook his head so violently the flames in the fire danced.

'I think he's nice,' Chloé volunteered with the honesty she was known for. 'He makes good hot chocolate!'

Jacques pulled a face.

'But Maman can't stand him. She's not allowed in the shop, you know.'

The old man slumped in his seat, ashamed at the way his friends were being treated by a member of his family and tormented by the fact that it was all his fault.

'She's thinking of casting a spell on him,' Chloé announced, which made Jacques sit bolt upright again with enthusiasm. 'To make him go home. But it involves ingredients. And you know what Maman is like with cooking! She'll probably mix the wrong things and . . . boom! Turn him into a frog or something. And then you'd have to put up with him hopping around here all day like this.'

Jacques started laughing as she did a quick impression of Fabian the amphibian, leaping around the table.

But when she sat back down, her face was serious.

'I told her she mustn't, but . . . ' She sighed, a heavy sound for such a small frame. 'She doesn't seem to listen to me lately. She's so busy.'

Her fingers started playing with the burn holes

81

that scarred the sunflowers on the bright plastic tablecloth, her bottom lip trembling. And for the first time since the arrival of his nephew, Jacques' concern was focused on someone other than the Parisian.

It must be tough, he thought. No father and a mother run off her feet trying to make ends meet.

He got up, knees creaking, and took a tentative hop towards the girl who was the closest he'd ever get to having grandchildren.

'Ribbit, ribbit,' he mouthed and she stifled a giggle.

He hopped past her.

'Ribbit, ribbit,' he mouthed again.

'Ribbit, ribbit,' she replied, in delight.

And when he hopped to the end of the table and pretended to fall over just like his hapless nephew, she laughed out loud, her voice carrying out of the bar and down the cellar stairs.

★ ★ ★

Fabian was concentrating on the two crates of beer he was carrying. He'd decided to get them while he had the chance otherwise Tante Josette would struggle up with them. He'd been trying to persuade her to leave all the heavy lifting to him but to no avail. Like earlier, when she'd come into the bar with the load of wood. He'd been embarrassed that the others would think he hadn't offered to help.

She was so stubborn, saying it was better if she didn't start to rely on him. As if she was expecting him to leave before long. Or hoping he would.

So he tried to pre-empt her, getting stock up from the cellar before it was really needed, and bringing in the firewood before she had the chance. Even then, she complained about tripping over the extra crates behind the bar and moaned that they were getting through the wood too fast.

He just couldn't win.

But he wasn't prepared to admit defeat just yet, he thought as he shifted the weight of the beer to negotiate the final few steps. And that was when he heard her.

Chloé. Saying something about turning someone into a frog.

He eased the crates onto the ground and peeked round the doorway. The young girl was at the table, no one else in sight.

Intrigued, he watched as she hopped around the room and then sat down again. She murmured into the fire, too quiet for him to hear, and then started giggling, her eyes wandering as though she was watching something. Or someone.

All the while saying 'Ribbit, ribbit'.

The girl was clearly insane. Just like her mother.

★　★　★

Josette heard the gales of laughter and knew that Jacques was up to something. She rushed into the bar, Annie on her heels, to see her husband leaping around the table like a frog while Chloé was rocking in her chair with merriment. And Fabian was standing in the cellar doorway. Staring.

'Chloé!' she said, a bit more sharply than she meant to. 'I think you may have had too much sugar, young lady. Don't you agree, Fabian?'

Chloé was quick to catch on, her hand flying to her mouth when she spotted the lanky figure opposite.

'Sorry, Josette. I was just playing.'

'And I know who with,' muttered Josette as she glared at Jacques, now back in his seat looking like butter wouldn't melt. He even had the audacity to throw her a wink! Whatever the pair of them had been up to, at least he was back to his normal self. First time she'd seen him like that in weeks.

'How's that coffee coming along?' demanded Annie, her craving forcing her to speak as clearly as possible and for once Fabian understood and started tweaking the machine into life.

'Make that two!' Christian strode in through the front door, his size instantly dwarfing the room. 'Just got time before I head home to change.'

'Got a hot date this afternoon then?' Josette teased.

Christian blushed. 'No! The bank manager. He's been good enough to see me on a Saturday.'

'Must be serrrious then,' quipped Annie, cursing her quick tongue when she saw her fellow farmer grow tense. She of all people

84

should know better than to pry. She made a mental note to cut down on the caffeine. After this one.

'Just routine,' he muttered and changed the subject. 'I thought I might catch Véronique here? Wondered if she wanted a trip into town?'

'She's up at the house, moping arrround. Drrriving me mad!'

'Why? What's the matter with her?' asked Josette as Fabian placed the drinks on the table.

'Says she's going stirrr crrrazy,' huffed Annie. 'Me and the dogs arrren't enough company forrr herrr.'

'I can see her point,' Christian said without thinking and then hastened to make amends. 'I mean . . . not that you're not good company, Annie . . . but you know . . . '

Annie's laugh cut across his blustering.

'No need to apologise. She's rrrright. She's too young to be stuck up therrre with me. She needs a place of herrr own and herrr job back.'

'Actually, that's partly why I dropped in,' he continued. 'I've just heard that one of the commune flats in the old school has become available. There's a council meeting next Friday night and I'm hoping to get approval for her to rent it.'

'Oh, that would be perfect,' said Josette. 'She'd be just round the corner. I can't believe how much I've missed her these last few weeks.'

'You're not the only one,' Christian agreed and then blushed again as he realised what he'd said. 'I mean, you know, it's just not the same in here without her . . . ' He faltered to a stop as he saw Fabian looking hurt.

'Well, you lot arrre welcome to herrr!' Annie barked. 'She does nothing but tell me off!'

'That's probably because you need it,' Christian retorted with a grin. 'Anyway, Josette, I'll pick you up about seven on Friday night, if that's okay?'

'Oh, well, I guess . . . '

'What's the matter?'

Josette glanced at Jacques, all smiles now that Christian was in the room, and then at Fabian who was picking up a pile of teaspoons he'd managed to knock to the floor. How could she leave them alone for an entire night while she was up in Fogas at a council meeting? It would be a disaster.

'I don't think I can make it.'

Christian raised an eyebrow. 'But Fabian can look after the shop.'

'Yes, I know, it's just . . . ' She couldn't think of a good enough excuse. Not one they'd believe. And if she told them the truth they would have her locked up! 'I don't want to leave Fabian on his own. He's still getting to grips with it all.'

'Don't you trust me, Tante Josette?' Fabian asked, his tone arid.

'No, it's not that . . . '

Chloé came to her aid.

'I could come down, Josette. Then Fabian wouldn't be lonely. Maman will probably be working anyway.'

Josette looked over at the child who was jerking her head towards the fireplace, her eyes alight with secret messages.

'That's not a bad idea,' said Christian. 'I could bring Véronique as well. She could have a look at the flat while she's here and be on hand if Fabian needs help with anything.'

'Okay. That might work,' Josette agreed reluctantly. Her enthusiasm for the plan wasn't helped by Jacques rubbing his hands in anticipation of an evening alone with his nephew.

'Right, that's settled. I'll give Véronique a call when I get back to the farm. Tell her about the flat and see if I can't persuade her to come into town while I'm at it.' Christian drained the last of his drink, smacking his lips as he finished it. 'God, Fabian, that's great coffee!'

'Yes,' Fabian replied with just the right amount of sarcasm. 'At least I can get that right.'

* * *

Véronique was slowly going mad. Apart from a trip to the hospital in St Girons and to church on Sundays, she hadn't been anywhere in weeks. She hadn't dared risk the market since she'd broken her leg, not trusting herself to be able to negotiate the narrow lanes between the stalls which were always packed. As the temperatures had been bitter the last few Saturdays she hadn't really minded.

But today was glorious, a day made for wandering along under the plane trees on the Champ de Mars, the smell of cheese and charcuterie mingling with the fragrance of freshly cooked paella and the mouth-watering aroma of rotisserie chicken. She never managed to complete an aisle without bumping into someone she knew and then they'd stand chatting, jostled to and fro by the crowds milling past, as they caught up on local news. When she finally got the shopping done, the morning was rounded off with a coffee at Le Bouchon and more often than not, she would meet half the commune there, sitting at the outside tables and watching the world go by.

Apart from Maman, who refused to go to the market. Had never been as far as Véronique could remember. Said it was an excuse for gossip.'

Which was exactly what Véronique was missing. She'd spent the morning watching in frustration as car after car went down the hill towards town while she was stranded here.

In a fortnight her cast would come off and then at least she could get away. She'd forgotten how lonely the farm made her feel. And the bad memories it brought with it of her unhappy childhood.

Her right hand touched the small crucifix that lay at her throat.

That was the other thing. Being stuck in the house with a leg in plaster gave her way too much time to think. To dwell on the past and the bullying she'd suffered at school. Even the holidays had been hell, with Maman too busy on the farm to spare time, and her tormentors content to spend the long days seeking her out for more abuse. All because she didn't know who her father was. And, according to their taunts, because her mother didn't know either.

One summer, when trying to escape the bullies, she'd discovered that the old church in La Rivière was unlocked. She'd pushed open the thick wooden door and had entered a sanctuary.

They'd never thought to look for her there.

She'd curled up on one of the rickety pews and cried herself to sleep. The curate had found her late that night when he came to lock up and when she'd explained, he'd given her the crucifix she wore now. And a key. The small church became her place of refuge.

When the curate had left in dramatic fashion several years later, confronted by a rifle and an angry husband, Véronique hadn't relinquished her key. Apart from Fabian Servat, whom she'd told one year when he was over on holiday, no one knew she had it. And no one knew that she spent most of her days sitting within the safety of the thick walls, planning her escape from Fogas.

As soon as she was old enough, she left for college in Toulouse. But after years of dreaming about a new life, she missed the mountains and pined for the slow rhythm and easy ways that were all she'd known. Plus she'd realised that the kids who'd plagued her were adults now too and most of them had moved away to find work. So when her studies were completed, she'd returned home and secured the job as postmistress, which came with a small flat provided by the commune, right opposite the church. She knew that people talked about her, called her pious, regarded her devotion warily. But she'd never felt the need to explain. She'd been happy, working and living in La Rivière. The fire on New Year's

89

Eve had put an end to that.

Now she was jobless and homeless and utterly despondent.

It had never been in her plans to live back at the farm and she was struggling to cope.

Although, she had to admit, she was getting on better with Maman than she'd expected. Ever since the fire, Maman seemed to have made more of an effort, getting new false teeth for one thing. But she still maintained her brusque demeanour and Véronique didn't feel she knew her any better than when she'd been a child. So much for the mother-daughter bond getting stronger with age! Maman talked more to the dogs than she did to Véronique.

Noticing the time on her alarm clock, she clumped across the bedroom on her crutches and sat on the windowsill looking out across the pasture to the road and the mountains beyond.

It was stunning.

The midday sun was glorious, glistening off the snowcapped peaks, and she could see a red kite circling lazily in the sky, wings spread wide as though soaking up this premature burst of spring.

Huh, she thought. Make the most of it, mister. There's snow coming!

Not that she could believe the weather forecast on a day like this. But she'd lived long enough in the mountains to know that winter wasn't over on the first sunny day. She remembered one year they'd had a blizzard in May which had caused all sorts of damage, trees coming into bud snapped in half by the weight of the snow, power lines brought down, people killed by falling branches.

The kite swooped low over the field in front of the house, the vibrant colour of its body intensified in the sunlight. Véronique followed it as it soared once more and then disappeared beyond the tree tops.

Christian had told her once that kites mated for life and that each spring they renewed their relationship with mid-air acrobatics, locking their talons together and spiralling towards the ground until they parted company at the last minute, just before they collided into the trees. How exhilarating that must be. Twisting and turning through the sky as one like that. Literally falling in love.

She heard a toot from the road and was just in time to see a blue Panda rattle past, a hand waving out of the driver's window.

He was early!

She threw an arm up in response but it was too late. The car was gone and anyway, he wouldn't have seen her up here.

Damn. She'd missed him. Watching the bloody kite.

She rested her head against the glass and let the warmth seep into her skin.

She really needed to get away from here. Her heart couldn't take much more.

★ ★ ★

'It's always bloody steeperrr than I rrrememberrr,' muttered Annie as she trudged up the

91

road beside Chloé who was wheeling her bike.

Christian had offered them a lift but she'd refused, partly out of habit but also because she didn't want to enter the house smelling of coffee. Not with Véronique there.

'We're nearly home,' chirped Chloé who was used to this hill. She normally only succeded in tackling the first couple of bends up from La Rivière and then she had to get off and walk, her legs not yet strong enough to cycle all the way home.

Annie paused to catch her breath and eased her bags onto the ground, aware that her heart was beating a little faster than normal as it struggled to cope with both the incline and the caffeine. She held a hand to her chest and felt the fluttering pulse beneath skin so thin now that she wondered how it contained the palpitating muscle at all. Feeling her years, she picked up her shopping and was about to continue when she heard a car, downhill and concealed by the bend.

Funny. It had been behind them all the way up. But it hadn't overtaken them yet.

'Keep in a bit Chloé, I think therrre might be someone coming.'

Chloé edged her bike in closer to the verge and Annie dropped back to walk in single file.

But still the car didn't appear.

Must have stopped for something.

They turned the last bend around to the left and out of curiosity, Annie hung back to see if anyone appeared on the stretch of road behind her. She was about to give up when the round headlights and snub nose of an old Renault crept around the corner. She just had time to glimpse a battered green body and to register the plates as out-of-town, when the car slammed into reverse and jerked back out of sight.

How bizarre.

'Come on Annie, slowcoach!'

Chloé was already halfway down the track that led to the farmhouse, frantically waving her on.

Must be lost, Annie thought as she resumed walking. Bloody tourists. Probably using one of those computerised map things. Only last week Christian had to rescue a couple from Toulouse who'd driven into the quarry, blindly following their blasted gadget, and had got their car stuck on a rock. Couldn't go forward, couldn't reverse. Christian had to pull them out with a tractor!

But as she reached the house, stepping over Chloé's bike which had been discarded right in front of the door, she was sure she could still hear the mechanical rattle coming from just round the bend.

She was about to look back again when she saw Véronique sitting at her bedroom window, her face pensive and pale. A wave of concern for her daughter engulfed her and as she entered the house, she forgot all about the car.

★　★　★

Véronique heard the clatter of feet in the kitchen and Chloé's excited voice mingling with the demented barking of the two dogs who worshipped her.

Maman had no doubt talked her into having lunch at the farm. She seemed to enjoy the girl's company. More so than she had done Véronique's when she was the same age.

But Véronique didn't feel bitter. She was simply glad that Maman wasn't on her own all the time. And Chloé was a great kid, full of life.

'Vérrronique? We'rrre having lunch.' Maman's voice came up the stairs.

'Down in a minute.'

Véronique bent to retrieve her crutches from the floor and then stood carefully, her good leg numb from sitting so long. As she was about to turn from the window she saw a vehicle edging up the road, a small, dark green van like the ones that used to come round delivering bread when she was a kid. There was nothing unusual about it. Apart from the fact that it was going so slowly and the front wing was bashed in.

It went past the entrance to the track and then the brake lights flicked on and the van reversed until it was level with the gate. She could just about make out the driver's head, twisted towards the house.

What on earth could have caught his attention, she wondered. There was nothing out there but grass. And Chloé's bike of course.

She moved to get a better view of the driver, but all she could see was a dark shadow. Then, as though he'd seen her watching him, there was a crashing of gears and the van spluttered off up the hill.

94

Strange.

'Vérrronique? Hurrrry up orrrr I'll feed it to the dogs!'

'I'm coming!' Véronique hobbled across the room, wondering if it would ever get any easier living with Maman. She somehow doubted it would.

6

Snow. Big fat flakes spiralling down from a grey blanket of cloud.

It had started the day before and hadn't let up, deep tracks marking the white surface of the road from the few cars that had braved it. Bernard Mirouze had been past a few times in the tractor, the snowplough fixed to the front clearing a path which was quickly covered behind him.

Josette had been praying fervently that the inclement weather would put off the inevitable. But it hadn't.

That morning, a white van fitted with snow chains had pulled up in front of the épicerie and the workmen had arrived.

'Are you sure you don't want to close for a couple of weeks?' the foreman was asking Fabian.

'We're quite sure,' she replied before her nephew could open his mouth. She turned from the window and faced the two men.

'It'll be very disruptive.' The foreman twisted the ends of his moustache and glanced at Fabian as though imploring him to make the old lady see sense.

'We've coped with worse,' she responded haughtily, drawing her cardigan about her and flouncing past them into the bar.

Not that it could be called the bar any more.

The three workmen and Fabian had toiled all morning and had transformed it into a shop with tins, bottles and jars piled high on the table, makeshift shelves erected against the walls, strings of saucisson hanging from a hook and the till placed next to the coffee machine. Poor Jacques was looking lost in the inglenook.

Still, it was only for two weeks. And then . . .

She dared not think about it. The plans Fabian had outlined were impressive but, at the same time, she was worried that they would lose something precious amongst the gleaming new surfaces and fancy display cases. And so she was putting up resistance, letting it be known that she wasn't totally on board, as Fabian liked to say.

Maybe she was more like Jacques than she'd realised. Now there was a thought!

'Where do you want the knife cabinets, Tante Josette?'

She pointed at the front door. 'Put the tall one over there next to the bread and the other one here, on the table.'

Fabian edged the wicker basket to the side to make room, trying not to smile when he saw the loaves piled on top of each other, their crusty surfaces dusted with flour, not a fingermark in sight. He'd been astounded when Josette had suddenly announced at the beginning of the week that she was willing to give the organic ones a try. He didn't know what had changed her mind, but the new baguettes were selling well.

He retreated into the shop where one of the

workmen was now busy pinning up a dust sheet to keep out the worst of the mess created by the renovations from the bar. The other two were carefully lifting the upright display case.

'Be careful with that!' he whispered. 'She'll have a fit if you break it.'

The older of the two gave him a wink and Fabian tried not to notice the smears his grease-covered fingers were leaving on the glass.

She'd be muttering for days. Still, it would give her something to do while the work commenced!

He looked around the space they'd just cleared, the true size of the épicerie apparent now the fridge was gone, the shelves were empty and the baskets of fruit and vegetables no longer cluttered the floor. It was big. And already a lot lighter.

During the move, they'd found a packet of old cigarettes down the back of the counter, a bar of soap under the fridge and a newspaper from August 1939, proclaiming war was imminent, wedged behind the dilapidated cheese cabinet that hung on the wall.

He wondered if Tante Josette had noticed the irony, seeing how hostile she was to the changes they were about to make. She'd been awkward about hiring men from outside the area, saying it was disloyal to the locals, and then when he'd found a local company who could fit them in right away, she'd said it was too sudden. When he'd finally talked her round, she'd refused to even contemplate closing the shop while the work progressed. Which was crazy. Perhaps she didn't appreciate how much dust would be generated by knocking down the back wall and opening up the épicerie into the bar.

But all the hassle was worth it. It was going to be unlike anything Fogas had ever known.

'Just this to go through now then,' said the foreman, moving towards the glass display case on the counter.

'I'll get it!' Fabian crossed the floor and slipped his hands under the wooden base. He lifted it gently and cradled it against his chest like a baby. 'She's very particular about this one.'

'As you wish,' muttered the foreman, rolling his eyes at the other men. 'All right if we get on with it then? Start knocking the wall down?'

Fabian nodded, and turned towards the door. One of the men held the sheet back, allowing him through and with his mind concentrating on the load he was carrying, he stepped into the bar.

Josette's head snapped up when she saw him. Or more importantly, saw what he was carrying.

'I'll take that!' Anxious to retrieve Jacques' most treasured possession from the clumsiest man she'd ever known, she lunged towards him.

What happened next was inevitable.

Fabian took a step to the side to avoid her and his heel caught in the trailing edge of the dust sheet. His left leg now static, the other leg somehow managed to wind itself around it as he staggered sideways and before Josette could avert the accident, he toppled over, arms spiralling windmill-like, the display case tossed up in the air.

Josette could only watch, the long table blocking her path, as Fabian crashed to the ground. Then a flash of movement came from the inglenook as Jacques leapt into life and threw himself across the room, arms outstretched to catch the case he had cherished for so long.

The seconds seemed like minutes as she saw it falling, falling, falling into his arms.

Then it plummeted straight through them and hit the wooden floor.

Silence followed, punctuated only by the dull thud of a sledge hammer against bricks and mortar from the shop next door.

Fabian groaned and sat up, holding his long chin which had taken the brunt of his tumble.

'Is it broken?' he mumbled and Josette nodded, not trusting herself to speak.

Jacques meanwhile, overcome with grief, sloped off towards the dust sheet and melted through the wall.

Poor man. He'd adored that cabinet. The day he'd bought it he'd been like a dog with two tails, or a man with ten knives!

'A bargain,' he'd proclaimed as he swaggered into the shop with the case in his arms. They hadn't been married long, hadn't got much money either. Which had made the thousand francs he'd spent on the knives seem excessive.

'Where did you get them?' she'd demanded, trying to be stern but undermined by his boyish enthusiasm.

'A salesman at the market. He was on his way back from a fair in Toulouse and only had one set left. I'd have been mad not to buy them.'

'Are they genuine?'

He'd turned a hurt look on her. 'What do you take me for? He let me handle them and everything. That's a Laguiole Damascus blade right there! Worth a fortune. He even took them to his van and cleaned them for me.'

The shop had become busy and they'd talked no more until that night when he'd placed the knives next to the till and declared they were not for sale. She'd questioned whether they could afford to keep them but he'd said they were an investment. To preserve their value, they were out of bounds to everyone and to safeguard them, he would have the only key. And from that day on, they had sat on the counter in their glass cabinet. She had never seen him open the case, but occasionally she would catch him looking down into it with a wistful expression.

Over the years that followed, she'd encouraged him to get them out, tried to persuade him to let Fabian have a look at them when he was there on holiday. But Jacques was resolute. They were not to be touched. And they hadn't been.

Until now.

The glass had smashed and the floor was littered with knives.

'I'm so sorry,' Fabian was saying as he bent down to pick them up.

She wanted to slap them out of his hands she was so angry with him.

'That's weird. Tante Josette . . . '

'What?' she snapped.

'Look!'

He was holding the Corsican Vendetta, the

handle etched with the trademark Moor's head. He pulled out the blade, a vicious slice of metal, and proceeded to stab his hand.

'What are you doing?' she screeched as the knife pressed into his palm.

And then she saw the blade buckle and break. 'I don't understand . . . '

'It's plastic. They all are.'

'WHAT?' She grabbed the knife and thrust her thumb against the steel. Warm. Soft. Pliant. 'But . . . but . . . '

Fabian was testing the others and shaking his head. 'The whole lot. Jesus. All these years.'

He handed her the Laguiole and she bent it between her fingers. It yielded instantly, more damask than Damascus.

'Do you think he knew?' Fabian was as stunned by the discovery as she was.

She started to shake her head. And then her kaleidoscope of memories shifted, as though jolted by this revelation, old patterns merging with new to form an entirely different picture of the last forty-six years.

'The bugger,' she muttered.

The movement of the dust sheet caught her eye and Jacques stood there, wringing his hands, his white hair now coated with building debris. She knew that look. Last time she'd seen it had been the morning after the Fogas fête in the summer of 1971 when he'd finally won the annual petanque tournament with Serge Papon. They'd proceeded to celebrate like the champions they thought they were. And the next morning he'd crawled home, full of remorse.

102

That had been for one night of misbehaviour. This was an entire lifetime's worth.

'I think,' she said to Fabian while her stare skewered her husband to the floor, 'it might be better if you gave me a bit of space.'

★ ★ ★

Up in Picarets the weather was just as bleak as in the valley below. And for Christian, standing at the edge of one of his fields, the future didn't look any better.

He was a failure. A failure as a farmer, a failure as a son. Just as well he was single, he thought bitterly. No doubt he'd end up a failure as a husband and father too.

He'd just got back from St Girons where he'd spent an hour with the accountant going over the year-end books, and for the first time since he'd taken over the farm, it had made a loss.

'No need to worry,' the accountant had said blithely. 'Most farmers around here operate at a loss.'

But Christian and his family weren't most farmers and the thought of having to break the news to Papa was what had brought him out in the snowstorm. He'd rather be out here than in the house, avoiding his father's eye whenever he asked how things had gone in town.

The visit to the bank manager the week before hadn't brought much comfort either. After much cajoling, Christian had secured an overdraft but the bank weren't keen to extend it too far. In fact, the bank manager had warned him that tough times were coming and the banks wouldn't be able to keep bailing out the farmers.

No matter how he viewed it, things weren't good.

He scratched his head, the motion catching the eye of the only occupant in the field, and the low toll of a cow bell sounded as Sarko, Christian's Limousin bull, looked up. He bellowed at the farmer, his breath condensing into soft clouds around his nostrils, as though to remind him that things weren't over yet.

Soon the cows in the field near the house would start calving and Christian would have another year of Russian roulette, hoping that the calves would all be born fit and well and able to put on meat, that cattle prices would soar and that his farm would remain free from bluetongue and TB, both of which had plagued the area in the last few years.

An outbreak of either disease would mean the end.

But even if they made it through the season without any calamities, the outcome of their hard work would always be the same. Lower and lower profit margins. If only they could get a fair price for their meat. It drove him mad when he visited the supermarket and saw steaks for sale at eighteen euros a kilo when he knew that he was only getting a fraction of that for his stock.

'Everything all right, Christian?' A small hand slipped inside the crook of his arm and his mother stood next to him, her head barely up to his chest.

'Fine, Maman,' he lied.

She pulled a face. 'You don't look it. Did you get bad news?'

Christian nodded and she grasped his arm tighter, her knuckles white.

'I don't want to tell Papa. Not until I've had a chance to think.'

'You're right. He'll only fret. Did the accountant give you any advice, any help on how to turn it round?'

Christian snorted. 'No. Just the bill.'

'So what are you . . . we . . . going to do?'

'I don't know. I'd quite like a second opinion on the accounts. Maybe we can make more cutbacks, save a bit of money that way.'

Josephine Dupuy laughed. 'I could stop trying to cook! I only burn everything anyway. But there is someone you could talk to. Someone who's good with figures.'

'Who?'

When she told him, Christian wondered why he hadn't thought of it before.

'You're a genius!' he proclaimed, kissing the top of her head before taking off towards the car.

'You're going now? In this?' Josephine gestured at the snow still falling around them. 'You'll miss your dinner.'

'That's what I'm hoping,' he replied with a grin as he backed out the car and slowly took off down the hill.

★   ★   ★

The woodpile behind the épicerie was cold but at least it was sheltered. Fabian hunkered down

105

into his jacket and stared out at the swirling flakes, the cat from the Auberge immediately jumping on to his lap.

He hadn't expected this, not after the burst of spring they'd had last week. He'd been sure the winter was over with the tips of daffodils peeking through the soil and he'd started looking forward to long rides up the mountains in the sunshine.

Instead, they had snow. Lots of it.

Of course the locals had warned him. René in particular had droned on about some old wives' tale, something about the winter not being over until the cuckoo has sung. Or was it that there would be more snow after the cuckoo had sung?

Whatever. Either way it involved a blasted cuckoo and according to everyone, the fat bird had yet to sing.

He pulled the cat closer into his body, stroking her in return for the warmth she generated.

'You escaping from home too?' he asked and she purred loudly in response.

When Josette had asked him to give her some space, his natural inclination had been to go for a ride, but with the weather, he was trapped. The shop was now a building site and the thought of being banished to his bedroom was too much. So he'd decided to brave the elements and seek solace amongst the wood. With the cat for company. And something else he'd confiscated off a young lad he'd caught stealing cigarette papers in the épicerie last week.

'Mind if I join you?'

Christian was looming over him, his hair and shoulders dusted white.

'Be my guest,' Fabian said, shaking his neighbour's hand. 'But you're not getting the cat!'

Christian laughed and sat down.

'Josette said I would find you out here.'

Fabian tipped his head in acknowledgement. 'She's angry with me.'

'I think she's more angry with herself. She told me about the knives.' A soft chuckle followed. 'Just as well Jacques is dead. I wouldn't want to face her right now.'

'Poor Tante Josette. It would have been better if I hadn't dropped them. Then she would never have known. Could have just kept on polishing the glass.'

'You weren't to know he'd been deceiving her all these years.'

'When do you think he found out?'

'That night probably. Opened the box and discovered his costly purchase was nothing but a lot of plastic with rocks in the bottom of the case to make it feel heavier.'

'No wonder he never let me play with them!' Fabian's face fell. 'I don't think it's just the knives though. I may have been pushing her too hard. Insisting on too many changes.'

Christian leaned back against the wood, taking time to consider his answer.

'I don't know. It hasn't helped that you took out the restraining order against Stephanie. She's well liked in the commune.' He paused, trying to gauge how much more he could say. 'It might help your cause if you lifted it.'

'I may have overreacted,' Fabian admitted. 'After all, she's gone nearly a month without

107

trying to kill me again!'

Christian's laugh sent a staccato of white breath into the cold air.

'You think that would do it?'

'It'd be a start. And don't forget, you've had some good ideas. The coffee machine is very popular and the new bread is fantastic . . . '

'But . . . ?'

'Well,' Christian continued, 'you need to remember that the épicerie hasn't changed in over fifty years. And for Josette, no matter how much she welcomes your innovations, she's torn by her loyalty to Jacques. You need to give her time. People around here don't do things in a hurry!'

'And you drove all the way down from Picarets in a blizzard to tell me that!'

'Not quite. I came down to ask you for advice.'

Fabian glanced at him in surprise.

'I've got some figures for you to look at, if you don't mind.'

★ ★ ★

'So that's about it.'

Twenty minutes was all it took for Fabian to see the full picture. And to explain it in crystal clear terms. Christian folded up the paperwork and slipped it back inside his jacket pocket.

'Christ,' he muttered, scratching his head. 'It's worse than I thought.'

'Sorry.' Fabian stroked the cat, uncomfortable to have been the one to tell the farmer the bad news.

'I'll have to sell the farm,' Christian said, his voice strangled. 'God, I could do with a drink.'

'So could I but the bar is out of bounds until further notice. However, I do have an alternative.' Fabian reached into his pocket and pulled out a plastic bag full of what looked like dry grass.

'Where did you get that?'

'Took it off some lad who was trying to steal from the shop. Told him I was going to hand it over to the police.' His slender fingers were already busy rolling a cigarette which he lit with a long drag and then passed to Christian.

'I haven't done this in years!' exclaimed the farmer as he inhaled and felt the smoke drift down into his lungs. 'We used to go up behind the cowsheds when we were kids. Papa caught us once and took the dope off us.'

'Probably did what we're doing now!'

'Yeah!'

They passed the joint between them in silence for a while as the cat dozed in the sweet scented air.

'Maybe this is the solution to your problems,' Fabian finally said.

'Hmm? Become a junkie?'

'No, diversify. Grow dope. In a big polytunnel like Stephanie has.'

Christian giggled. 'Might be a bit obvious. Most of the growers in this area at least hide it in the woods.'

'You could pretend they were tomato plants.'

But Christian wasn't listening. Through a haze of inertia, he was trying to focus on something

109

Fabian had just said.

'You might be on to something there,' he declared. 'Think I'll walk down to see Paul at the Auberge once I've had a look at this flat for Véronique. Get dinner down there while I'm at it. I'm starving all of a sudden!'

He extended his hand once more and grasped Fabian's tightly.

'Thanks. You staying out here?'

Fabian nodded. 'Just a bit longer. Give Josette a chance to calm down.'

He watched the big man wander off down the garden towards the épicerie, white flakes dancing around him as he went. Then he stubbed out the cigarette in the snow, popped the butt in his pocket and lifted the sleeping cat off his lap.

Time to face the music.

★   ★   ★

The situation was so absurd, Josette didn't know whether to laugh or cry.

She'd spent the last half-hour berating Jacques, her voice in a low hiss to avoid the builders overhearing, which simply meant she had to repeat everything as her husband's hearing was as selective as it had been in life.

'And don't cup your ear at me! I know you can hear.' She prodded the fire with venom, the flames spitting in reply which made Jacques recoil in his seat. 'You should count yourself lucky that you're already dead!' She brandished the poker at him.

Which was when Fabian walked in.

110

'Tante Josette?' He looked alarmed to see his aunt wielding a weapon at an empty inglenook. 'What are you doing?'

'Just trying to loosen my shoulders. Bit stiff. Think it's the cold.' She laid the poker down and shot Jacques a dirty look before she straightened up. 'Did Christian find you?'

Fabian nodded, his hands rifling through the pile of stock on the table.

'What did he want?'

'Oh nothing much. A chat,' he said, still rummaging.

'What are you looking for?'

'Chocolate. I was sure we had some.'

'Chocolate? Thought you didn't eat it,' she said as she fished out a bar of Milka and handed it to him.

He tore open the packet greedily and started eating.

'Are you okay?' he asked after the first mouthful. 'About the knives I mean?'

Her lips tightened and she couldn't help but look at her husband who was willing her to say yes.

But Fabian didn't wait for her reply.

'Perhaps it's for the best anyway,' he gabbled. 'Kind of symbolic maybe?'

'In what way?'

'Well, maybe now you don't need to feel as loyal to Oncle Jacques. Maybe that was what was stopping you from embracing the future. Breaking that cabinet and finding out that the knives were all fakes, it kind of means you're free now. Free to change.'

He wandered off towards the stairs munching his chocolate, leaving her open-mouthed and her thoughts in turmoil.

He was right. This had been cathartic. She no longer had to worry about Jacques' opinion or about betraying him by moving forward. Now she could indulge in a bit of that blue sky thinking Fabian was always going on about. Think outside the box, whatever that meant.

She laughed, a low throaty chuckle, and sat down next to Jacques.

'Seems like your nephew might be right for once,' she whispered. 'You're forgiven, you rascal.'

He leaned forward, eyes alight, and she felt a cool breeze of air on her skin as he kissed her on the cheek.

'Any more of that chocolate, Tante Josette?'

Josette leapt up, her face burning, but it didn't matter. Fabian hadn't seen anything. He'd already found another bar of Milka and was sloping back out of the room, leaving her and Jacques giggling like adolescents in his wake.

7

'Now are you sure you'll be all right?' Josette asked for the fourth time later that evening and Chloé, Fabian and Véronique answered in unison.

'Yes!'

'Come on, Josette. The council meeting is only going to last a few hours and what could possibly go wrong?' Christian placed a hand under her elbow and steered her towards the front door. She twisted round at the last minute to give Jacques a meaningful stare but he was sitting, very contrite, in the inglenook.

'Don't worry about the fire, Tante Josette. I'll make sure it doesn't go out,' Fabian said, misunderstanding her concern.

Before she could reply, Christian had ushered her out into the night and the last thing she saw as the door closed behind her was Jacques grinning at Chloé and rubbing his hands.

'Lord help me,' she muttered.

'Sorry?' Christian asked as he got into the car beside her.

'I said Lord it's cold.'

'You're not wrong there. Let's hope this baby can make it up the hill with chains on.' He patted the steering wheel affectionately and then turned the key in the ignition.

The car rattled round the corner, the engine already straining, and was soon out of earshot.

'Thought she'd never go!' said Fabian. 'Now, who's for a coffee. Or hot chocolate?'

Chloé's hand shot into the air.

'Sounds great. I'll have a coffee and then nip down to have a look at that flat.' Véronique settled herself at the table where Chloé was already spreading out her school books.

'Goodness, you're keen,' Véronique laughed. 'It's only just the start of half-term and you're doing your homework on the first night?'

Chloé nodded solemnly. 'It gets it out of the way.'

'What are you doing?'

'An essay. On my family.' Chloé grimaced and Véronique understood.

'Don't you like writing about your family?' asked Fabian tactlessly as he placed her hot chocolate before her.

'There's not much to write about. I only have Maman.'

Fabian cursed inwardly. That joint he'd had with Christian seemed to have loosened his tongue.

Véronique reached across to the girl who was chewing on the end of her pencil.

'I didn't like writing about my family either!' she confided. 'So I used to make stuff up about my dad. Pretend he was a film star or a pilot.'

Chloé's eyes widened. 'Didn't you get told off?'

Véronique grinned. 'Oh yes. But then no one could tell me it wasn't true.'

'So you didn't know who your dad was either?'

'No. Still don't.' Véronique managed to keep her tone light.

'Doesn't it bother you?'

'Sometimes. Father's Day. Stuff like that.' She shrugged, aware that Fabian could hear every word and knew the truth.

'So you think it would be all right if I did the same?' asked Chloé.

'Well, what would you write if you could?'

Chloé sat back in her chair and crossed her arms behind her head, the pencil sticking out of her mouth.

'He'd be an acrobat!' she said. 'With long legs and silky black hair. And he'd be from Paris.'

'That's very detailed,' said Fabian as he hung the cycling kit he'd washed that day on the back of a chair to dry, a lock of hair falling across his face as he bent over. 'Sounds like you have someone in mind.'

'I do!' Chloé watched him walk back to the bar and Véronique smothered a smile behind her mug of coffee.

'Right,' she said as she put down the empty mug. 'I won't be long.'

She pulled her coat on and hobbled across the floor.

'Do you need a hand?' Fabian offered.

'No. It's stopped snowing at last and besides, it's best if I view it alone.'

She opened the door and let herself out into the sharp night air, the stars outshone by the crystals that covered the pavement in the moonlight. She took a deep breath and carefully inched down the road, keeping into the edge where the snow was less icy.

Christian had picked her up that evening, full

of praise for the flat in the old school which he'd seen earlier in the day. According to him it was just the thing she needed, ideal in every way. And he hadn't understood why she hadn't shared his enthusiasm.

But then he didn't know her connection with the building, the horrible memories it held for her.

She saw it ahead, its snow-draped roof outlined against the mountain behind, a single light glowing in one of the arched windows on the top floor.

She felt herself beginning to shake and knew it wasn't from the cold.

'This is ridiculous,' she berated herself and forced her feet through the gateway that had been the entrance to hell for so much of her life.

★ ★ ★

'Two more hot chocolates it is then!' Fabian said as he started mixing powder in mugs.

'Can I have a peek next door while you make them?' asked Chloé.

'Don't see why not. But don't touch anything. And don't get your clothes dirty. Last thing I need is your mother angry at me!'

Chloé motioned for Jacques to join her and the two of them slipped under the dust sheet and through the door into the shop.

'It's huge!' Chloé exclaimed, marvelling at the space which yawned before her. She carefully climbed over the mound of rubble where the back of the épicerie used to be and peered into

116

the storeroom beyond. That too had been emptied, Fabian having carried everything down to the cellar until the work was over. In a corner, he'd stacked the shelves he'd taken down which were destined for the fire, and all that remained were a couple of calendars, the most up to date being 1975, and a faded enamel plaque covered in debris propped against the wall.

Chloé picked up the plaque and blew on it, a swirl of dust enveloping Jacques who started sneezing, staggered backwards and promptly fell over a pile of bricks making Chloé laugh. It was like watching one of the Max Linder movies that Maman sometimes took her to see in Toulouse: all action and no sound.

Jacques shook his head vigorously, dislodging bits of mortar from his hair, and then slowly got back to his feet, rubbing his backside dramatically.

'Are you okay?' she giggled.

He glowered at her from under dusty eyebrows and leaned over her shoulder to look at what she was holding.

'It's beautiful,' she said, twisting it so he could see it better.

The central image was a little girl who was reaching up to write on a wall, a basket of food at her feet. Across the top the words *Chocolat Menier* stretched from side to side. Chloé blew on the surface again, this time holding it away from Jacques, and the words the girl was writing became clear.

Beware of imitations!

'Do you think I could have this?' Chloé asked,

her fingers tracing the outline of the child.

But before Jacques could answer, the muffled sound of voices in the bar filtered through to them.

' . . . do you know her?' came the twang of a stranger with a northern accent.

'Stephanie Morvan . . . ' The rest of Fabian's reply was drowned out by the coffee machine as it gave one of its periodic gurgles.

'Could be . . . has a daughter . . . some advice on organic gardening.'

Even with her ear fixed firmly to the door, Chloé couldn't catch everything that was being said, but it was enough.

'He's asking about Maman. And me!' she whispered at Jacques.

'That's her,' they heard Fabian continue. 'She works at the Auberge . . . open a garden centre . . . '

Filled with curiosity, Jacques motioned for Chloé to stay where she was while he melted through the wall, holding his breath as he slipped between the bricks, having ingested enough debris for one night thanks to Chloé's dusting techniques.

He emerged blinking into the bright lights of the bar, and could see the man Fabian was talking to. He was short with straggly black hair sticking out from beneath a baseball cap, his legs stocky, encased in a pair of Le Chameau St Hubert hunting boots, and his shoulders broad beneath the camouflage jacket he was wearing.

'Been hunting?' Fabian asked, thinking Josette

would be proud of him, making small talk with a customer.

'You could say that,' came the enigmatic reply as the man pointed at a poster behind the bar for the locally brewed La Brouche beer which Fabian had persuaded Josette to start selling. 'I'll take four of those and a packet of Gauloises.'

Fabian mentally rolled his eyes. What was it with people around here?

'Sorry, we don't have any Gauloises. Would Marlboro Lights do?'

The man snorted his derision. 'Just the beer.'

'Right. Back in a minute.' Fabian disappeared down the stairs to the cellar and the man turned round, his gaze piercing Jacques as he hovered behind him.

And what a gaze it was.

Jacques shuddered as ice-blue eyes, ringed with dark circles and glazed with venom, stared straight through him.

With the calculated air of a hunter, the man stepped quickly, quietly, over to the fire and plucked one of Fabian's cycling gloves off the chair where it was drying. Then he crossed silently to the coat stand, his hand slipping into each of the pockets of Fabian's jacket in turn. A sneer twisted his face as he pulled out what looked like a cigarette butt from one of them.

'Just the thing,' he muttered as he stuffed both items into his rucksack and when Fabian came back up the stairs, beer in hand, the man was standing nonchalantly at the bar, running the edge of his thumb along the blade of his knife, an ugly block of metal and wood with

119

no poetry to it at all.

Jacques couldn't make sense of it. If someone was going to steal, why not steal something of value?

'There you go,' said Fabian as he took the customer's money and handed him his change. 'Have a nice night.'

'Oh, I will, I will.' The man picked up the beer and slipped out into the dark leaving Jacques with his heart thundering.

There was something not right about the stranger. He didn't look like the type who'd be interested in organic gardening, not with the hunting boots and the brutal Muela knife that was made only for killing. So why did he ask about Stephanie and Chloé and then take some of Fabian's belongings?

The man was an impostor. And all of Jacques' long experience, in life and death, was warning he would bring trouble.

He floated back through the wall to where Chloé was rubbing her right ear, numb from being pushed against the door so long.

'Has he gone?' she whispered and Jacques nodded.

'I couldn't catch it all. Who was he?'

Jacques shrugged, a frown pulling his bushy eyebrows together.

'Think!' he admonished himself tapping a knuckle against his forehead. He had to raise the alarm, but how? Then he had a flash of inspiration.

The plaque.

He gestured at the oblong sign that Chloé was

120

still clutching to her chest and she turned it so he could see. She watched as his ghostly finger underlined the words the girl was scrawling in thick crayon.

''Beware of imitations,'' she read, looking at him for an explanation. But now he was pointing at the wall. The wall that separated the shop from the bar.

Despite her aversion to school, Chloé was by far the brightest child in her class and her brain was already doing somersaults, trying to make a connection between Jacques' mimes.

'The man in the bar?' she offered.

He nodded and then jabbed a finger at the writing on the plaque once more.

'You mean him? He's an imitation?'

Jacques clapped at her cleverness.

'So we should be wary of him?'

Jacques' face was sombre as he tipped his head in confirmation.

'But,' said Chloé, her voice quivering with concern. 'I don't know what he looks like!'

And Jacques felt a shiver race up his spine. The heavy tread of a man in hunting boots had just walked over his grave.

★　★　★

Christian was getting more and more frustrated. The council meeting was supposed to be a formality, a simple vote on two items and a preliminary discussion on the budget for the year.

But as always, things in Fogas never went to plan.

121

'Quite frankly,' came the pompous accent of Pascal Souquet from the head of the table, 'I fail to see the necessity for yet another commercial venture in Fogas. We already have the épicerie and the Auberge.'

'No thanks to you!' barked René Piquemal making Pascal's face tighten with annoyance.

It was the first proper meeting of the Conseil Municipal since the controversy surrounding the purchase of the Auberge by the British couple had been settled and tempers were running high. The atmosphere wasn't helped by the fact that Pascal had eschewed the informality that normally reigned and insisted that everyone sat in their designated seats, according to their rank in the election. Which meant he was at the top of the table as deputy mayor. And, as the other deputy, Christian was forced to sit next to him.

'Oh come, come, René,' patronised Geneviève Souquet, cousin of Pascal and a second-home owner from Toulouse who only graced the commune with her presence on a handful of days a year. And to attend council meetings. 'I seem to remember you voting to close the place too.'

René squirmed under the accuracy of her remark, embarrassed into silence by the role he had played in what was a dark period in the history of Fogas.

'I think we need to move on,' said Christian, unable to bite his tongue any longer. 'What happened over the Auberge is in the past and it won't help to dwell on it.'

He looked around the U-shaped table where

the councillors were sitting, his eyes resting in particular on Bernard Mirouze who was trying to avoid his gaze, thumbing through a hunting magazine on the table in front of him.

A couple of months ago, on the night Sarko the bull was let out of his enclosure, Christian would have killed the person responsible if he could have got his hands on them. Now he was pretty sure the chubby man facing him had been involved but he had no way of proving it. And even if he did, he knew that the *cantonnier* had been a mere tool, wielded by a masterful hand. One that wasn't present this evening.

'And in the absence of our mayor, Serge Papon, who has entrusted me with deputising for him, I have the right to propose that we proceed to the vote.'

'Actually, you don't.'

The voice came from the public gallery beyond the table.

'What do you mean, Fatima?'

A sour-faced woman rose from amongst the crowd of locals who had attended the session, their numbers swollen in the hope of seeing some action given the simmering tension that existed between the eleven members of the council.

She smiled at the farmer with all the warmth of a cobra drawing back to strike.

'You don't have the right to propose the vote. Pascal does.' She gestured at her husband to underline her point.

Christian gripped the table. He really didn't need this. Not today. He had enough battles of his own without getting embroiled in more commune disputes.

'Serge Papon left me in charge when he took his leave of absence in January. I have witnesses to prove it.'

'Yes!' René piped up. 'I was there. I heard it myself.'

'I don't care if Jesus Christ himself was there,' continued Fatima, her voice sharp. 'It doesn't count.'

'Perhaps you'd care to enlighten us then?' Christian asked.

'According to the Code Général, Article L2122-17,' Fatima Souquet began, holding up a thick paperback and René groaned, dropping his head into his hands.

'It's always the bloody Code with you, Fatima,' he grumbled but she ignored him and continued, reading aloud from the book at an open page.

''In the case of absence, suspension, revocation or any other cause, the mayor is temporarily replaced in his role by a deputy . . . ''

She paused, a finger holding her place.

'Where's the problem then? Christian is a deputy,' said Monique Sentenac, unwittingly walking straight into Fatima's trap.

'I haven't finished,' came the reply. '' . . . the mayor is temporarily replaced in his role by a deputy, *in the order of their appointment.*''

She slapped the book shut with a triumphant smile. 'So, in adherence with the Code, as Pascal was voted in as deputy first, *he* is the mayor in the absence of Serge Papon.'

'But we've never been that rigid here,' commented Alain Rougé who had served on the council for decades. 'The mayor has never insisted that we stick to the rule book. Not over the little stuff.'

'Well, that says a lot about how the commune has been run for the last twenty-five years,' Fatima sniffed.

'Says more about your uptight tendencies,' muttered René. 'Bet she even has a Code for the bedroom!'

Muffled laughter swept the room but Christian had heard enough. Normally a placid man, his worries over the future of the farm, not helped by a fuggy head following the joint with Fabian earlier, had served to make him much more irritable than usual.

He got slowly to his feet, his face dangerously flushed, and the low murmur which had been circling grew as the villagers in the public gallery strained to get a better view.

'Is that how you think we should run the council then, Fatima?' he asked, the menace in his voice carrying over the noise and silencing it. 'According to the Code?'

Fatima tilted her chin in defiance, ignoring the worried looks from Josette and René who knew the farmer far better than she, and knew that she was heading for trouble.

'Yes! And then we might actually get some proper governance around here.'

'Then,' came the soft response as he stared down at her, 'perhaps you could turn to Article L2121-8 and read it out for us.'

The only sound was the frantic turning of pages as Fatima thumbed backwards through the book.

'Here we are. It says 'In communes with three thousand five hundred inhabitants or more, the council must establish Rules of Procedure . . . ''

She looked up from the Code. 'What does that have to do with anything? It doesn't even apply to us. We barely have a hundred people — '

A loud thud interrupted her as Christian threw a thick sheaf of stapled pages down on the table in front of the other deputy.

'Read the title, Pascal,' he thundered, making him flinch.

''Rules of Procedure for the Conseil Municipal of Fogas,'' Pascal squeaked.

'You see, Fatima,' Christian continued. 'Mayor Serge Papon is a bit better at governing us than you think. He established these rules years ago even though it wasn't compulsory. Now could you turn to page four, Pascal, item eighteen?'

Pascal cast a worried glance at his wife as he rifled through the pages which were creased with age and battered with use and then, in a voice pitched slightly higher than normal, he began to read.

''All council sessions are to be open to the public. The public are to refrain from all manner of intervention and to maintain silence at all times . . . '' He halted, trepidation on his face at the wrath so visible on his wife's.

'So, Fatima, given that you have yet to attain public office, I think this applies to you,'

126

Christian said calmly while René gleefully wagged a finger at her and made *shhh* noises.

'Where did you get that?' hissed Fatima, unable to contain herself.

'I was given it the day I was elected. I've no doubt Pascal has a copy too. Haven't you seen it?'

Pascal's gulp was audible. As was the slamming of the door as Fatima whirled out of the meeting, a loud cheer from René greeting her departure.

'Now, Pascal,' Christian said as he wearily resumed his seat. 'Seeing as you're in charge, could you call a vote please? And then we might be able to get home some time tonight.'

★ ★ ★

While Jacques and Chloé were eavesdropping on the man in the bar and Christian was putting Fatima Souquet in her place, Véronique was wrestling with her own demons.

She'd thought it would be difficult. But not as bad as this.

The walk up the stairs to the flat on the top floor had taken all of her resolve, her every step haunted by flashbacks of her much younger self being chased up the very same route, satchel trailing from her hands, hounded by the kids behind her. But turning the key and entering the apartment had been even worse.

It was her old classroom.

She'd known that. What she hadn't foreseen was that she would be filled with the same paralysis she'd experienced every day of her school life.

Ten minutes she'd been in there and she hadn't got beyond the doorway.

Her palms were sweating, the hair at the nape of her neck was matted and stuck to her, and her legs were quivering like a new born lamb's.

'For heaven's sake, get a grip!' she said out loud, her voice rocking around the bare walls, sounding distinctly like her mother's. 'It's just a bloody flat.'

She took a tentative step forward.

No one shouted. No one jeered.

One foot slowly in front of the other she crossed the room to the back corner where she'd spent her days, alone at her desk, no one willing to sit next to her.

They'd been the last students at the school, a group of fifteen children aged between six and eleven, all taught in the one classroom by the same teacher, Madame Eychenne. Petite and shrill, her resemblance to Edith Piaf having earned her the nickname Sparrow long before Véronique's time, she was an educator who refused to embrace the hippy tendencies of the seventies and ruled her class through fear.

The slightest misdemeanour brought punishment and Véronique had suffered as much as the rest. Rapped knuckles, slapped legs, even the bigger boys weren't exempt. And no one dared go home and tell or they'd receive another blow from a parent who'd learnt from the best of teachers.

Once during break when the bullying grew too

much, Véronique had hurtled into the classroom seeking protection and Madame Eychenne had screamed at her to stop running. When a tearful Véronique had tried to explain her predicament, words mangled by hiccups of distress, she'd been curtly told to grow a backbone and sent back outside. After that, she didn't bother complaining but spent her days wishing the school and Madame Eychenne into oblivion. Her wish was granted, albeit too late for her to benefit.

By the time Véronique left to go to secondary school in Seix, numbers had dwindled and a year later the remaining students were transferred to the larger premises up the mountain in the neighbouring commune of Sarrat. Madame Eychenne retired but died six months later and a decade after that, the abandoned building in La Rivière, the setting of Véronique's torment, had been developed into flats.

Could she really contemplate living here?

She looked out of the window in what would be her lounge, the open bell tower of the church lit up and visible over the roof of the épicerie and behind it, the mountains.

It was just a collection of rooms, that was all. With a good view, great access to the village and, when the post office was rebuilt, right round the corner from work. Plus the commune owned the flat so her rent would be subsidised.

She forced herself to inspect the rest of the small apartment and was pleased to find a decent-sized kitchen and bathroom, even if the bedroom was a bit on the cramped side. Not like she had to share it!

129

Christian was right. She'd be mad not to take it.

Over time she'd make it her own space and erase the bad memories until one day she'd be able to walk through the gate and not hear the word 'bastard' ringing around the playground.

Her throat tightened and before she could stop herself, she was crying, her forehead slumped against the cold glass of the window.

It didn't matter how many pictures she put up or cushions she placed on the sofa. Even with a vase of flowers in the window or the smell of baking coming from the oven, nothing would change.

This building would always remind her of the fact that she didn't have a father. And that was what she would have to live with if she moved in.

But Véronique didn't bear the Estaque name for nothing.

With a few curt words to herself that would have made Madame Eychenne proud, she pulled herself upright and wiped her eyes on her sleeve.

If that was the only thing standing between her and this apartment, then she would just have to do something about it. But what?

She let her gaze wander out over the village and beyond to the dark mass of Cap de Bouirex while her mind raced. And in the shadows of what was to become her home, she finally hit on a plan. One that would possibly solve her problems forever.

★　★　★

The interior of the Panda was unusually quiet as Christian and Josette made their way home from the town hall, the full moon spotlighting the treacherous road which wound down the mountain from Fogas to La Rivière. If Josette had given it thought, she would have attributed Christian's reticence to concentration as he negotiated the bends covered in thick snow, the Panda occasionally sliding despite the chains. Likewise, Christian, if asked, would have said that Josette was worn out from all the commotion at the council meeting.

But neither would have been right.

Josette's silence was caused by an overwhelming sensation that she would return to find the épicerie nothing but a pile of cinders and ash with Jacques wandering aimlessly over it, wringing his hands. She wasn't an expert in the lifecycle of ghosts but she was pretty sure they couldn't die and it would be just like him to cause an accident that left him homeless. As for Fabian and the others, she didn't even dare think about it.

She'd been an idiot for agreeing to go to the meeting. It hadn't even been worth it, a bunch of adults arguing over arcane protocol. When they'd finally got around to voting, Stephanie's project had been approved by a good majority, no one had contested Véronique being allocated the vacant flat, and the planning permission for Philippe Galy's barn conversion had got the green light. It would now be forwarded to the relevant authorities in St Girons for further consideration.

131

The discussions over the budget, however, had not run so smoothly. With Christian allowing Pascal to take charge, the debate had waffled on without direction until she'd almost walked out, so desperate was she to get back to the épicerie. She'd actually found herself wishing it was Serge Papon's ample backside that filled the chair at the top of the table and not the scrawny derrière of his incompetent deputy.

Thankfully, word was that the mayor would return before the next meeting. But whether Josette would be attending would all depend on what she encountered when they finally got down to the village.

She grasped her handbag more tightly and willed Christian to hurry despite the conditions.

'Is my driving making you nervous?' asked Christian, seeing her knuckles tense out of the corner of his eye.

'No, not at all. Just looking forward to getting home.'

'Huh. Glad one of us is,' muttered Christian.

Josette saw his worried profile in the flash of moonlight coming through the bare branches of the trees lining the narrow gorge.

'Is everything okay?'

'No. Not at all. It's the farm.'

'What about the farm?' Josette twisted in her seat to see him properly, concerned by the defeat in his voice.

He cast a glance at her as though deciding how much to say. Then he sighed in resignation.

'Look, Papa and Maman don't know the full details yet so not a word, all right?'

Josette nodded, her own fears forgotten by the unusual intensity in the young man's voice.

'The farm is in trouble. Financial trouble.'

'But you can turn it around. There's a whole season ahead of you.'

Christian gave a dry smile. 'Thanks for the faith, Josette, but I think the writing is on the wall. I can only see one way out of this.'

'You're not going to . . . '

'Sell? Probably. I'll wait until after the summer and then make a decision.'

The silence returned but this time much heavier than before.

'You can't,' Josette finally whispered. 'It just wouldn't be right.'

Christian shrugged. 'I've looked at all the options. The bank doesn't want to know. And as for diversifying, I've talked to Paul at the Auberge about supplying him directly with meat but even if I'm able to get something like that going, it won't be enough to subsidise the farm. And by the time I get it off the ground . . . '

'But what will you do?'

'Don't know. Try to find work somewhere. Move to Toulouse maybe.'

'And your parents?'

'They have the house Stephanie's renting. They could move in there. Or buy something with the money the farm brings in. I hear property with mountain views goes for a good price these days despite the recession.'

Josette could hear the bitterness in his voice and knew how much this was hurting him.

'You should have said,' she murmured, laying

her hand on his arm. 'You shouldn't be carrying this around all by yourself.'

'It's not like you don't have problems of your own.'

'Yes, but even so. I'm sure Fabian and I will come to an agreement eventually. This . . . this is so much more important.'

'Fabian's got some good ideas you know,' Christian suggested gently. 'He's what's needed around here. A breath of fresh air. A bit of ingenuity. Maybe if I'd been more like him, I wouldn't be in the trouble I am.' He rubbed his forehead in frustration. 'That's what made me so angry at the meeting. People like Pascal and his cronies who want to keep the place mothballed in antiquity so they can marvel at how quaint it all is even as the very heart of the commune is dying around them. Fabian's not like that. He certainly helped me sort things out.'

'Fabian?' Josette asked sharply. 'You've spoken to Fabian about this?'

'Yes,' Christian said warily. 'He went over the figures with me earlier today. Helped me see the light. Or the dark, depending on how you look at it!'

Josette didn't respond and in the silence that accompanied them for the remainder of the journey, Christian was unable to work out if she was annoyed or just surprised.

★   ★   ★

Véronique closed the door of the apartment behind her and carefully made her way down the steps to the concrete yard, no longer the home of kids playing hopscotch or throwing rugby balls. Now it housed the commune tractor and snow-plough, along with containers of grit and salt for the roads.

She edged gingerly around the side of the building towards the gate and in the distance she heard the ping of the bell on the barn door carry across the snow-laden quiet. A squat figure in a camouflage jacket was walking towards a small van, its colour indistinct in the white light of the moon but it looked similar to the one she'd seen the other day up at the farm.

Intrigued, she hurried to get a better view but her crutches kept sinking into the snow and slowing her down. She was just at the gate as the vehicle approached, driver slouched in his seat.

Despite the conditions, it raced past so she didn't see much of the man behind the wheel but as it disappeared around the bend towards Massat, tipping precariously over to the right as it took the corner at speed, she was convinced it was the same van. A dark green Renault 4 Fourgonnette, the front wing dented and smeared with blue paint, and the registration ending in 29. Which department was that? She seemed to think it was one of the northern ones. Somewhere in Brittany maybe?

She'd ask Fabian when she got back, she decided, and she was within crutch-swinging distance of the bar when she heard the familiar splutter of a car engine and Christian pulled up.

Her heart lifted as he clambered out of the

Panda, legs and arms seeming to explode from the small interior.

'See, Josette,' he said as he helped his passenger out of the car and across the snow. 'Your beloved épicerie is still standing!'

Josette didn't take the time to reply, such was her haste to get inside and check that everything was as it should be.

Then Christian noticed Véronique standing in the shadows.

'Véronique!' he exclaimed with the eagerness of a puppy. 'How was the flat?'

'Perfect,' she lied, making her way carefully towards him. 'Simply perfect.'

His face lit up and he enveloped her in a bear hug, his enthusiasm crushing the top of her crutches into her ribs. But she didn't complain; the discomfort when he released her was more acute.

'I knew you'd like it. Think this calls for a celebratory drink,' he declared, holding open the door.

And yet again, as Christian and Véronique slipped into the warmth of the bar, a Fogas resident allowed the dark green van with the out-of-town number plates to slip into the dusty unused corner of her consciousness.

8

'Just there. No, there. Great.'

René placed the TV exactly where Véronique wanted it, rubbing his back as he straightened up.

'And the couch?' Christian asked.

'Between the windows.'

Christian and Paul lowered the sofa to the floor and then in unspoken agreement, promptly flopped on to it, while René switched on the TV.

'Hey!' admonished Véronique. 'No slacking. There's half a van load left to bring up.'

Christian groaned and dragged himself to his feet, hauling Paul up after him.

'How can a woman who lost everything in a fire two months ago have accumulated so much stuff since?' he mused.

'Women!' declared Paul, his English-accented French providing even more emphasis. 'They are same everywhere. Magnet for junk.'

Véronique gave him a friendly clip around the ear before herding the three of them down the stairs.

She still couldn't get over how liberating it was to be without her cast. Not that she was ready to run up the hill to Fogas any time soon, her leg noticeably weaker following its internment. But getting rid of the crutches was a great start. And the doctor had said that as long as she did the exercises he'd given her, there should be no

137

long-term damage. He'd even said she could drive. Which she intended to make the most of in the next few weeks.

'You are not finishing yet?'

Véronique looked up to see Lorna, her arms filled with a bundled up blanket, walking through the gate with Annie. They were both watching René's plump backside emerge from the interior of the van, followed by the rest of him struggling with two chairs and a mirror.

'You need to get betterrr help!' scoffed Annie.

'She's got what she paid for,' René muttered before stomping back up the stairs with his awkward load while Paul and Christian followed carrying a dining table.

'Sounds like the worrrkerrrs could do with a brrreak.' Annie held out the basket she was carrying for her daughter to inspect. 'Got two flasks of coffee off Fabian and Lorrrna has made chocolate cake.'

'We even bring cups and plates,' added Lorna.

'How thoughtful!'

'Did I hear you say coffee?' The dishevelled plumber scowled over the banister rail at them.

'You gets out of bed the other side this morning, no?' laughed Lorna.

'He's given up smoking,' whispered Véronique. 'That's why he's in such a bad mood.'

'I'm in a bad mood because I hurt my back lifting all your belongings!' René retorted as he took the basket from Annie, his nose quivering like a hunting dog on a scent. 'Can I smell . . . '

'Chocolate cake. I makes it this morning so it is still hot. Perhaps it is better to waiting . . . '

But René already had the cake out on the table, his Opinel in hand, and was cutting large chunks while the other two men looked on, drooling.

Véronique rolled her eyes in mock exasperation as Lorna stood in the doorway, taking in the room.

'It is lovely,' she exclaimed and Annie nodded her head in agreement.

The floorboards were partially covered by a huge rug that Annie had provided and the couch, which Alain Rougé had been going to throw out, fitted snugly between the two tall arched windows which dominated the space. Potted plants, courtesy of Stephanie, brightened the corners of the flat and one wall was taken up by an old dresser Josette had donated, its shelves carved with intricate scrolls.

'Where do you buying everything?' asked Lorna as she ran her hand over the polished wood of the table, the light streaming through the window bringing out hues of honey in its glossy surface.

'I can't afford new so in the trocs mostly,' explained Véronique.

'Trocs?'

'They're places where you can buy and sell things,' mumbled Christian through a mouthful of cake. 'Usually furniture. You can get some great bargains.'

Lorna's eyes lit up.

'See,' Paul moaned, knowing that his next day off would be spent trailing around trocs. 'Magnet for junk!'

Lorna ignored him and turned to Véronique.

139

'I bring you something back,' she said and laid the bundle she'd been carrying on the table. 'I think she is needing to come home.'

Puzzled, Véronique started to unwrap the blanket and when she caught sight of the saintly face that lay within its folds, she felt her throat constrict.

'St Germaine!'

She lifted up the statue of the devout shepherdess which had saved her life the night of the fire.

'See she hasn't imprrroved with age!' commented Annie as the sunlight caught the vivid scar around the saint's neck where Christian had performed rudimentary surgery and glued her head back on after her ordeal in the church. Slightly the worse for wear with a wonky shepherd's crook and deformed lamb, the battered statue nevertheless represented something hopeful to Véronique and she had lent it to Lorna and Paul in their darkest hour, hoping the saint would bring them luck. Now, its presence in the flat made all the difference.

She reached up and placed the statue on the top of the dresser.

'Thanks,' she said to Lorna. 'But are you sure you don't mind giving her back?'

Annie snorted into her sleeve.

'Prrrobably glad to! That thing will have been frrrightening off the guests. Now how about that bloody coffee.'

Véronique laughed and then realised she'd never heard the sound of her own laughter in that room before.

'You should have a house warming,' urged René, whose bad mood seemed to have been alleviated by the two slices of cake he'd consumed. 'Really celebrate your new home.'

'Time enough when she gets back,' said Annie as she poured the coffee.

'Gets back? You off somewhere, Véronique?' Christian asked.

Annie cackled. 'You haven't told them?'

Véronique shook her head, her cheeks crimson.

'She's going away forrr a week. Won't say wherrre. Think it's got something to do with that firrreman, Majorrr Gaillarrrd myself!'

'Maman!' Véronique protested, her eyes darting towards Christian who had turned and was staring out of the window as though oblivious to the banter.

'Well, he does keep calling,' continued Annie, her face full of mischief. 'Been haunting us since the inspection at the Auberrrge. I was beginning to think I might have to starrrt setting the dogs loose when I wasn't therrre!'

René and Paul chuckled while Véronique groaned, any reservations she'd had about leaving the farm instantly quashed.

'Prrrobably why she was so keen to move out,' Annie finished off with her usual perception and amidst the laughter, Christian strode out of the room.

'You're in a bit of a rush,' hollered René after him.

'No point dallying,' a terse reply floated up from the bottom of the stairs. 'Some of us have

141

proper work to get to.'

And with that, they cleared up the remnants of their coffee break and began unloading the rest of Véronique's belongings, some of them with heavier hearts than others.

★ ★ ★

Stephanie's heart, in contrast, was as light as a feather. She was floating on air. Dancing among the snowdrops. Head over heels . . .

'Stop right there!' she said out loud as her daydreams threatened to go too far.

But even so, she couldn't erase the grin that had spread itself across her face the night before and had yet to be shifted.

Pierre was coming down to see her.

Coming all the way from Bordeaux for the opening of her garden centre in two months' time.

She'd been wondering whether to invite him, as he'd been such a help to her from the outset. But in the end, it was he who'd suggested it. And she'd been delighted to say yes.

They'd only known each other a month but there was something about him. He was a passionate organic gardener for a start and a keen botanist. She got the sense that he was as excited about seeing the Pyrenean meadows in full bloom as he was about meeting her, hoping to catch a glimpse of a bee orchid while he was down here. Although when she'd told him it might be too early for the orchids to be in bloom, he'd said never mind, he might come again later in the summer.

They'd agreed three days was long enough for a first visit. She hadn't needed to broach the awkward subject of accommodation as he'd asked for the number of the Auberge and had booked his room straight away. Which suited her as she wasn't comfortable with someone staying in the house. Especially as she had yet to raise the subject with Chloé.

God, how was she going to do that?

Chloé would be marrying them off before they'd even had a chance to get to know each other properly.

Stephanie changed gears and the blue van shuddered as she came to a halt at the junction with the main road, the Auberge opposite, window boxes filled with cheerful pansies and the menu board already in place outside covered with Lorna's neat angular writing, so different to the cursive script of a French hand. But at least it was legible.

She checked her watch. Still not midday. She flipped on the indicator and turned right. She just about had time to have a peek at the garden centre before she went to work.

After weeks of backbreaking labour by her and Chloé, the land had finally been cleared and Christian had helped bring the polytunnel down from Picarets. She really needed two but until she saw a bit of return on her investment, she couldn't afford to splash out on a new one, even with the loan that she had just had approved. Especially as she still had to settle up with Fabian for the damage to his bike.

Maybe she should go over to the shop and speak to him about it. She felt bad for not having paid him and from what Christian had said, he was thinking about revoking the restraining order which would make her life a lot easier. So it wouldn't hurt to call in and tell him she was fully intending to pay. It just might take a while.

If she turned on the charm, he might even waive the bill!

Chuckling softly, she got out of the van and stood for a moment taking in the efforts of her hard work. The plot was long and narrow, widening out as it stretched towards the bridge on one side and the car park on the other. Gone were all the shrubs and bushes that had cluttered the area, the brambles now replaced with open spaces that were yet to be filled with plants. And in the centre, stood the polytunnel, looking lonely.

When the fence was erected along the front she would start to plant the rest of it. Until then, although crime wasn't big in the area, she didn't want to risk anyone walking off with her stock.

She walked towards her business, the thrill of pride she'd experienced the day she'd taken possession of the land no less today despite the long hours and the lack of time off. It was beautiful. A little oasis with the river running past at the back, curving around as it flowed down the mountain from Massat and raced towards the weir next to the Auberge, where the roar of cascading water filled the morning air.

'You did a good job, Steph,' she thought to

herself as she stepped on to the grass and her foot sank into the ground, water welling around her shoes.

'What the . . . ?'

The plot was flooded.

The river? But it hadn't rained. And the snowmelt hadn't started yet. She picked her way across to the polytunnel, worried sick at what she might find. If the plants were water logged she may as well give up.

But she'd been lucky. The water was lapping at the door but hadn't yet penetrated, the ground inside still dry.

God, if she hadn't thought to check it. She clenched her jaw at the prospect.

What was the cause though, she wondered as she carried on towards the river, the pools of water lessening with each step.

How bizarre.

The area nearest to the riverbanks was dry. The water seemed to be coming from the road. Which didn't make sense at all.

Unless . . .

She raced across the land, her legs spattered with mud as she splashed her way towards the tap.

It was on. Full. Gushing water pumping out of its spout.

Someone had left the tap on. Deliberately? Accidentally?

She turned it off, tightening it as much as she could, her hands cold in the water which was lapping around the base of it. And that was when she saw the evidence, floating there, telling her exactly who had done this even if she didn't know why.

She fished it out of the puddle and with rage in her eyes, stormed across the road towards the épicerie.

★ ★ ★

The bar was peaceful. The morning business had been frantic, people rushing in on their way to the market. But now, finally, they had reached that lull which lay between mid-morning and midday every Saturday and Josette was glad of the quiet.

After a week of having workmen hammering away next door, it was lovely to be able to enjoy a bit of tranquillity. She wouldn't mind so much if they were making good progress but already they'd extended the timetable from a fortnight to three weeks which hadn't pleased her. Or Fabian. He'd muttered something about local builders, some dry comment about their priorities when they'd announced they were taking Wednesday off to go hunting as it was the last week of the season.

'Wouldn't get that if we'd hired the lads from Toulouse,' he'd stated.

Maybe he was right. The thought of having renovations going on until mid-March filled her with dismay. And soon they would begin knocking through from the shop to make the big archway that would unite the two rooms. That, she was dreading.

'Didn't know helping Vérrronique move in would

146

be such thirrrsty worrrk!' Annie announced as she adjusted her position on her chair by the fire and pointedly tapped her empty cup.

'Do you want another coffee then?' asked Fabian, with a smile. A month and a half after his arrival and finally his ears had tuned in to the special frequency that was Annie Estaque.

'Brrrilliant idea!'

Josette cast a worried glance at her friend and sidled up to Fabian behind the counter.

'Don't you think we ought to ration her?' she whispered. 'She seems to be a bit addicted and it can't be good for her. All that caffeine at her age.'

'Don't worry about it, Tante Josette.' Fabian twisted the filter into place and put a cup underneath it.

'I do worry about it,' hissed Josette. 'It's not all about the profit, you know!'

Fabian gave her a hurt look. 'I know. That's why I've made this.'

He turned the bag of coffee he'd used so she could see it.

Annie's Blend.

'I don't understand.'

'I've been diluting her drinks for the last week, gradually reducing the strength day by day. What she's having right now is virtually caffeine free. But she doesn't know it.'

Josette stared at the label and then looked at her nephew. Really looked at him. His sensitive face was watching her nervously, eyes wary below his dark fringe.

She hadn't given him a chance, she thought.

Not since she'd walked in the door and found him on the floor. And here he was watching over Annie, quietly and with no fuss.

She reached out a hand and stroked his cheek with affection.

'That,' she said, 'is quite possibly the nicest thing anyone has ever done.'

'Yeah, well if she ever finds out, I'm telling her it was your idea!' he quipped as he poured hot milk into the cup and took it over to the table. He was a step away when the door was flung open by a wild-eyed Stephanie who marched into the room, Fabian firmly fixed in her sights.

'Everything okay, Stephanie?' asked Josette as the cup Fabian was holding started to rattle in its saucer.

'Everything . . . is . . . far . . . from . . . okay . . . ' she retorted, the words clipped and measured as though she was holding something back while her green eyes bore into the tall Parisian.

'I'll take that.' Annie reached out and grabbed the cup, tutting at the wasted coffee which was now swilling around the saucer.

'Are these yours?' Stephanie threw two items onto the table, Fabian flinching as her arm rose. He edged cautiously forward to get a better view.

'That's my cycling glove,' he said. 'Where did you get that?'

Stephanie took a deep breath, her powers of self-control at full stretch.

'Don't mess with me, Fabian. You know full well where I found it. And that was next to it!'

She pointed at the sodden cigarette butt. 'Yours too I suppose?'

He was about to shake his head when he remembered. The afternoon with Christian, smoking in the snow. But how . . . ?

He crossed the bar to where his jacket was hanging on the coat stand and frantically checked the pockets. Nothing.

How bizarre.

'Well?' Stephanie barked.

'They do appear to be mine,' he began. 'But where did you find them?'

Stephanie made a noise of disgust.

'What is it?' asked Josette. 'What's happened?'

'Someone turned the tap on across the road last night. Pretty much flooded the whole place. If I hadn't checked this morning I would have lost all of the stock in the polytunnel.'

'But what does that have to do with Fabian?'

'I found both of those over there.'

'But it wasn't me . . . ' spluttered Fabian.

'Right! You were probably so stoned you don't even remember,' retorted Stephanie. 'You know, I was planning on coming over to see you today. To try and put our bad start behind us. But after this . . . ' She threw her arms in the air. 'What's the point? Just stay away from me and from my daughter. She's not allowed in here any more and you are to have nothing to do with either of us. You hear me? NOTHING!'

And with that she was gone, the door slamming in her wake.

'I didn't do it!' Fabian said into the silence that was left behind.

Annie was watching him carefully.

'So why was yourrr glove left therrre?'

'I don't know. I must have dropped it outside when I came in off the bike.'

'And what about the joint?' asked Josette. 'You acknowledge that was yours too?'

'It could be,' he mumbled, knowing she wouldn't approve. 'I confiscated it off that kid who was trying to steal the other day. Then after I dropped the knives . . . ' He shrugged.

'Where?'

'Up at the woodshed.'

'The day Christian called in? Did he . . . ?'

Fabian just looked at the ground and Josette knew he was telling the truth. That was the day Christian had come to him for help. She could see why he thought Fabian was wonderful if they'd been getting high out in the snow!

'So if you didn't do it,' mused Annie, 'who did?'

'I don't know,' said Fabian. 'But I don't think Stephanie is going to believe me. No one around here is going to believe me!'

He turned an accusatory look at Josette but she was too busy watching Jacques who was standing next to the door into the épicerie, the usual patina of dust coating him. He seemed to spend all his time now at the window in the work zone, oblivious to the noise, watching the road as if on the lookout for something, so she was surprised by his appearance in the bar.

Now however, he was gesturing at her. Pointing at Fabian and trying to tell her something.

'Actually, Fabian,' she said, keeping an eye on her husband's reaction, 'I believe you.'

Fabian's eyebrows shot up in amazement while Jacques gave her a big smile.

'It's all a bit strrrange,' Annie was saying and Josette couldn't have agreed more. What on earth had happened to make her husband take the part of his nephew? She watched as Jacques melted back through the wall and Fabian started stoking the fire.

Something was going on in the commune and whatever it was, it didn't feel right.

★ ★ ★

'But I don't understand why he would do such a thing,' said Lorna, placing a tray of salmon and spinach tarts in the oven.

Stephanie had no reply. It made absolutely no sense. Fabian didn't strike her as someone who ever let go so the mere fact that he'd admitted to smoking a joint had surprised her. But the image of him staggering around out of his skull wasn't one she could easily envisage now that she'd had time to calm down and consider things rationally.

He was too uptight. Too controlled.

So what had happened?

She finished washing the radishes she'd brought down from her garden and started on the potatoes. Inspired by a conversation with Christian about the possibility of supplying them with beef direct from his farm, Lorna and Paul had approached Stephanie about providing vegetables for the Auberge and she'd been happy

151

to agree. At the moment it was only on a small scale but, in the future, it could really supplement her other work. When she had time, she'd catch up with Christian and thank him in person for his great idea.

Time. It was a luxury at the moment. If she wasn't working at the Auberge she was gardening or on the computer trying to iron out last-minute problems. Poor Chloé was beginning to think she didn't have a mother. Stephanie had even had to turn down a very lucrative offer from the yoga centre last week. They'd rung up begging her to take some classes over the summer but she'd declined. If all went to plan, she would be too busy in the garden centre.

'So when is the big day?' asked Lorna, now carefully pouring crème brûlée into small ramekins. Stephanie watched her with admiration as she moved from one part of the kitchen to another, working tirelessly, her concentration spread over all the aspects of the meals she was about to start serving. Stephanie knew she would never be able to do it, have her focus so divided and yet be so ordered.

'I must to open before May eleventh. But it is difficult. Zere is still so much to do.'

'Couldn't you delay a bit?' asked Paul as he peeled and chopped the pile of potatoes.

'No, zat is when everyone buys zeir plants. If I am later, it is a disaster!'

'What's so important about the eleventh of May?' he mused, munching on a radish.

'It is ze start of ze three days of icy saints. After zat, we plant.'

152

Paul was looking at her, a radish raised halfway to his mouth.

'The what?'

'*Les saints de glace*. We believe zat after zese days pass, zere will be no damage from ice.'

'I think she means frost,' Lorna said to a still puzzled Paul.

'Frost, yes of course! So, I must to open before zese days, or else the door will 'ave shut after ze 'orse 'as run away.'

'Is there anything we can do to help?' asked Lorna, her attention now on the lamb tajine which was simmering slowly on the stove, filling the air with tantalising aromas.

'Perhaps when I move down ze rest of my stock? But now, maybe it is enough to stop your 'usband eating all of my radishes!'

Lorna laughed and slapped Paul's outstretched hand which was reaching for yet another while Stephanie headed into the restaurant to open up. She flipped the sign on the door to *Ouvert* and through the glass she saw the unmistakable figure of Fabian go past on his bike, stick legs pumping furiously as he went up the road towards Picarets.

So, if it wasn't him who turned on the tap, Stephanie wondered as she watched the rangy silhouette disappear into the trees, who on earth was it?

★ ★ ★

Heart pounding. Breath coming in gasps. Sunglasses misting up.

153

Fabian pushed harder on the pedals, determined to exorcise his bad mood through the effort of getting up the hill to Picarets in record time. Well, his record time.

He felt his legs starting to complain, the steep incline demanding more than they could give but he knew it wasn't much longer. A few more rotations of the wheel and he was around the bend, on the false plateau that passed in front of the Estaque farmhouse.

He eased off as the road began to level out, taking the time to gulp down oxygen, his new heart rate monitor telling him he was in the red zone.

Like he needed telling!

He fiddled with the screen to see the altimeter: 800 metres. Not bad. He'd finally given up waiting for Stephanie to pay him for the damage she'd caused and had bought himself a new Garmin cycle computer which could tell him how fast he'd ridden uphill, the speed of his descent, the distance he'd covered. It did pretty much everything except turn the pedals. He'd bought a new wheel at the same time but it didn't seem to make him any faster than the old one!

Stephanie Morvan.

Even though he'd been determined not to, he found himself thinking about her.

What had he ever done to make her so determined to hate him? She didn't seem to apply logic to any of her decisions. Her first course of action was always exactly that: action, and usually of a violent nature. No time for contemplation. For rational thought.

For example, what possible motive could he have for turning on the tap and flooding her business? *He* wasn't the one who'd tried to kill someone. Twice!

Perhaps that was it? Maybe she'd convinced herself that he was so annoyed, he'd decided to take his revenge on her?

But that simply didn't make sense in Fabian's world, a universe governed by the application of reason, the following of ordered systems. Even his decision to move to Fogas, although seemingly a fit of reckless abandon, had been analysed and dissected until it met with approval.

He'd been accused by one of the few girlfriends he'd had of being a cold fish. And although hurt at the time, in retrospect, he'd begun to think she might be right. Passion was something he didn't subscribe to.

He stood on the pedals as the road kicked up again, leaving the plateau behind and entering the forest once more, clumps of snow still lingering in pockets where the sun didn't penetrate. He was just wondering how long it would be before the higher mountain passes were reopened when the crack of a rifle sounded from the steep hillside to his left, startling him.

Hunters!

That was something he'd not had to contend with around the boulevards of Paris. Thankfully this was the last day of the season but it no doubt meant the woods were crawling with overgrown boys with deadly toys creeping amongst the undergrowth, making the most of it.

Having heard René's tales of hunting mishaps, Fabian settled back in the saddle and kept his attention as much on the forest as on the road ahead. It would be just his luck to get shot. And sure enough, the bushes were shaking, there was a streak of black, the snap of saplings and then a full grown boar crashed on to the tarmac right in front of him.

It was difficult to say who was the more surprised as Fabian came to an abrupt stop while the boar shook its head, long tusks stark white against its dark bristles.

Shit! Fabian's brain had already calculated and dismissed the option of turning tail, the boar being too close. And going past was out of the question.

So he stood there, one foot on the ground, his breath coming in short bursts as the boar sniffed the air and then glared at him.

Pepper spray. In his rear pocket. He'd bought it before he came to the Pyrenees, having read that it was useful against the occasional aggressive dog. But would it work on seventy kilos of angry pig?

He inched his hand towards his back but as his fingers closed around the cylinder, the boar took off, plunging down the precipitous slope to the right, impervious to the danger.

Fabian followed its descent until the beast disappeared from view and then he recommenced his ride. He'd turned the pedals twice when he heard the tinkle of a small bell and the bushes rustled again. This time a hunting dog landed almost under his front wheel.

'Woof!' the beagle greeted him, ears flapping as he raced up and down the road, nose pushed to the tarmac, the bell at his throat jingling. 'Woof!'

He circled back to the bike and promptly rolled over for a belly rub.

'Some hunting dog you are!' said Fabian, bending down to pat the soft fur.

'OUCH! Ow! OUCH! Ow!'

Fabian glanced round at the loud exclamations and was amazed to see the bushes stirring once more, this time moved by a much bigger force, a much larger animal. He caught a glimpse of bright orange and camouflage in quick rotation and then the shape of a man materialised tumbling head over sizeable backside out of the forest and on to the ground.

'Merde!' Bernard Mirouze exclaimed as he straightened his hunting beret and staggered to his feet, his rifle dangling from his shoulder. 'Did you see which way it went?'

'What?' asked Fabian innocently while he continued petting the dog.

'The boar. Where did it go?'

'Oh, the boar. It went that way,' he said and pointed back up the embankment to his left.

Bernard stared mournfully at the steep hillside he'd just descended.

'Are you sure?' he asked, his voice weary.

'Definitely. It came down on the road over there and then went back up the mountain.'

'Damn it!' Bernard snatched off his beret and scratched his head which was covered in leaves

157

and debris from his fall. His mobile sounded and he answered it with resignation.

'Is it there, Bernard?' an authoritative voice issued from the phone.

Bernard looked down at his dog, now writhing around on the ground in ecstasy at the attention Fabian was lavishing on it. Then he looked up at the hill and gave a sigh.

'No,' he muttered, turning his back on Fabian. 'No sign of it. Think I'll call it a day and head for the car.'

'Okay. See you back at the lodge.'

Bernard turned back to Fabian with an apologetic shrug.

'Kind of hard to get the enthusiasm up so late in the season,' he mumbled and Fabian nodded. 'Plus I have the softest hunting dog in the world!'

He scooped the beagle up into a warm embrace.

'We're neither of us much good at hunting, are we, Serge?' he said, giving it a few pats before putting it back on the ground. He bade Fabian farewell, hitched up his trousers and started the long hike down the road, Serge the beagle yapping at his heels.

Fabian cycled up the last stretch of hill and was still chuckling when he arrived in Picarets. Knowing it would be impossible to go much higher with the snow and reluctant to go as far as Christian's grandmother's house which he now knew to be Stephanie's, he rode to the end of the village intending to turn.

On another day, he might not have noticed.

On another day, he might have ridden that bit further and been a bit more curious.

But she'd warned him to stay out of her business.

So when he saw, just visible in the distance, a man coming out of Stephanie's garden, the same thickset man who'd been in the bar asking about her, he made a mental note but nothing more.

He simply wheeled his bike around and began the journey home, eyes alert for boars or hunters dropping out of the surrounding forest.

9

Tuesday. It wasn't Chloé's favourite day. But it also wasn't the worst. The week was two days old, there was no school on Wednesdays, and then only Thursday and Friday remained before the weekend.

And as it was the afternoon and the school day was already over, then this particular Tuesday was getting better and better.

'How many raps today, Chloé?' asked Nicolas Rogalle as he kicked a ball along the road with his twin brother.

'Only two,' announced Chloé with pride. 'And no extra homework.'

Her teacher, Madame Soum, fought a losing battle with Chloé's wandering attention every day, rapping her desk with a ruler whenever the girl's mind was wooed out of the window by the vast expanse of the mountains that filled the view from her seat. It wasn't her fault if the inherent promise of those peaks held so much more allure than the sound of Madame Soum's voice droning on about the history of the revolution or the intricacies of grammar.

'That's 'cos it was maths,' muttered Max with disdain as he hoofed the football up the hill ahead of them and waited for it to roll back down. 'When I'm older I'm never going to use maths. Ever!'

'Yeah,' grumbled his brother in agreement.

'Who needs to know what seven times seven is anyway?'

'Well, I like it. It makes sense.' Chloé took a swipe at the ball and it ballooned into the air, landing in the trees off to the side.

'You kick like a girl!' jeered Max as he jogged off to retrieve it.

'That's 'cos I am a girl, dimwit!' Chloé retorted and Nicolas giggled.

'He's just jealous that's all.'

'Am not!' Max protested, cheeks flaming as he thrust an arm at his twin.

'Are too!' flung back Nicolas as he retaliated with a thump.

'Not!' Shove.

'Are too.' Thump.

Within seconds the two boys were rolling around on the ground, their school bags discarded in a heap, as they pummelled each other in a routine that Chloé was inured to after years of walking home with them. She kept on with her slow pace, knowing that soon they would tire of their fighting and dash after her, just like Annie's dogs when she went out in the fields with them.

But today was different.

To begin with, Max seemed intent on pulverising his twin, probably after a day of frustration at the mercy of multiplication tables and long division. In fact, he may well have continued if it hadn't been for the sound of a car coming up the road behind them.

And that was the second thing.

The vehicle stopped alongside the boys, who'd

managed to get to their feet and rescue their bags before it ran over them, and the driver was speaking to them out of the window.

She could see Max nodding and then the passenger door opened and he hopped in while Nicolas was waving at Chloé to join them.

It wasn't unusual. They often got lifts home after the school bus dropped them at the lay-by opposite the Auberge. And who could blame them, the walk all the way up to Picarets being so long for such young legs.

But Chloé could feel her feet reluctantly heading down the hill. There was something wrong. She didn't know what.

'Come on, sissy, you walk like a girl!' jeered Max.

It was all it took. Goaded by his jibes she ran the remaining few yards to the van, despite her better instincts.

'I'm having front seat,' declared Nicolas and so Chloé climbed in the back next to Max, getting nothing more than a glimpse of the driver's profile, baseball cap thrust low over his face, before Nicolas slammed the door shut with a finality that made her shiver.

And with a crunch of gears, the dark green Renault 4 Fourgonnette set off up the hill.

★ ★ ★

'When's Véronique back then?'

'Frrriday. If she comes back! Might decide to stay away with this Majorrr Gaillarrrd!'

'Where have they gone?' asked Josette as she

162

placed the last of Annie's shopping in a bag for her.

'Don't know. She was verrry secrrretive about it all.'

'Véronique?' joined in Fabian who was staggering into the bar with several crates of beer. 'I know where she's gone.'

The two women waited expectantly but he simply placed the crates down and started towards the cellar stairs once more.

'Hang on a minute!' Josette exclaimed. 'You can't say that and then walk off! Where has she gone?'

'Oh, sorry. Somewhere over near Perpignan. St Paul de something or other.'

'Near Perpignan?' Josette demanded of his back as it disappeared from view. 'Are you sure?'

'Very,' came a muffled reply from down below. 'She borrowed my car.'

'Well,' declared Josette as she turned back to Annie. 'Not that exotic after all! She's only just gone down the road. Thought she might have gone to Paris or the Alps or somewhere romantic!'

But Annie didn't respond. If Josette hadn't known better thanks to Fabian's secret blend, she might have thought that the coffee her friend had consumed just minutes before had been one shot of caffeine too far.

'You all right, Annie? You've gone terribly pale.'

'Fine. How much do I owe you?'

Josette totted up the bill on a scrap of paper and then took the money from Annie's shaking

163

hand and placed it in the till.

'You sure you're up to walking home? Do you want me to get Christian to drive you back?'

'Stop fussing!' Annie barked. Then she said a curt goodbye and left.

Josette watched her with concern, debating whether she ought to call Christian anyway. It was almost as if Annie was in shock. She was just stretching her hand out for the phone when she heard an almighty crash from the cellar, followed by loud curses, and she turned her eyes to the heavens.

'Can you put another crate of beer on that order, Tante Josette?'

She stifled her instinctive reply and picked up her pencil. By the time she looked back out of the window, the sturdy shape of Annie was turning up towards Picarets. Maybe the walk will do her good, thought Josette and instead of reaching for the phone, she picked up the broom instead.

'And could you throw down the broom? I seem to have had an accident.'

It took all of Josette's patience not to hurl it down the stairs at him.

★   ★   ★

St Paul de Fenouillet!

Annie was a fair way up the hill before she could breathe properly.

St Paul de Fenouillet! It had to be. Of all places.

She paused but her legs were shaking so badly,

164

she knew the only solution was to get home and close the door. And hope that this was all a bad dream.

But maybe she was reacting over nothing? Maybe Véronique was simply on a romantic break somewhere towards the Mediterranean?

Annie wasn't convinced. It was too much of a coincidence. Too much to believe that Véronique, out of all the options open to her, had chosen to go to the very same area where Annie's cousins lived, cousins Véronique had never met.

The winter cold melted away and Annie was back there again, standing amongst the interminable rows of vines which arched over the hillside, the heat unbearable and her back breaking as she bent to pick the fat grapes. Her swollen feet shuffled her forward while her baby kicked and turned inside her as she yearned to be home amongst the mountain pastures. Her exile had been agony and she'd been amazed when the harvest had been turned into wine and declared an excellent vintage, so sure was she that her bitterness would have soured the grapes. But it had been necessary. She was a single mother. Far better to have the stigma of a solitary pregnancy left amongst the arid lands of St Paul de Fenouillet than carried around the valleys of Fogas.

A shrill wind came through the trees, bringing Annie sharply back to the present as she turned up her collar and walked a bit faster.

If Véronique had gone there, what would she discover? Nothing. Annie had remained resolutely stubborn when pestered by her relatives to reveal the identity of the man who had fathered her child. A passing fair worker, was the only reply she ever gave. And no one had known any different. Apart from one other. And she was now dead.

But what if there was some clue she'd overlooked. Something that would lead Véronique right back here to her father?

The farmhouse came into view and Annie shifted her shopping into her other hand.

No point fretting. Véronique would return knowing everything or nothing at all and either way, it was time that Annie sorted this.

Soon, she promised, looking up at the heavens. I will tell them both soon.

She let herself into the house and closed the door on the world behind her.

* * *

'Where you from?'

'Here and there.'

'How old's this car?'

'Older than you.'

'How fast does it go?'

'Fast enough.'

While his brother peppered the driver with questions, Nicolas reached forward to inspect the contents of the glove box. A strong arm shot out, thick fingers encircling his wrist and making him flinch.

'Leave it alone.'

'Sorry,' Nicolas squeaked as he sat back in his seat, eyes enormous.

'Where you been?' Max continued without missing a beat.

'Nowhere special.'

'Where you going?'

'Never you mind.'

Chloé shifted her position on the rough blanket which covered the floor of metal panelling in the back of the van. She was starting to feel really sick. The interior was stuffy with an overpowering smell of damp dog and strong cigarettes and the twists and turns on the mountain road were throwing her from side to side.

But she was an acrobat, capable of turning ten somersaults in a row without getting too dizzy, the cartwheel queen at school. So it wasn't motion sickness that was tying her stomach in knots.

It was the cold stare of the driver.

He hadn't taken his eyes off her the whole way, not when harangued by stupid Max or even when telling off Nicolas.

At first she'd thought he was simply looking in the mirror to see if there was traffic behind. But the rear windows had been blacked-out and it was impossible to see through them. So she'd moved and his gaze had followed her.

Now she was starting to sweat, beads of fear forming along her hairline and on her neck where her unruly black curls exploded over her collar.

She swallowed, trying to get some moisture back into her dry throat, and concentrated on the slice of road she could see through the windscreen between Nicolas and the driver. The edge of the Estaque farm slipped by.

Not far now and she'd be able to get out.

'You married?'

'Yes.'

'Kids?'

'Yes.'

'How many?'

'One.'

'Boy or girl?'

'Just here!' Nicolas announced as they drew level with the lime tree that dominated the tiny square in Picarets.

Normally when they had a lift Chloé got dropped off further on, saving her the extra walk through the village and up the hill to her house. But not today. She had no desire to be alone with this man.

Nicolas got out and Chloé was about to follow him, eager to escape, when she realised her bag had slid towards the rear of the van. She stretched her arm out and grabbed the straps but she was too slow. Max had already hopped over her, flipped the front seat back up and slammed the door shut behind him as was usual.

Chloé panicked. She was trapped.

Her eyes caught the icy blue gaze of the driver in the mirror and then she saw his hand slide the gear lever and the van started to move.

Do something! React!

She thrust herself off the floor and over the passenger seat in a forward roll and as her legs followed through, striking the man on the head, her fingers were already reaching for the door.

Safety. A cold blast of fresh air on her face and she was scrabbling across the seat towards the tarmac.

But one of her legs, her left leg, wouldn't move. It was trapped, a ring of iron gripped around her ankle as his fingers dug deeper into her flesh.

'You're not going anywhere, Chloé!'

She froze.

He knew her name.

She turned to stare at him, panting with fear as he grabbed hold of her shoulder and started to pull her towards him, back into the van.

That was when she noticed the tattoo on the inside of his wrist. Several lines of black and white with what looked like arrows in the top left corner. It meant nothing to Chloé as her mind sought a way out of her nightmare. But it offered a target.

She twisted within his grasp and sank her beautiful white teeth, her strong white teeth, into the centre of the tattoo, putting all the might of her fear behind it.

The man howled, letting go of her as he whipped his arm out of her mouth, and she pushed away from him, executing a flawless backward roll out of the van and on to the road. Before he could even open his door she was on her feet and running, heading into the cluster of trees that lay behind the houses. She didn't stop, her breath rasping in her chest as she hurtled towards the safety of home.

★ ★ ★

169

'So it's really not that difficult.' Stephanie pushed the pile of papers towards Christian who was regarding them as if they held the answer to life.

'And how soon can you start selling produce as organic?'

'Usually within three years. It might take a bit longer with livestock but it shouldn't, not if you follow the guidelines. So are you really thinking of going ahead with it?'

The farmer shrugged. 'Possibly. Fabian gave me the idea of diversifying so I'm just checking out options at the moment.'

'Fabian? He suggested you should sell meat to the Auberge?'

'In a roundabout way, yes.' Christian gave a chuckle. 'We were both a bit out of it at the time, smoking a joint he'd confiscated from some lad in the shop.'

'So he was telling the truth,' mused Stephanie.

'Telling the truth about what?'

'Nothing. Doesn't matter.'

The front door of the little cottage crashed open and Chloé burst in, red-cheeked and out of breath. She flung her bag to the floor and raced up the stairs.

'Chloé!' Stephanie shouted after her, feet thundering overhead. 'How many times do I have to tell you? Don't run in the house!'

The sound of her bedroom door slamming echoed in response and Stephanie sighed.

'Sorry about that. She's still cross with me for banning her from the bar.'

'Can't see her hero, Fabian?'

Stephanie nodded. 'It's like I can't get

anything right with her at the moment.'

'Maybe making peace with Fabian would help?' he suggested. 'The poor kid does seem to idolise him.'

'Tell me about it! She's convinced he's Jules Léotard reincarnate! Probably up there talking to her poster of him right now!'

'Well, I'd best be off. Thanks for the help,' Christian said as he gathered up the information Stephanie had got for him. 'I'll get it back to you soon.'

'Say hello to your parents for me.'

'Just so you know,' he said as he leaned down to kiss her farewell. 'Maman's threatening to have you round for dinner again soon. Says she's ordered some smoke alarms from some travelling salesman so we don't need to worry about her burning the place down this time!'

Stephanie laughed and slapped him on the arm. 'Her cooking's not that bad!' she reproached him.

Christian merely winked and made for the door, the cottage seeming to expand back to its normal size as his broad shape departed as though the dense matter of his body had warped time and space around it.

Stephanie watched him drive off and then stood for a few moments, listening.

Silence.

Whatever was up with Chloé, she was very quiet.

She'd give her a bit of time to herself and then go and see what was the matter. And in the meantime, she'd finish her reply to Pierre.

Stephanie was wrong. Chloé wasn't addressing the life-sized poster of Jules Léotard that hung above her bed, his graceful profile staring wistfully out of the window at the oak tree in the garden.

Instead she was looking at the enamel plaque that Jacques had given her.

'Beware of imitations,' she whispered to the little girl who was stretching to reach the piece of wall she was writing on. 'Beware of imitations.'

She should tell Maman what had happened in the van. But what if she was wrong? She'd bitten the man so hard, she'd seen red rivulets colouring the stripes on his tattoo as she'd fled. Plus she'd kicked him in the head. She'd be in trouble for sure.

But what if she was right? What if it had been him? The man Jacques had warned her about.

She didn't know what to do and Jules Léotard offered no help. She needed to talk to someone. But not Maman, who was too busy to listen properly. And she couldn't talk to Jacques as she wasn't allowed in the bar any more.

Which ruled out Fabian too.

It was so unfair.

She was left with Christian or Annie but Chloé knew they would tell Maman and Maman would tell her off for being silly.

So it was up to her.

At least now she knew what he looked like. She would just have to keep watch like Jacques was doing down in the épicerie. And maybe between them they could avert the danger.

She lifted the plaque off the wall and curled up on the bed and within minutes, as the rush of adrenaline took its toll on her young body, she was fast asleep.

★ ★ ★

Stephanie didn't know what woke her. A rattling shutter perhaps. The screech of a passing owl. She opened her eyes and sat up in bed, aware of a warmth in the house, like she'd left the woodburner roaring. She sniffed the air, alert to the danger of fire. But it wasn't that.

Curious, she got up and as she crossed the bedroom she felt the draught from the open window.

That was weird!

It was warm. Summer warm. On a night in early March.

She pulled the window fully open, unlatched the shutters and poked her head outside.

'Oh my God,' she murmured with a smile. 'Finally, after all these years!'

She rushed to Chloé's room where the child was fast asleep, lying as Stephanie had found her earlier that night, curled up on the bed holding tight to the old advertising plaque she'd found at the épicerie. Stephanie had covered her up, loathe to wake her, thinking she would be down in time for dinner. But Chloé had slept on and Stephanie had let her.

Now though she stirred in her dreams as though tussling with an invisible adversary and when her mother gently shook her, her eyes shot open, luminous with fear.

'Maman!'

'It's all right, love.' Stephanie drew her daughter towards her. 'It's just a silly nightmare. Nothing to worry about.'

She felt the rapid heartbeats slow beneath her palm as she stroked the small back and marvelled, not for the first time, at the inherent power of motherhood. How long, she wondered, before a simple cuddle would no longer be enough to soothe her daughter's fears?

'Okay?' she asked and Chloé nodded.

'Come on then. I want to show you something.'

She led her down the stairs and outside to the bench in the back garden where she sat down, Chloé on her lap, a blanket wrapped around them.

'What is it, Maman?' asked Chloé, as through her sleepy haze she began to register the unusual temperature of the night air.

'Look up!'

Chloé rested her head against Maman's shoulder and saw the clouds above racing through the sky as though in a gale. But she could feel only a gentle breeze that lapped around them, cocooning them in its warm embrace.

'It's amazing!'

'Last time I felt it this strong, we'd just arrived and you were tiny,' said Maman as she kissed Chloé's forehead. 'I thought the world was coming to an end!'

She laughed softly at the memory.

'I ran all the way up to Christian's in my pyjamas with you in my arms. They must have thought I was mad! Now I know better.'

'But what is it?'

'Its proper name is the foehn. Others like to call it the Witches' Wind.'

'Why do they call it that?'

'They blame it for bad things, think it brings misfortune.'

Chloé shuddered. 'Do you believe that?'

Maman shook her head. 'No, my love. I think it's a good thing and sometimes I even think it was what brought us here.'

But Chloé wasn't convinced. She watched the clouds tumbling far above her and in their scattered shapes, she thought she could see the outline of terrible things to come.

* * *

So, thought Christian as he stood on the hillside above the farm. The foehn was blowing again. Luckily their valley wound from east to west so they were spared the full brunt of the dry wind which was howling down the slopes of the mountains, devouring any remaining snow.

He'd had trouble getting to sleep, plagued by worries over the future of the business. Then, when he'd finally drifted off, he'd been haunted by disturbed dreams where he was being chased by a man in a fireman's uniform. He'd woken up in a foul mood, like the one he'd been in since Annie had announced Véronique was going on holiday with Major Gaillard, Chief Fire Inspector for the department of Ariège.

He couldn't work out whether his irritation was caused by Véronique's departure or by his reaction to it. Why on earth should he be bothered where she went and with whom she chose to go? It was beyond him. Véronique Estaque of all people. Sure, they'd become friends during the skulduggery that had surrounded the sale of the Auberge. But nothing more. Even though he'd caught a glimpse of her shapely backside once. Naked.

A smile curved his lips at the memory.

Knowing then that any chance of a restful night had evaded him, he'd come outside and been enveloped in the zephyr that was circling the house.

It had to be at least twenty degrees.

He gave a thought for his fellow farmers in the neighbouring north-south valley who weren't going to be so fortunate. Last time it had roared through like this, the ski station above Seix had been badly hit, ski lifts pulled out of the ground and buildings battered. They'd had to close early because of the damage. Plus there hadn't been any snow left!

Satan's Wind, Grand-père had called it. He'd told stories of folk in the Alps going crazy because of it, killing people, committing suicide.

Christian wasn't sure he believed all those old wives' tales.

He was far more concerned about forest fires, a much more likely outcome of the arid air and rising temperatures.

He cast his eyes around the hills that encircled the farm. No sparks. No flames.

Perhaps they'd been blessed this time and the suffering that his elders associated with the wind would pass them by.

Or maybe, he thought ruefully as he looked down at the small cluster of buildings that weighed so heavily on his shoulders, maybe it was already here!

10

Dust! Everywhere! In the cracks between the floorboards, on the makeshift shelves, a dull veneer covering the table and even Fabian's beloved coffee machine.

It was impossible to keep the place clean no matter how she tried.

Josette shook her duster out of the door of the bar, watching the emerging cloud of dirt drift off into the spring sunshine.

Over a month since the start of the renovations and completion was still a long way off. She was beginning to wish she'd never seen Fabian's fancy plans and had never agreed to the changes.

Of course, he argued that the hold-ups were all the fault of the local builders and to some extent he was right. After taking that Wednesday off to chase wild boar across the mountainside, they'd announced that they would not be in for three days in mid-March because the fishing season had opened.

Finally, last week, they'd seemed to really put their backs into it and the wall between the bar and the shop had been knocked through. Which meant even more mess and she'd had to close for four whole days! An event unheard of in Fogas.

Blasted builders!

They'd gone off for the weekend after demolishing the wall between the two rooms

178

without even bothering to tidy up. It had been Fabian who'd rigged up the plastic tarpaulin over the new archway, thus shielding the worst of the worksite from view in the bar. But it didn't stop the white debris drifting through and coating each and every surface, including Jacques who spent his entire time sneezing. And staring out of the épicerie window.

Josette picked up the broom which never seemed to be out of her hands these days and began sweeping the floor. Not that there was much point. The workmen would be here soon and the whole thing would start all over again.

Today of all days, she really didn't want to have to deal with it.

She felt her mood sour. She'd had about as much of this renovation lark as she could take.

★ ★ ★

Sunshine. Beautiful, glorious sunshine pouring over her face and into her bones.

Chloé held her arms aloft and felt the warmth cascading down on to her.

It felt even better, knowing that she shouldn't be here.

She'd made the decision that morning when she'd woken up and seen the blue sky stretched taut across the mountains, not a cloud marring its expanse. It was Monday and the thought of suffering hours of droning dictation under the watch of Madame Soum when she could be outside in this had been more than she could contemplate. So rather than subject herself to

179

the agonies of transposing texts from present to past or working on feminine and masculine agreements, she'd opted for a day off.

A surreptitious one of course.

Aided in her scheming by the Rogalle twins, veterans in the art of truancy, she'd walked down to the main road with them as normal so that everyone saw her going to school. But when the minibus came into view, she hid in the thicket of trees at the back of the lay-by and heard Nicolas informing the driver that she was ill. The small red bus had pulled off, Max making faces at her from the rear window, and she'd been free!

Well almost.

The help of the twins had come at a cost: their maths homework for the next week. But that was nothing compared to the exhilaration she felt at having an entire day to herself, without the confines of school and with the sun beaming down on her.

When she was sure the bus had gone, she'd quickly scrambled out of the bushes and across to the path that led up to Picarets. Normally in the winter they all used the road to get up and down on foot as the path was treacherous in the colder months when the dead leaves formed a slippery mush underfoot. But today she had no choice. If she went back up the road there was a good chance she would meet Maman driving down and then she would be in trouble. So with slight trepidation, she'd entered the forest.

It was the first time she'd been alone since the 'incident'. That was how Chloé had taken to referring to it as three weeks on, she still didn't understand what had happened in the green van. She'd not seen it again, or the driver, and with every day that passed, it seemed as though she might have sunk her teeth into an innocent man. But at night, when she turned out the light and lay vulnerable in those seconds when her eyes had yet to adjust to the dark, her trembling heart overruled her head and told her to be alert, be on guard and be afraid.

It had told her the same thing that morning as the trees closed around her, cutting off the sunlight. She'd shifted her bag across her body to leave her hands free and began clambering up the steep path, her steps rapid despite the terrain as her nerves drove her forwards.

Forty minutes later and she was in a clearing above the village, her head thrown back, her arms held high and the sunshine draped around her. The walk up had been uneventful, apart from nearly bumping into Christian at the first point where the winding road cut through the more direct path. She'd burst out of the trees at speed and heard the car at the last moment, throwing herself to the ground as the blue Panda came into sight round a bend. He'd not noticed her in the shadows but she'd been more careful after that, taking her time whenever she had to leave the cover of the forest to cross the tarmac.

She looked down on the houses below, in particular the small cottage just before the village boundary. No blue van. Which meant Chloé had at least until lunch-time before Maman got back. Now, how should she spend her morning? Her eyes came to rest on the lush grass in Christian's field further up the road, the new growth a temptation of vibrant green, and a grin spread across her face.

She knew exactly what was called for.

★ ★ ★

Jacques was tired. His legs ached, his back was sore and his eyesight was blurred. Plus he was finding it hard to breathe with all the dust. He shifted his weight slightly, trying to ease his discomfort but in a couple of minutes it was just as bad and he knew he needed to sit down.

Over a month he'd been keeping vigil. And in all that time he'd seen nothing.

Well, actually, he'd seen plenty! Thanks to Josette leaving the shutters open for him even at night he'd witnessed René having a sneaky cigarette in the alley by the post office, Bernard Mirouze kissing his new hunting dog when he thought no one could see, Pascal Souquet getting into a car with someone in the dead of night and Véronique's face glowing after Christian gave her a hug.

But not once had he seen the man who'd come into the bar asking about Stephanie and Chloé.

And all he had for his trouble were varicose veins and creaky knee joints.

That's it, he decided. Time to call it a day.

So he drifted across the empty room where the workmen's tools littered the floor and floated under the new arch, through the tarpaulin and into the bar.

'Good of you to show your face!' Josette greeted him as he sank on to his seat in the inglenook. She gave him an expectant look but he returned a weary smile, his head suddenly heavy and his eyelids drooping. Within seconds he was asleep.

'Huh!' snorted Josette as she watched her sleeping husband with affection. He'd forgotten the date. No change there then, dead or alive. 'Fine company you are!'

'Who's fine company?' Fabian's voice came from the doorway, making her jump.

'I was just talking to myself,' she said, trying to sound nonchalant.

He gave her his doctor's smile, the one that was tinged with wariness, and she knew he was contemplating her sanity. After all, it wasn't the first time he'd walked into a room and caught her talking to thin air. Now that Fabian was permanently underfoot, she was finding it harder and harder to be alone with Jacques and so the other night, unable to sleep, she'd crept downstairs and sat by the dying embers of the fire, hot chocolate in hand, chatting to her husband.

Of course Jacques couldn't reply. But it gave her comfort. Discussing things with him. She'd been so engrossed in a onesided conversation about the changes that were taking place around them that she didn't hear the creak of a floorboard behind her until it was too late.

Fabian. She'd fallen silent and hadn't moved, pretended that she didn't know he was there while she covertly watched his reflection in the

183

shuttered window. And she'd seen him giving her that look, the one he was giving her now, full of concern and apprehension. Then he'd simply turned around and quietly gone back to bed. He hadn't mentioned it the next morning and neither had she. But she knew he was thinking about it now.

'Everything all right, Tante Josette?' he asked lightly.

'Fine,' she bit back, on the defensive. 'Would be even better if I wasn't fighting a losing battle against the builders.'

'Talking of which, they've just called.'

'And?'

'They're not coming today.'

'What?' Josette had a sharp edge to her voice.

'They've got another job down in St Girons which they can't put off any longer. Said they hadn't expected this to take so long.'

'So when are they intending to come back?'

'In two weeks.'

'*Two weeks?*' Josette exclaimed, waking Jacques in the process. 'That's ridiculous!'

'But there is a bit of good news. The builders have agreed to knock out the fireplace for free in return for the delays.' Fabian beamed at his aunt.

'Knock out the *fireplace?*'

Fabian pointed at the inglenook where Jacques was listening, mouth open in horror. 'I've asked the builders to install a wood-burner, state of the art.'

'I don't remember agreeing to that.'

'It's a surprise,' Fabian replied hesitantly, his smile slipping as he sensed her annoyance. 'I

184

thought it would save you a lot of work. Be more cost efficient too. I'm paying for it with the money from the wine I found in the cellar. Turns out it was a particularly good vintage of Bordeaux and we made quite a bit at auction!'

Josette felt an icy calm descend.

'*We* made quite a bit?' she asked with menace. 'Perhaps that *we* is something *we* ought to discuss,' Josette continued. 'It's two months now since you arrived and in that time, there's been nothing but upheaval.'

Fabian blinked. 'I thought . . . it seemed to be going well . . . '

'Going well? You call this going well?' She waved a hand at the bar which was overcrowded with stock. 'Or the fact that you're intending to rip out the inglenook without so much as consulting me. How on earth is that going well?'

'I wouldn't have done it without asking you. I just thought the place needed modernising.'

'You just thought!' Josette spat. 'You just thought you'd walk in here and turn my life upside down so that you can live out some fantasy of country living now that you can't hack it in the city any more. Well, I'll tell you something, young man. I've had enough. Had enough of your cost saving exercises and your obsession with profit and progress and your endless spreadsheets! So you can pack your bags and head back to Paris and just leave me and . . . '

She cast a look at the figure in the fireplace and her shoulders slumped. How could she ever explain to Fabian what his presence had done to

185

her life? Her and Jacques' lives?

' . . . just leave me in peace. Please.' She pulled off the apron she was wearing and tossed it on the table and as she brushed past him and up the stairs, Fabian thought he saw tears in her eyes.

'Me and my big mouth!' he muttered as he collapsed on to a chair, head in his hands.

'What's yourrr big mouth done this time?' Annie growled as she walked in.

Fabian looked up, despair on his face. 'I've upset Tante Josette. Really upset her.'

And he told her about the argument.

Annie listened in silence and then tipped her head to one side, thinking about all manner of things, not least the fact that the coffee machine belonged to Fabian and if he went . . .

'Leave it with me,' she said. 'You go out on yourrr bike and clearrr yourrr head and I'll sorrrt this out. It's not like Josette to make a fuss overrr nothing. Therrre must be something else botherrring herrr.'

Fabian got to his feet and on an impulse, he threw his arms around the small wiry frame of Annie Estaque, planting a kiss on her leathery cheek.

'Thanks, Annie. I don't want to have to leave.'

'And I don't want you to have to leave eitherrr,' said Annie, surprised to find that she actually meant it and only partly because of the excellent coffee. 'Now buggerrr off and give us women some space.'

Stephanie felt like she'd been reborn. She was sitting on the grass on a hillside up above Picarets and the bright sunlight was adding to her growing sense of optimism.

Life was good.

The garden centre was on schedule for an early May opening and the inspection process for the organic certification was already under way. With the burst of spring weather over the last few weeks, her young plants were doing well and she would have enough stock to see her through the summer. But she knew it wouldn't be long before she needed more. And that would require additional space which was why she was spending her morning looking at a field that was possibly for rent.

She'd driven up out of the village but instead of turning off at the old quarry road, she went straight on, the strip of tarmac getting narrower and narrower until it gave way to an unmade surface which was pitted and damaged from the winter frosts. The van bounced along for a few minutes and then the road ended in a turning circle, surrounded by forest.

When she'd got out of the van and seen how dense the trees were, she'd been sceptical but she'd followed the instructions she'd been given by André Dupuy, Christian's father, and soon she was on a path which took her further into the heart of the woods. She passed the ruins of several houses, stone walls crumbling, young oaks now spreading their branches where the slate roofs had been, and she was impressed by the way the people of this land had once

187

inhabited it to the full. But the introduction of electricity had rendered the Ariège's abundant supply of water-power redundant, stripping the region of its employment and then its youth. And the resulting years of depopulation had changed the department from being somewhere at the heart of French industry, to being a relatively unknown backwater.

Something which suited Stephanie just fine, given her circumstances.

A few minutes more on the path and she'd emerged into a clearing. It wasn't large enough to take a big herd of cattle or sheep but it was ideal for a polytunnel or two. And the land looked good, a gently sloping square of grass surrounded by woods on three sides, purple and yellow crocuses dotted about. It had been well kept by the owner who no longer had the energy for the long walk to bring animals across from Fogas just to graze this patch in Picarets that had been inherited long ago.

It was a recurring problem in the commune which was geographically split in two by the deep mountain valleys, one that was having a very visible impact on the landscape. Over time, as people moved away and the population aged, the well maintained fields that Annie's generation remembered from their childhoods had degenerated, often owned by someone too elderly or too far away to look after them. As a result, they became overgrown and were soon reclaimed by the forest, the only evidence that they were once cultivated being the tumbling walls of stone that marked the edge of the

188

terraces which climbed the hillside.

Thus when Stephanie had started making enquiries about the possibility of renting extra land, she'd been besieged by offers from older residents and second home owners desperate for someone to take care of their plots. She'd viewed a couple of sites but they'd been too difficult to reach by car or were over the other side of Fogas. But this one was just right!

And the views were breathtaking. She could see down to the valley floor below and then trace the trees all the way up the opposite side until her eyes reached the horizon of snowcapped peaks which rose from behind the hill. Red kites were circling lazily in the cobalt sky, their occasional cry piercing the silence. Stephanie sat down on the grass, feeling a slight tinge of damp which came with spring sunshine, and marvelled at how well her life was going.

If she could make enough money from her early plant sales, she'd be able to get a polytunnel set up here and expand her stock. Of course, it depended on the rent. But André had said he didn't think it would be much.

She closed her eyes and let the warmth of the sun wash over her, quietening her mind. A few moments of calm, and then she would get on with her day.

* * *

'I'm such an old fool!' said Josette as she mopped up the last of her tears with the tissue Annie had handed her and put her glasses back

189

on. 'I don't know what came over me.'

'Sharrring yourr space with someone can do that. Me and Vérrronique nearrrly came to blows when she was up at the farrrm!'

Josette chuckled, already feeling better after five minutes of Estaque counselling. 'Thanks, Annie. You're a good friend.'

'Huh! Don't be so surrre. It's just the coffee machine I'm prrrotecting! Now you get yourrr-self sorrrted and I'll go down and mind the shop forrr a bit.'

Josette gazed at her reflection in the faded mirror on her dressing table as Annie made her way downstairs. Her face was slightly puffy and her cheeks were flushed but other than that there was no evidence that she'd been upset.

Was it her age, she wondered as she traced the fine lines radiating out from the corners of her eyes. Was that why she'd reacted so badly to Fabian's suggestion about the fireplace? Had she become one of those women she used to scorn, who clung to the past like a shield against the future?

She sighed, disturbing the thin cover of plaster dust on the marble surface. It had even got up here! No wonder she wasn't herself. But taking it out on Fabian had been unfair. Especially after they'd been getting on so well lately.

Only the week before, when the épicerie had been closed for the renovation work and she hadn't known what to do with herself, Fabian had suggested they drive up to Col d'Agnes for a picnic. It had been glorious weather, really warm, so she'd agreed and they'd had a wonderful day.

She couldn't remember the last time she'd gone up there. Not since she helped out with the transhumance, herding sheep and cattle up to the higher pastures for the summer. Must be thirty years ago! She'd forgotten how beautiful the high meadows were, the views dominated by the rugged peaks of the Pyrenees in one direction and the plains stretching out to Toulouse in the other. And it had made her wistful to explore more of the area which she'd once known so intimately.

After she'd married and began working in the shop, her world had become defined by the walls that surrounded it and she rarely got out. A trip to St Girons now and then for the market with a neighbour, but that was about it. And since Jacques died, it had been more difficult. She'd had to find cover for the épicerie and then she'd been reliant on lifts from friends as there was no bus service.

Which was another crackpot idea Fabian had had while they were up there.

When she'd acknowledged that she'd like to see more of the place but couldn't get around, he'd suggested that she learn to drive! Just like that. As though she was eighteen or something.

She'd thought it was the mountain air going to his city head but he'd kept on about it, saying how easy it was and how he'd help her with the theory. He'd even ordered the books for her to start studying for the test.

She glanced out of the bedroom window to the garage down the road which had remained closed since the summer before. Inside was a

191

brand new Peugeot 308, a deep cherry colour like a lollipop on wheels. The back seats still had the protective coverings on from the garage and there were barely two thousand kilometres on the clock. She'd talked Jacques into treating himself to it this time last year, his first brand new car, and then a few months later he was dead.

She hadn't had the heart to part with it and had been contemplating giving it to Christian. But Fabian had got her thinking. Maybe he was right. Maybe she could learn to drive. If only to see the shock on Jacques' face when she backed that beautiful shiny car out of the garage!

And that was why having Fabian around was a good thing. She'd known from the day he'd arrived and announced his intention to stay that they would have to come to some kind of arrangement. The alternative didn't bear thinking about; a house and business literally split in half like her cousin's house up in Massat. He'd inherited it along with another cousin and as neither could agree as to what to do with it, they'd built an internal wall right up the middle, dividing it into two. Crazy! Even some of the windows had been halved by their ridiculous solution and it had resulted in a house that was virtually uninhabitable.

So the only choice, given that she couldn't leave Jacques behind, was to try and make this work. And so far, if she was honest, it was Fabian who'd done most of the trying.

She took a deep breath and straightened her shoulders. When he came in from his bike ride

192

she would sit down with him and they would sort something out. It was just that she needed a bit more space. Space to talk to Jacques, that was all, so they could share days like today. Special days.

She gave her eyes one last dab and started down the stairs.

* * *

Jacques was frustrated. He'd witnessed the argument between Josette and his nephew and had been genuinely horrified at the thought of losing the inglenook. But that paled into insignificance when he'd had to watch his wife leave the room in tears and he'd been unable to follow. He didn't understand why he couldn't go beyond the bar and the épicerie. He didn't understand much about this second existence where he found himself. But he did know that the minute he went to cross the threshold towards the stairs, he started to feel faint as though losing the tentative grip he had on what now constituted his reality.

So he'd been left downstairs feeling useless when he'd suddenly noticed the calendar.

March 30th.

She'd even ringed it in a big red circle. He slapped his forehead. What an idiot! He'd been so caught up in watching out for the man in camouflage that he'd lost track of time. No wonder she'd blown up at Fabian. She'd been upset.

But what could he do? The only talent left to

him in this afterlife was a ridiculous ability to move air. He could make the fire dance by breathing on it and make paper flutter by exhaling hard. But that was it. Pathetic really. He was a ghostly version of one of those leaf-blower thingies that Bernard Mirouze had been pestering the council to buy every autumn.

He sniffed in derision at his own inadequacies and a sneeze rocked him back on his feet causing the dust on the surface of the bar to ripple. Which was when inspiration struck. Taking a deep breath, he got to work.

He was standing back admiring his handiwork several minutes later when Annie Estaque came down the stairs. And picked up a duster.

She wiped it across the counter of the bar and completely destroyed what had taken him considerable time to create.

Not to be defeated, he went over to the table and tried again, getting dizzy with the effort. But no sooner had he straightened up than she was behind him, her yellow cloth flicking across the surface and destroying yet another masterpiece.

Annoyed now, he moved over to the upright knife cabinet near the door. He inhaled and began again. And just as he finished, a sturdy hand flashed in front of his face and his work disappeared.

He was fit to kill her as she bustled around, gathering up all the dust in the place. He was going to have to give up. Then, just as he heard Josette's footfall on the stairs, he had a brainwave. He slipped under the table and leaned in over one of the chairs. He expanded

194

his lungs and began, working as quickly as he could.

'Oh, Annie! There's no need to dust!' Josette said as she came into the room and saw her hard at work.

'Everrry little helps. And I'll take a coffee by way of thanks!'

Josette turned to start making the drinks which was when she noticed Jacques emerging from under the table looking very red in the cheeks for a ghost.

She raised an eyebrow at him and he gestured for her to join him, casting a nervous glance at Annie as she advanced with her duster.

'I'll just clean off the chairrrs, and then I'm done.'

Jacques waved his arms in distress, his body crouched protectively over the chair he was standing next to.

'Don't worry about them!' Josette replied as she rushed over, making Annie halt in her tracks.

'Arrre you surrre?' Annie regarded her friend quizzically.

'Quite,' said Josette as she pulled out the chair Jacques had been trying so hard to defend.

'That's weirrrd!' The two of them regarded the beautifully formed heart that had been drawn in the dust on the wooden seat. 'Bloody hearrrts all overrr the place in herrre. I just cleaned up thrrree otherrrs!'

Josette smothered a smile and looked up at her husband who was pointing at the calendar and blowing her kisses.

He'd remembered.

Annie moved forward with her duster ready but Josette put a hand on her arm.

'Leave it. Let's have our coffee and a box of those chocolates left over from Valentine's Day.'

'What arrre we celebrrrating?' asked Annie as she happily discarded her cloth.

'It's our wedding anniversary. Would have been fifty years today.'

'Bloody hell!' muttered Annie, impressed. 'Think that merrrits morrre than just a coffee, don't you?'

As she reached towards the brandy on the top shelf of the bar, Jacques sat back down in the inglenook, exhausted by his morning's work.

'Herrre's to you, Josette,' toasted Annie as they clinked glasses. 'And to Jacques, wherrreverrr he is.'

Josette smiled into her drink, knowing exactly where her husband was as she saw his chest start to rise and fall in a familiar rhythm. She'd talk to Fabian about the fireplace. Persuade him to change his mind. It was the least she could do for the old romantic.

11

Chloé had died and gone to heaven. Not literally of course, but an acre of green grass, abundant sunshine and the freedom to be an acrobat was about as good as it could get in the mind of the nine-year-old.

She stretched to her full height at the road end of Christian's field, her hands reaching for the sky as she drew her body upright. Then, in an explosion of power, she pounded across the ground and pushed off. Front handspring, hands solid beneath her, landed and into a cartwheel, legs arcing overhead, and down into a front flip, airborne for a second and then bare feet planted into the grass to spring backwards into a reverse flip, the world spinning the other way momentarily, her momentum carrying her into a back handspring to finish, her landing executed faultlessly. Straight into a pile of cow dung.

'Ugh!' She leapt sideways, frantically wiping her toes in a clean section of grass, trying to get the brown muck off her.

But it wasn't enough to mar her day. After months of practice, she'd finally mastered the reverse flip. She reached for her bag and fished out a pencil and the battered tome that was her acrobatic bible.

The Art of Gymnastics for Boys and Girls
She'd found it languishing beneath a pile of *Asterix* comic books in the second-hand

bookshop in St Girons a year ago when she'd gone to town with Annie. It had taken all her pocket money and a secret loan from her companion to buy it but it had been worth it. Although it was ancient, printed some time before even Annie had been born, the diagrams were clear and the techniques worked and Chloé spent long evenings under the bedclothes with a torch, studying it from cover to cover.

She flicked through the yellowed pages to the one showing the back flip and put a tick beside it. Next up, the aerial cartwheel.

Chloé had tried this a few times before without any success but if she wanted to achieve her dreams, then she had to be able to master such moves. She dropped the book beside her bag, stretched, flexed her neck and then gave it her best shot.

With a running start she hit her take-off spot and catapulted her legs high into the air above her head, arms tucked close by her sides but just as she thought she might have got it, she felt gravity pulling her down long before she'd got her feet into the right position.

Whump!

She collapsed on her back on the grass, the air knocked from her lungs, and lay there for a minute while the earth readjusted itself on its axis.

She'd never get into Cirque du Soleil at this rate.

It was her sole focus in life. Joining a circus.

She couldn't remember what had started this obsession, couldn't remember a time when she hadn't wanted to be a trapeze artist. Maman had never approved, even in the early days when she'd found Chloé twisting her dolls into cartwheels and suspending them from the ceiling on a length of rope. When Chloé had started experimenting herself, Maman had hit the roof and declared that under no circumstances was Chloé to perform acrobatics. There was no explanation given, only the rule laid down.

But it was asking too much of the young girl whose dreams were filled with big tops and high wires and the roar of the crowd. It was something she couldn't explain, this impulse to hurl herself into the air, to tumble through space and then grab the safety of a metal bar. And so, in her only ever act of rebellion, Chloé had simply decided that this edict applied only when her mother was present. From then on, she sought out places where she could practise in secret like behind Annie's barn or here, in Christian's field, and she continued to hone her skills. So far she'd mastered the art of tumbling, with one or two exceptions, but she knew that soon she would have to start raising her game. Literally.

The next step was to lift her acrobatics off the ground and into the air. She'd already tried once or twice, using a low hanging branch of the oak tree in the garden but it hadn't really worked. Chloé had fallen off in a heap and had nothing but grazed hands and knees to show for it.

A quick look at her watch told her Maman was due home in half an hour. Time for another couple of attempts at the aerial cartwheel before she had to disappear.

She stood up, facing the road, stretched her limbs once more and prepared to have another go. She was oblivious to the movement in the field behind her, a shape emerging from the copse of ash trees. Oblivious to the angry brown eyes which were fixed on her. She had no idea of the dire straits she was in.

★　★　★

Fabian got as far as the unmade road that tapered off into the forest above Picarets before lifting his head. He'd stormed up the hill, concentrating only on his cadence and unaware of his surroundings as he forced his muscles to keep going. When he finally ran out of tarmac, he stopped, slumped over the handlebars breathing hard, and checked his cycle computer.

The stats were astounding. Only two months of riding these lower hills and already he was fitter, his legs were stronger and he was itching to tackle some more serious mountains.

His timing was perfect as the snow was fast disappearing from the high passes and even Col d'Agnes had been rideable the other day when he'd taken Tante Josette up there, just a few patches of white clinging to the hillsides on the hairpin bends that didn't get the sun.

Tante Josette. Thinking about her made him cringe.

She'd been right in what she'd said. He hadn't really looked at his plans from her angle, just

200

presumed that, as a widow, she'd be glad of some company around the place. It hadn't occurred to him that she might not appreciate him turning up. But then, he wasn't very good at seeing things from other people's perspectives. It wasn't that he was selfish. Just that he had difficulty relating to other people's experiences. Even had problems relating to his own sometimes. Another thing an ex-girlfriend had kindly informed him of before she flounced out of his apartment, spare keys thrown on the coffee table.

He'd really messed things up. Pushed Tante Josette so far that he'd probably wrecked all chances of them working together at the épicerie. And as she showed no signs of wanting to give it up and he didn't have the heart to force her to accept his inheritance, it was looking like he might have to head back to Paris.

The notion terrified him.

He wasn't worried about the financial side of things as he had enough saved from his days in banking to last a while until he found another job. But the thought of spending long evenings on his own in his ultra-modern apartment, his solitary reflection staring back at him from the pristine metal and glass surfaces, filled him with a sadness he'd never experienced before.

He'd got used to things here. Most things! He still had to fight the urge to chivvy customers out of the shop when they stood too long chatting, holding up the person behind. And he didn't think he would ever get used to Fogas Time where tomorrow at ten could mean two days

201

later in the afternoon. And then only if you were lucky!

But the slow pace of life had seeped into his bones. He'd become as bad as Tante Josette, lingering over tasks, making the work fit around the day, whatever the day turned out to be, instead of shoehorning it into a prescribed half-hour and not taking the time to notice the daffodils that were coming up across the road, or to play with Tomate, the cat from the Auberge that seemed to have taken a liking to him. He'd also noticed the Ariégeois accent creeping back into his voice like an old friend he'd been ignoring, sidling around the edges of his precise Parisian intonation and slipping consonants in places his mother would never have approved of.

But what surprised him more than anything was the fact that he would miss the people. In two short months he'd got to know them, had become part of the community. He'd even begun to understand Annie Estaque! If he went back to Paris now he would only find out second-hand if Christian managed to keep his farm, only get snippets of news about Stephanie's new business and he might never know if René found a way to stay off the cigarettes.

He really didn't want to think about it.

He turned his bike around and started freewheeling down the hill, convinced that it might be his last ride in the Pyrenees for a long time. And if that was the case, he was going to make the most of it.

Crouching low over the handlebars, bum pushed to the back of the saddle, he felt the bike accelerate beneath him, trees flashing past on either side. The first bend came at him fast and he shifted his weight on to his outside leg, inside leg raised, followed the curve and then out of it on to the straight. Just time to change position, weight transferring, and then he was turning the other way. Three more hairpins in quick succession, Fabian rode them with exhilaration, heart leaping in excitement. He exited the last one and the long stretch that led down to Picarets lay before him, Christian's farm visible on the left.

God, this was magical. The rush of air on his face, the thrill of the speed. He was Laurent Jalabert, King of the Mountains, wearing the polka-dot jersey in the Tour de France and racing to victory on Bastille Day, his cycle computer soaring upwards to hit fifty-five kilometres per hour.

That's when he saw Chloé. She was standing in a field, arms raised above her head, eyes focused forward. Even though he was travelling very fast, he could see that she was in immense danger. And that she had no idea.

Shit!

He didn't think he'd be able to stop in time.

★   ★   ★

Stephanie had been so tempted to take the day off and play truant. The sun had almost seduced her with its warmth, enticing her to lie down in the pasture, kick off her shoes and close her eyes.

On any other day, she would have bitten that

203

apple. But she had an appointment with the bank manager that afternoon and she wanted to check on the garden centre before she went so, with great reluctance, she'd turned her back on the sundrenched clearing and headed for home.

She took her time driving back over the unmade road, trying to avoid the worst of the potholes, afraid that with every jolt and rattle she was leaving half of the van on the ground. She picked up a bit of pace once she hit the tarmac but still took it fairly easy out of respect for the hairpins and the ravine that lay below them. So it was that she exited the last bend just in time to see a cyclist in the road some distance ahead of her. He was going at speed, body flat along the bar of the bike. Then suddenly he was braking and skidding and shouting at someone in the field to his left.

Which was when she noticed Chloé and the world faded into nothing.

★   ★   ★

Fabian pulled hard on the brakes, both hands gripping tight as though his life depended on it, because Chloé's life did depend on it. His bike seemed to buckle beneath him, the back wheel kicking out into the road and then his left foot was on the tarmac, right foot unclipping from the pedal as he thrust the bike to one side and began running, his long legs carrying him towards the field.

'Stand still, Chloé!' he yelled, not really having

204

any expertise in situations like this.

Chloé raised a hand as though to greet him and then she heard it. Behind her. A snorting sound.

He saw her turn her head and freeze, her arm stuck in the air, her greeting incomplete as she finally comprehended the predicament she was in.

Sarko, Christian's prize Limousin bull, was in the field with her, strands of wire draped over his colossal shoulders and a fence post trailing behind him.

'Fabiiiiaaaannn, help!' she screamed as the Parisian leapt over the electric fence, a shot of pain zapping his trailing left calf where it touched, making the leg collapse under him as he landed on the other side.

'Don't move, Chloé!' he said again as he picked himself up and ran towards her, trying to assess the situation.

The bull had lowered his massive forehead and was pawing the ground, froth issuing from his mouth. And his focus was totally on Chloé.

Even for Fabian, a city kid born and bred, this didn't look good.

Not having read the manual on how to deter an imminent attack from an enraged beast, he went on his instincts.

He needed to distract the bull. How?

He started waving his arms manically above his head as he ran. But Sarko was ignoring him.

'Fabiiiiaaaannn, please! Hurry!'

Throw something.

What?

He was in an empty field. Empty apart from the bull.

His shoes!

Still moving forward, he hopped a few steps and undid the Velcro straps on first one and then the other. Within firing distance now, he took aim and released, a silver cycling shoe sailing through the air, landing on Sarko's broad back.

Not a flicker. He might as well have been tickled by a fly, brown eyes focused on Chloé who was standing totally still, her scared breaths audible to Fabian across the distance that remained between them.

'Second time lucky!' he called out as he let fly with the other shoe. It arched over the field and struck the bull firmly on the forehead, the cleat drawing blood.

Sarko tossed his head from side to side and bellowed, turning his malevolent gaze on Fabian.

'Come on!' Fabian urged. 'Tackle someone your own size!'

The bull pawed the ground again, shoulders hunched, thick veins standing out on his muscular neck.

Christ! It was going to take him at his word!

Then the earth started to tremble as a tonne of prime beast came charging across the pasture, the sun glinting off the sharp points of the lowered horns.

Cycling jacket.

Fabian's fingers fumbled with the zip, then he was pulling out his right arm, his left, the bull getting ever closer, then the jacket was free and he was a matador, twirling a cape of red and black as the animal thundered straight at him, the stretch of grass that separated them getting shorter by the second.

And then it was upon him. Not fooled by Fabian's jacket hanging out to the right. Aiming for the Parisian's chest. Fabian threw himself to the side as with a rank smell of sweat, which Fabian couldn't be sure wasn't his, the bull stormed past, close enough to feel the warmth emanating from its heaving flanks. Too close.

'He's turning, Fabian!' Chloé's voice cracked on his name. 'He's coming back!'

Fabian didn't need telling. From where he lay sprawled he could see it circle round, snorting, head lowered. He scrambled to his feet.

This time. He had to get it right. If he did, then their escape route would be clear. If he didn't . . .

He felt his body go cold, fingers devoid of blood as he gripped the collar of the cycling jacket. In front of him. That's where he had to hold it. No other choice. Sarko was too wily to fall for anything else.

He forced himself to concentrate on the bull. One stride. Another. Hooves travelling at speed. Two more strides and . . .

Here.

Fabian pirouetted, twisting his body away to the left, leaving Sarko with nothing but red and black nylon as a target. A horn pierced the thin fabric and the animal was gone, down the field, Fabian's hands empty and the sour odour of fear in his nostrils as the bull raced away.

Seizing his chance, Fabian shouted to Chloé

207

and she came to life, running towards him, her arms open wide. He scooped her up and raced with her to safety, the bull roaring behind him. He didn't have time to look, legs hurtling across the grass, Chloé panting in his ear, his arms aching under her weight. Only when he'd dropped her over the electric fence and thrown himself after her did he glance back.

Sarko had tossed the jacket on the ground and was gouging it with his horns, tearing it into thin strips. He'd also managed to trample one of the cycling shoes into the mud and Fabian had no desire to rescue the other one.

As the adrenaline levels lowered, Fabian's shattered nerves turned, as always, to numbers and unbidden, an Excel spreadsheet opened in his mind:

Assos ultimate cycling jacket	torn by bull	€280
Sidi Carbon Lite shoes	trampled by bull	€330
Assos thermic socks	covered in cowshit	€35

Then he heard a crunch of metal and the squeal of brakes.

'Maman,' shouted Chloé, who had recovered from the shock faster than her rescuer. 'Fabian saved my life!'

But Fabian wasn't really paying attention. He was too busy staring at his bike. His beautiful carbon fibre bike.

He heard a door slam and the patter of feet and he was aware that Stephanie had clasped Chloé to her chest.

'Is anything broken?' she demanded, her hands running over every inch of her daughter. 'Are you sure you're not hurt?'

'Fabian rescued me!' Chloé said again, jumping up and down with excitement.

In contrast, Fabian was motionless, fixated on the spinning front wheel of his beloved machine, the only part of the bike now visible. Automatically he started to fill in the details.

Time Vxr Proteam bike frame	mangled by blue van	

But before he could complete the last column he felt gentle hands on his cheeks drawing his face down and on an inhalation of wild flowers and incense, soft lips touched his own and a shock akin to that he'd got when leaping the electric fence shot along every nerve in his body.

'I can never thank you enough,' Stephanie said as she pulled away.

'Uh?' Fabian was blinking rapidly, not accustomed to the bright light that surrounded him.

'Maman!' Chloé's voice had an urgency that made Stephanie turn. She was pointing at the van. Or more specifically, what lay beneath it.

'Oh *shit*!' Stephanie's hands flew to her face. 'Your bike. Oh my God. I'm so sorry. I've destroyed your bike.'

'Uh?' Fabian tried to focus on what she was saying but her mouth mesmerised him, his eyes transfixed by the delicious red lips that had felt so surprisingly cool and tasted faintly of honey.

'How much was it worth?' she asked in a small

voice, dreading the response.

'Oh that!' Fabian forced himself to glance at the shattered carbon. He tried to access his spreadsheet but his internal processor was paralysed by the curve of Stephanie's body as she bent over and attempted to free the bike, T-shirt taut over her chest, skirt shaped tight over her thighs as she tugged at the fractured frame. His gaze rested on the beautiful hollows below her bare ankles and he had to fight the urge to run his hands down her legs and let his thumb and forefinger nestle in the tempting indentations. And for the first time in Fabian's life, the numbers didn't materialise.

Time Vxr Proteam bike frame	mangled by blue van	#VALUE!

'I'll buy you a new one,' she said as she straightened up, her face white.

'Don't worry about it,' he heard himself reply. 'Chloé's more important than my old bike.'

It must have been the right thing to say as Stephanie stretched up on tiptoe and kissed him again.

Chloé, standing to one side, watched on with a grin as Fabian's long arms enclosed Maman in an embrace. Almost getting killed by Sarko had definitely been worth it!

★ ★ ★

'Bitch!'

High on the hillside above the field which had

been the scene of such dramatic events, a man lowered his binoculars, his piercing blue eyes still focused on the three people below.

'You'll pay for this,' he muttered, as he threw his cigarette butt to the floor and ground it into the soil with the heel of his boot. 'Not long now, my darling Stephanie, and you'll pay.'

He slung the binoculars over his shoulder and walked off into the trees, his camouflage jacket hiding him from the casual observer.

12

Apple trees bursting with blossom, bees flitting from flower to flower, irises standing regal along the roadside, calves in the pastures across the river and the sunshine beaming down on it all.

Spring had truly arrived in Fogas and Véronique couldn't care less.

Standing at the kitchen window in her apartment, she was in a foul mood, one that had descended a couple of days into her trip to St Paul de Fenouillet and hadn't left her since.

She'd arrived at the small town nestled amongst the vineyards full of optimism, thinking she might at last discover something about her past. Thanks to the internet and the few bits and pieces she'd gleaned from Maman over the years, she'd tracked down her mother's cousins and they'd been overjoyed to meet her, welcoming her to their home on the hillside overlooking the vines they'd tended for generations, each passing year marked by a row of bottles in the cellar.

But in the week that she'd been their guest, not one of them had been able to cast any light on the mystery of her father.

Gerard and Marc, who now ran the family business, had been next to useless, barely remembering the short sojourn Maman had spent there. They'd been in their late teens at the time and more concerned with girls and rugby than some cousin who'd got herself into a mess.

Marie, their sister, hadn't offered much more. She remembered Annie with affection, had spent long days working in the fields with her and had been eager to help when the baby was born. But her mother, Yvette, hadn't been keen for her daughter to get too familiar with the ways of motherhood at such a young age, and from someone who'd approached it from the most unorthodox of angles, and so gradually she'd spent less and less time with her cousin.

Which left Yvette, the woman who'd agreed to take in the niece who had become pregnant out of wedlock. Now in her late seventies and a widow of many years, she passed her days sitting at the window of the grand farmhouse that had once been her domain but was now run by her daughter-in-law whom she couldn't stand. She'd been only too pleased to take Véronique's arm and walk with her amongst the vines, telling her tales of harvests long past and listing all the things her sons were doing wrong with the business. But when pressed for information about Annie's pregnancy, she revealed only one thing.

Véronique's father had been a passing fair worker.

Yvette had told her this in the unflinching manner that Véronique knew she herself had inherited but as she struggled to adapt to this latest piece in the puzzle that was her parentage, she sensed there was something more, something that remained unsaid.

'That's it?' she'd asked, trying to hide her

213

shock. So much for all the essays she'd written at school about her father being a pilot or a film star. He'd been nothing more than casual labour and an even more casual fling. 'That's all you know?'

Yvette had stopped, her thin frame leaning heavily on Véronique's arm.

'That's all Annie told me.' She squinted into the bright light as she surveyed the lands stretching before her.

'But you think there's more to it?' Véronique could hear the hope in her own voice.

'Ah!' Yvette turned to her, eyes dancing now. 'Now that would be speculation!'

She bent down to a vine and inspected its bare stems which had just been pruned. Before long it would be covered with buds, but now, in the slanting sunlight, the abundance of grapes seemed a long way off.

'Look,' said Yvette and her frail hand took hold of Véronique's, trailing her finger up the length of the stem.

'It's wet!' declared Véronique as her finger came away covered in small droplets.

Yvette nodded. 'It's the tears of the vine. Happens every spring when they come back to life.'

She straightened up, her back creaking.

'They say a vine must suffer to produce the best fruit,' she said. 'All I know about your mother's time here is that she suffered. More so than I would have thought over some passing fling.'

'Do you think she's not telling the truth?'

Yvette put a wrinkled hand to Véronique's cheek.

'I don't know for certain, child. But perhaps you should be looking closer to home.'

So Véronique had returned to the valleys of Fogas even more confused than before.

She really needed to ask Maman outright. But that took more courage than Véronique had and would create more pressure than she thought their relationship could bear.

It wasn't like she'd had the chance anyway. She'd been back three weeks and in that time she'd only seen Maman a handful of times, each one of them in passing, and not once had Maman asked her about her trip. Which Véronique was profoundly grateful for, as she'd been mortified when Maman had started broadcasting that she was off for a romantic liaison with Major Gaillard. She deliberately hadn't told Maman where she was going and had been happy for her to presume the dashing fireman was involved. Just hadn't expected her normally tight-lipped mother to start telling all and sundry. Especially not Christian Dupuy.

Although he hadn't seemed bothered.

That was another person she hadn't really seen since she got back. Now that she was no longer behind the desk in the post office on a daily basis, Véronique was finding that her contact with the community was dwindling. And it was driving her mad.

She'd been in touch with La Poste to ask them when they thought the post office would reopen but they'd not given her a straight answer, saying that until the mayor was back, there was nothing they could do. Despite having insisted on wielding power as second in command, Pascal Souquet had proven no more helpful, muttering something about a possible visit from a delegation to assess viability. He'd ushered her out of his office before she could ask any questions.

So now she was stuck, twiddling her thumbs, waiting for Mayor Serge Papon to return and trying to find the courage to ask her mother about her past.

She opened the window and reached out to latch a shutter that had come loose and the heady scent of wisteria blossom floated up to her from the trellis below.

She slammed the window shut. Spring was not what she was in the mood for.

★   ★   ★

Long limbs strewn across the woodpile, head tipped back and bathed in sunshine, Fabian felt as though he was made from liquid mercury, not a bit of calcium in him to give his body some structure.

She'd melted him. Turned his bones to mush. And then walked away.

He inhaled deeply and held his breath, letting the warm spring air drift smoke-like into his veins, his eyes closed but his senses alert to the season. He could smell the soft perfume of blossom wafting over from the orchard behind the garden and hear a bee buzzing past as tiny lizard feet pattered over the concrete, rustling through the dried-out leaves that remained on the ground. And as he exhaled, a faint taste of honey came to him as though her lips were still resting against his.

It was fitting. To be in love at the time of year when life is starting all over again. Only trouble was, the object of his desire didn't feel the same.

He'd been left stunned by the affection Stephanie had bestowed on him up at Christian's field. Only five days ago and yet his life before seemed indistinct as though viewed through some age-darkened lens. Her kisses had seared him, awakened something he hadn't known existed.

But for Stephanie, it had been just a kiss, given in a moment of gratitude, nothing more. He'd realised this pretty quickly as she'd reversed the van off the bike and then hopped out to stow the mangled frame in the back. She'd been all quick movements and energy as usual while he'd stood there, his eyes locked on to her like a malfunctioning missile guidance system, able to track but unable to move.

'Are you okay, Fabian?' he'd heard Chloé ask and she'd slipped a small hand in his.

He'd managed to nod, nothing more and she'd led him to the van.

'Maman can do that,' she said as she settled him in and pulled the seat belt round him. 'Make you feel dizzy.'

'All set?' asked Stephanie as she got in next to him and her hand brushed his leg as she put the van in gear, sending a trace of fire up his thigh.

Then she'd paused and pointed across to a beige lump in the middle of the field they'd just exited. 'What's that?'

'My school bag.'

Stephanie twisted around to see her daughter. 'What's in it?'

'A book.'

'What book?'

'Just a book.'

Stephanie gave Chloé a long, hard look and then started to get out of the van.

'Where are you going?' Chloé asked.

'To get your precious acrobat book.'

'What?' Fabian surfaced from his stupor. 'Are you mad? There's a bull in that field in case you didn't notice!'

'I know but he's down the other end now and seeing as he's so engrossed in tearing your jacket to shreds, I might get away with it.'

'Maman, don't,' Chloé pleaded. 'It's not worth it.'

'Not worth it? You carry that thing everywhere and don't think I don't know about your night-time reading sessions!'

Chloé's eyes widened. Maman had known all this time!

Stephanie walked purposefully towards the field but before she got to the electric fence, Fabian had thrown off his seat belt and was one side of her.

'I'll go!' he commanded, holding her back with his arm. 'You just distract that beast if he starts to come towards me, okay?'

'Are you sure?'

'Of course I'm not sure! You'd have to be an idiot to go back in a field with a raging bull when you've escaped once.'

'Then why are you doing it?' Stephanie looked up at him and he couldn't help but notice that her eyes were the same colour as dew-covered moss in the morning sunlight.

'Because I'm an idiot.' And with that he hopped across the strand of wire before he could change his mind.

He'd made it there and back without Sarko even turning around, but even so, Fabian's heart had thundered in fear and also anticipation. Would he get the same reward as before?

But she hadn't moved when he'd handed her the bag. Almost as if she knew the damage she'd already caused to his delicate circuitry. She'd simply patted his arm, her gaze holding his for a brief second.

Chloé however had leapt on him and covered him in kisses, declared that he was officially her hero and had promised him ringside seats for her first public performance.

They'd dropped him back at the épicerie and he'd known then that his future lay in this small commune that had captured his heart. He hadn't even wanted to get out of the van. How on earth could he contemplate going back to Paris?

He'd entered the bar prepared to do anything Tante Josette asked of him in order to safeguard his life here. But it hadn't been like that. They'd closed early and had sat at the big table to discuss the possibilities open to them.

To his delighted surprise, Tante Josette had

told him she wanted him to stay, that she'd grown to appreciate his help. Her only stipulation was that he left the inglenook alone. Sentimental value, she'd said. Something about it being Oncle Jacques' favourite place to sit. She'd agreed to consider a wood-burner in the future, but for the time being, they would leave it as is.

However, they'd both acknowledged that in order to make their situation work, they needed more space.

It was Tante Josette who'd suggested he move out. She'd already found somewhere for him to rent, his enthusiasm for the proposal increasing when he discovered it was old Monsieur Papon's house up in Picarets.

So everything was sorted. He'd even come up with a fantastic idea for the money that the wine auction had brought in now that ripping out the fireplace wasn't an option. Tante Josette would love it and it was only fitting seeing as Oncle Jacques had bought the wine in the first place.

And to top it all, he was in love with the most amazing woman in the world.

He felt a thud on his chest as Tomate the cat arrived, purring loudly, her claws sinking into his legs as she settled. But he didn't feel the pinpricks of feline adoration. Nothing could penetrate the mellow cloud of well-being that surrounded him.

He took a deep breath. In three days' time he would move up to his new home and be even closer to Stephanie. A smile rippled across his face.

Christian Dupuy pulled up outside the épicerie just in time to catch a flash of afternoon sunlight reflecting off a closing window in the old school.

Véronique.

He threw up an arm in welcome, not able to see if she responded as the sun was bouncing off the glass, and then he made his way towards the bar.

He felt guilty that he hadn't made the effort to visit her since she got back a few weeks ago. But to tell the truth, he didn't have the inclination to witness her breathless excitement as she regaled him about her romantic rendezvous with the gallant Major Gaillard. Personally, he failed to see the attraction. The man was old enough to be her father and going bald to boot.

Maybe that was it, he mused as he paused, hand on the door handle. You couldn't really blame her for looking for a father figure. But the Major of all people, with that hideous moustache . . .

Not that it was any of his business.

He shook his head, as much to dispel the thoughts swirling around his brain as to luxuriate in the thick, blond curls that were his crowning glory, and then he entered the bar.

'Bonjour, Christian!' Josette called out, a smile of welcome on her face as he stooped to kiss her.

'You seem cheerful. Full of the joys of spring?'

'Something like that!'

'What about the work?' Christian tipped his

221

head in the direction of the blue tarpaulin that still covered the new entranceway to the shop.

'Pouf!' Josette waved a dismissive hand in reply. 'They're supposed to be back with us in a week's time but I'm not holding my breath. Did your mother get my message about the smoke alarms?'

Christian nodded. 'She said to tell you that she hasn't heard back from the salesman yet but when she does, she'll get him to call.'

'I suppose she's got a big order in?' asked Josette with a roguish grin, Christian's mother being well known for her astounding ability to make fire out of a boeuf bourguignon.

'No doubt! But she's beginning to wonder where they've got to. It's been a month since the bloke called in.'

'He's probably on the Med celebrating the deal of his life!'

'Probably! Luckily she didn't pay him up front.' Christian looked around the empty room. 'So, where's your sidekick?'

'Up in the woodshed. You here to see him?'

'Just want to run some revised figures past him.'

'Well don't go smoking anything funny out there!' she warned him. 'Got him into all sorts of trouble last time.'

Christian raised his hands in mock surrender and then wandered through to the back door. He could see Fabian sprawled on a pile of logs, his head thrown back to catch the sun, a soppy smile plastered across his face and Tomate lying across his legs. It certainly looked as though the

222

Parisian was under the influence of something more than oxygen.

'Bonjour, Fabian.'

The young man's eyes flew open and his limbs jerked in surprise, depositing the cat on to the ground.

'Oh! Christian!'

'Not who you were dreaming of?'

Fabian blushed. 'Is it that obvious?'

'I thought you'd confiscated some more dope.' Christian sat down. 'So who's the lucky lady?'

Fabian scrunched up his face as though debating whether to say. 'Promise you won't laugh?'

'Promise.'

'Stephanie Morvan.'

Christian let out a bellow that ricocheted around the back garden and up into the trees.

'Sorry!' He held up a hand of apology at Fabian's wounded expression. 'Couldn't help it. Stephanie Morvan. Are you insane?'

'Totally.' Fabian hung his head in despair. 'I know she's out of my league. But . . . '

'She'll eat you for breakfast.'

'I know.'

'You'll never know what mood she's in and whatever you guess, it'll be wrong.'

'I know.'

'And she has a wicked temper.'

'I know.'

'Well in that case, I wish you all the best!'

'It's not that simple,' Fabian protested. 'She doesn't love me back.'

'Ahhhh!' Christian leaned back against the

wood and closed his eyes. 'Can't help you there, my friend.'

'She kissed me. When I rescued Chloé. And it changed my whole existence. Now I can't stop thinking about her.'

Christian stayed silent, listening to the sounds of the season as birds of prey screeched in the skies above and the cat chased scuttling lizards across the yard.

'I know I'm wasting my time,' Fabian declared mournfully. 'But I wouldn't swap this feeling for the world. You know what I mean?'

'No, actually I don't.' Christian scratched his head, disturbed by all this talk of romance, and reached into his pocket for the revised accounts.

'You've never been in love?' asked Fabian incredulously. 'Not once?'

'Never,' came the terse reply.

'Wow! I mean, it's the first time for me. Never felt like this before. But you . . . ' he shrugged. 'Just thought you would have had loads of girlfriends.'

Christian drummed his fingers impatiently. What was it with everyone recently? The whole of Fogas seemed to be loved up. Apart from him. Not that he had much opportunity what with the farm taking all his time and now she was seeing . . .

He slammed the door abruptly on that thought and turned to Fabian, papers in hand.

'Do you think you could have a quick look at these numbers and let me know if I've made a difference?' he asked, his voice clipped.

'I'll do it now if you like?'

'No need!' The farmer was already standing, eager to be away in case what Fabian had caught was contagious. 'I'll drop in later.'

And with that he was off down the garden, willing his thoughts on to other things but a small part of his mind conscious that the whole time he'd been listening to Fabian, he'd been thinking about Véronique.

Now what was that all about?

★   ★   ★

Véronique had seen the blue Panda pull up and had waved back but she didn't think her gesture had been noticed. She'd fought the temptation to go down to the épicerie on some fabricated errand, doing a bit of housework instead, and was about to curl up with a book when she heard heavy footsteps on the stairs, followed by a resounding knock at the door.

'Christian!' she exclaimed when she saw him standing on the doorstep.

'Bonjour, Véronique!' He kissed her cheeks and she stood back to let him enter.

'Would you like a coffee?'

'That'd be great,' he said and she noticed he was awkward, his huge hands twisting the jacket that he'd taken off.

'Make yourself at home,' she suggested, realising it was the first time he'd visited her in her own place. They'd only really got to know each other in the last six months, their friendship forged in the battle over the Auberge. No wonder he was a bit nervous.

'Been talking to Fabian,' Christian began as he settled into the armchair. 'He's fallen in love. With Stephanie of all people!'

Véronique laughed as she handed him his coffee, noticing how tiny the espresso cup looked in his grasp. 'Yes, I heard. Josette says he's dropped all talk of profit and loss. All he cares about now is getting Stephanie to go out with him!'

'Huh!' Christian tossed his head in scorn and a scowl darkened his features. 'Suppose you've been harpooned by that bugger Cupid too?'

'Me?' Véronique's voice rose in surprise and her cheeks went pink.

'Well, you have just spent a week with Major Goatherd.'

'Gaillard. His name is Major Gaillard.'

'Whatever. Did you have a good time?' he asked, his voice sounding more abrupt than he'd intended.

Véronique rose from the sofa and busied herself rearranging ornaments on the dresser while she pondered her response. Could she trust him to keep her secret?

'Judging by your silence it was a resounding success!' muttered Christian. He drank his coffee in one gulp, the acrid taste suiting his sour mood, and stood to go, kicking himself for having come over in the first place. He'd known he wasn't in the right frame of mind to hear more love talk.

He shrugged on his jacket and strode towards the door.

'I didn't go away with him.'

She spoke so quietly he almost didn't hear. 'Sorry?'

'Major Goatherd . . . Gaillard. I didn't go away with him.'

'Then why did Annie . . . ' Christian tailed off, confused.

'I didn't want her to know where I was going. Why I was going.'

Christian watched her begin to pace up and down the rug as he tried to ignore his thumping heart. Finally she stopped and turned to face him, tears visible.

'I went to find my father.' She hung her head and wiped away a teardrop with her sleeve.

'And did you find him?' he asked gently, unsure what to do, the hands that had been restlessly twisting his jacket now hanging uselessly by his side.

'No. Not a trace.' She made a face. 'Found a good wine supplier for the Auberge though!'

He laughed and pulled her into a clumsy hug.

'Come on,' he said. 'Get your coat and let's go sample some of this beer from St Girons that Fabian is plugging. Maybe listening to him mope around will make us both feel better.'

'What have you got to be upset about?' Véronique asked as she grabbed her purse off the table.

Christian scratched his head.

'Nothing, really,' he responded with honesty. 'Not any more.'

As they walked down the road he refused to let himself contemplate the reasons behind his reply.

'I'm telling you it's him!' René announced with authority and licked the end of his pencil before staring once more at the blank sheet of paper in front of him.

'But how can you be so sure?' asked Josette as she passed the magazine she'd been reading to Annie.

'Male intuition!'

'Is there any such thing?'

René scowled as the door opened and Christian and Véronique walked in.

'Here's the man to tell you,' René said as he shook hands with the farmer.

'Tell you what?' Christian took off his jacket and settled in at the end of the table which was the only space free of stock. 'Two beers please, Josette. Those fancy ones from the brewery in town.'

'Rrrené rrreckons he has male intuition,' Annie scoffed as she kissed her daughter. 'Whateverrr that is.'

'Well whatever it is, it's bound to be worse than the female version,' quipped Véronique, sitting next to her mother.

René snatched the magazine from Annie and thrust it under Christian's nose, pointing at a paragraph that had been circled.

'Read that and tell me who you think it is.'

Christian obliged.

' "Ariège Romeo, 45,75kg, athletic type with own property, seeks young woman to share his life. Must love beagles." '

He lowered the page and stared at René, a grin on his face.

'Where did you get this?'

'He left it in the car. We went fishing together this morning.'

'Who is it?' asked Véronique, taking the magazine from Christian and flicking to the front to check the title.

Christian looked at the three women, all of them nonplussed.

'You can't guess?'

They shook their heads.

'He drives a tractor, loves hunting and always wears an orange beret.'

'No! It can't be . . . ' Josette began.

'If it is he's lying about his weight!' countered Annie.

'Bernard Mirouze?' screeched Véronique in delight. 'He put a lonely hearts notice in *Le Chasseur Français*?'

René was now rocking with mirth.

'I don't know how you recognised him from that description,' continued Josette. '*Athletic* isn't the word I would have used.'

'And he's got to be at least 90kg!' said Véronique as she passed the advert to Annie who cast an eye over it and snorted.

'Bloody idiot! No wonderrr you knew it was him. That's his telephone numberrr at the bottom!'

'But what a weird place to put his advert, in a hunting magazine of all things.' Josette skimmed through the pages which were filled with advice on stalking deer and tracking boar.

'It's where he got his dog from,' Christian said.

'And look how that's turned out!' René said with a laugh.

'Wonder if he's had any luck,' Véronique mused as Josette set her beer before her.

'Well if he hasn't, he's about to!' René licked his pencil and began writing. ''Dear Ariège Romeo . . .''

'You're not!' Véronique admonished, while Christian started giggling.

'Too bloody right I am. Need something to keep me amused now I'm off the cigarettes. And anyway, do him good to have a reply. Imagine if he didn't get one at all.'

'I think that's cruel, don't you Fabian?' Josette asked as her nephew moped into the room.

'What's cruel?'

'Sending a fake reply to a lonely hearts advert.'

Fabian propped his elbows on the bar and regarded René with disapproval. 'You shouldn't mess with people's emotions like that.'

René's eyebrows shot up. 'Oh la la! Hark at him.'

'He's in love,' Véronique explained and Fabian blushed. 'With Stephanie.'

René dropped his pencil and stared at the young man in horror.

'Are you mad?'

'I've already had this conversation with him,' explained Christian.

'But . . . but . . . she'll eat him alive.'

'He knows.'

'She'll trample all over his heart and send it

back to him crushed and broken like his bike.'

'He knows.'

'And no other woman will ever measure up afterwards.'

'Like I said, René. He knows.'

René shook his head in despair, aghast at the future that lay ahead for the Parisian.

'I can't help it,' Fabian exclaimed. 'I'm in love.'

'Bonjour!' The door swung open letting in a gust of fresh air and Paul entered. 'Why you all are having long faces?'

'Fabian's in love!' announced Josette as she got up to serve him.

'And it is to make him unhappy?' he queried. 'But I am thinking the French are the expert lovers?'

'Oh we are!' boasted René. 'It's just Fabian that isn't. And besides, he's Parisian so he doesn't count.'

'So why is he like this?'

'He's in love with Stephanie.'

'Stephanie?' Paul's voice rose an octave. 'Our Stephanie? From the Auberge?'

Everyone in the bar nodded sombrely.

'But she will eating him up!'

'He knows!' came a chorus of voices.

'She will breaking his heart.'

'He knows!'

'And she will poisoning him with her cooking!'

'What?' Fabian looked up.

'She can not cooking,' Paul informed him, shaking his head at the memory of his one and only taste of her fare. 'She is terrible.'

'I didn't know that.'

'But none of this matters, no?'

Fabian shook his head.

'Then you are really in love!' Paul slapped him on the back, whether in congratulation or commiseration was unclear.

'But how do I make her mine?'

René let out a bark of laughter. 'Why are you asking him? He's English! What do they know about love?'

'You thought they knew buggerrr all about cooking not too long ago but now you'rrre down at the Auberrrge all the time!' Annie retorted.

'But this is different! Everyone knows the French are the most romantic nation on the planet. It's in our genes!' René smoothed his moustache and stuck out his chest, making Véronique choke on her beer. 'Go on, Paul. Say something romantic!'

'Five lengths of saucisson please, Josette,' Paul said, his eyes dancing with merriment while everyone laughed.

'See! He can't. The English know nothing about love.'

Paul put the shopping in his bag and then turned to Fabian.

'So, what am I knowing about love? Only that it is the most beautiful of dreams,' he said, his rich voice silencing the room. 'But the worst of nightmares.'

'Oh, that's lovely!' gushed Josette. 'Say something else!'

The Englishman took a moment to get the French right and then began again.

'Love comforts like sunshine after it rains.'

'More!' said Véronique, her face alight.

Paul gave a flourish and then continued.

'Love from one side hurts,' he said as Fabian nodded furiously in agreement. 'But love from two sides heals.'

'Ahhhh.' Josette clapped her hands and even Annie was looking misty eyed as Paul picked up his shopping to go.

'And finally,' he said. 'The last of English advice.'

He put an arm around Fabian and spoke slowly, so as not to mangle the words written so long ago in another language.

'She is beautiful and so to be chased. She is woman and so to be won!'

He said his goodbyes and let himself out of the now silent bar as his French neighbours digested their lesson in love.

'That was amazing!' sighed Josette as she cleared up the glasses. 'Who'd have thought the English could be so romantic. And to make it up just like that. Incredible! Don't you think, René!'

'Uh?' René looked up from the piece of paper he'd been scribbling on furiously.

'What are you writing?' asked Véronique, craning her neck to see.

'No point wasting it. I'm putting it in the letter to Bernard. What was the last bit again?'

Véronique clipped him around the ear while outside Paul was walking back to the Auberge, wondering if his poor translations had caused Shakespeare to rotate in his grave.

233

By the time the grand discussion on romance had concluded and its participants had made their way home, the stunning spring day had yielded to night, the chill in the air reminding people that summer was still a long way off. The hours passed and as midnight approached, La Rivière lay wrapped in calm, windows shuttered, lights out.

There was no one to see the dark figure slinking along the alley that led from the church to the épicerie, hugging tight to the walls and the shadows. No one to hear its careful footfall as it darted across the road and on to the patch of land that had been so lovingly tended.

If someone had been there, they might have seen the glint of light refracting off a blade, heard the soft swish of metal cutting through plastic.

But even if they had, they would have thought it nothing more than a cow down at the riverside, in search of a late-night drink. After all, this was Fogas. Nothing bad ever happened in Fogas.

13

'Chloé! Get your bum down here or I'm leaving without you!'

Stephanie heard a flurry of footsteps in response and then the heavy tread of her daughter coming down the stairs.

'Have you got everything?'

Chloé nodded, rucksack slung across her shoulder.

'Now be good, you hear me?' Stephanie warned as she tucked a stray black curl behind a freshly scrubbed ear. 'No getting into trouble.'

Chloé opened her mouth to protest but Maman simply raised an eyebrow and Chloé held her peace.

She'd got off lightly over the truancy. Maman had been so relieved her only child hadn't come to a gruesome end impaled on Sarko's horns that Chloé hadn't really been admonished. She'd had a lecture about the importance of education and Maman made her write a letter of apology to Madame Soum at the school but that was it.

Of course, this slight inconvenience was greatly outweighed by the status she now had amongst her classmates, none of whom had witnessed the event, thereby giving Chloé free rein to embellish. Max and Nicolas Rogalle were particularly enthralled and had made Chloé retell the story every morning since, on their way to school. They'd even waived her obligation to

235

do their maths homework, so honoured were they to be the walking companions of a real-life matador.

But the best part about Chloé's flirtation with death was that Maman had finally relented when it came to practising somersaults. It transpired that she'd known all along about Chloé's antics, about the acrobatic sessions behind Annie's barn and the book which she used to train. Now Maman wanted no more secrets. She'd made Chloé promise never to use Christian's field again, which Chloé was more than willing to agree to given what had happened, and had granted permission instead for her to use the back garden.

'Have you got your book?'

Chloé patted her bag which contained her manual on gymnastics, all the more treasured now that it had been rescued by the heroic Fabian, and Stephanie stroked her hair with affection.

'And your toothbrush?'

Another pat of the bag.

'Only a couple more weeks, love, and then things will get back to normal.'

'I know, Maman. It's fine. And anyway, Annie said she'd help me with my aerial cart-wheels . . .'

Stephanie clamped a hand over her daughter's mouth. 'I don't want to hear about it, all right? Otherwise I'll just have images of you in a pile of broken bones all day.'

Chloé grinned behind the hand.

'Now get in the car before I change my mind

and tie you to the table!'

Stephanie closed the door behind them and watched her daughter skip down the path towards the van. All these years she'd been trying to stop the inevitable, attempting to prevent something that was preordained, and it had taken the incident with the bull to make her accept the truth: Chloé was an acrobat, pure and simple.

The thought filled Stephanie with a mixture of pride and apprehension. She was proud that her daughter had inherited her father's abilities but apprehensive about where they might take her. And the questions they would bring.

★   ★   ★

'Have you got everything?'

Fabian nodded and patted his rucksack.

'You haven't forgotten your toothbrush or your pyjamas?'

He laughed and gave his aunt a hug.

'I'm thirty-five, Tante Josette! I think I'm old enough to take care of myself now.'

He threw the bag on to the passenger seat of his car, the rest filled with bits of old furniture, pots and pans and crockery that he'd been given once people heard he was moving into the house in Picarets. There was no room for a bike, which didn't matter as his beautiful Time bicycle was beyond repair and he was about to look for a new one.

'Are you sure you don't want to take the bed from your room?' fretted Josette.

237

'Stop fussing!'

'Huh!' Josette plumped herself up with indignation. 'I'm just worried about you.'

'Thought you couldn't wait to get rid of me!' teased Fabian as they went back into the bar.

'You know it's not like that,' she protested with a quick glance at Jacques who was looking sad in the inglenook. 'It's just . . . '

Fabian put an arm around her thin shoulders and kissed her cheek. 'I know. I really do. Now how about we have a cup of coffee and you help me choose my next bike before I head up the hill?'

He took a seat and started thumbing through a catalogue while Josette got to grips with the coffee machine.

★ ★ ★

Stephanie waited until Chloé's mop of black hair disappeared behind Annie's door and then she drove on. It was another beautiful day, the azure sky marred by only a few wisps of cloud, the sunshine streaming down on the green pastures. Even the trees in the forest were starting to bud, some already showing signs of leaves. Soon the clumps of mistletoe that festooned the bare branches all winter would be hidden again until the autumn.

It was the kind of day where being cooped up inside in the Auberge would be difficult to bear.

Still, it was a good job and she loved working with Lorna and Paul. Her English was improving, although not as rapidly as they were learning French, but that was fine. They tended to communicate in a mixture of the two now anyway.

All in all, everything was going very well. She had money coming in from the Auberge and in less than a month her business would open and provide another source of income. Before long she might even be able to afford proper gymnastic lessons for Chloé.

She shook her head at the idea. The fact she was even contemplating it!

And of course the other good news had been that Fabian had lifted the restraining order against her and astoundingly had waived the bill for the damages to his bike too. He'd come to see her at the Auberge the day after the incident with Sarko, Lorna laughing at him as he stood in the doorway shifting his weight from foot to foot like an awkward teen. When he'd managed to get the words out, he told her that she didn't need to compensate him. For either accident!

It was such a relief. She'd been cutting it fine in the financial department, what with rent due, more stock needed and the fence still to put up around the garden centre. Plus she had payments to make on the small loan she'd secured to set up the business. So when he'd said she didn't need to pay him, she'd almost kissed him again. But something held her back. He'd seemed so vulnerable, like a moth flitting around a candle.

She'd thanked him profusely and given him a brief hug instead, much to Lorna's amusement. The Englishwoman was convinced Fabian had a crush on Stephanie and if she was right, even better that things were kept platonic!

Which instantly brought Pierre to mind, the familiar tingle of nerves pinpricking her skin in response.

Only four weeks until he was here. She'd got to the point where she didn't know which she was looking forward to most: the grand opening or his visit. Of course, she still had to tell Chloé, a task she wasn't relishing. Especially now the child seemed to think Fabian was perfect father material.

Still, Stephanie had to admit, she owed Fabian more than she could ever pay. She shuddered, not wanting to contemplate what might have happened if he hadn't been there.

She was torn from her morbid thoughts as a deer leapt gracefully out of the trees to the right, followed by a faun, legs almost too long for its body, and Stephanie slammed on the brakes. They darted across the road in front of her and off into the forest on her left.

'Beautiful!' she sighed as she followed their flight until they were lost in the foliage.

It was like an omen. A metaphor for herself and Chloé maybe, she mused as she drove off. She was still thinking about it when she got to the junction opposite the Auberge and turned right towards the épicerie. And if she'd been aware of the man in hunting apparel using binoculars to track her progress from his hiding place on the path behind the village, she might have appreciated just how apt her metaphor was.

'I don't understand. Are you telling me it's three thousand euros and you don't even get the wheels?'

Josette was looking at the bike catalogue, her face aghast.

'It's made of carbon,' Fabian said defensively.

'So are pencils and they don't cost that much!'

'It's top of the range. That's why.'

'But it doesn't make sense. It doesn't get you any faster from A to B.'

'It can do. If you're any good.'

'And are you? Three thousand euros worth of good?'

Fabian took the catalogue from her. 'You don't understand,' he muttered.

'Too right I don't! It's insane paying that kind of money for a bike. Especially with your record around these parts. Only here ten weeks and you've already got through two of them.'

'That wasn't my fault!'

'No, I'll give you that. But even so, it's extravagant to say the least.' Josette got up and cleared their cups on to the bar. 'Can't you get something cheaper?'

'I don't want something cheaper,' sulked Fabian.

Josette shook her head at the spendthrift nature of the younger generation, sharing a knowing look with her husband. She'd just turned back to berate Fabian further when the door swung open and Stephanie stood swaying in the doorway.

'What is it?' Josette called out in alarm at the young woman's pale features.

Stephanie staggered forward, close to collapse, and Fabian leapt to his feet and thrust an arm around her, leading her to a chair.

'Are you hurt?' he asked with concern.

She stared at him, her eyes out of focus.

'The garden centre . . . '

'What about it?'

'Someone . . . someone has . . . ' She shook her head and covered her face with her hands, unable to continue.

'Keep an eye on her,' said Fabian as he left the bar and crossed the road.

He didn't have to go far. A few steps and he could see the full extent of the damage.

'Christ!'

The polytunnel had been ripped apart, probably by a knife, and the plastic sheets hung in tattered strips, the ground beneath them strewn with broken pots and up-turned plants, roots exposed, stems snapped. The perpetrators had even upended the water butt Stephanie used to collect rain water which normally stood just by the entrance, the soil around it now sodden.

Judging by the number of beer bottles which littered the floor, most smashed, glass glittering underfoot, it had been the work of some drunken yobs. And yet, thought Fabian, he hadn't heard any noise last night and his bedroom was directly opposite.

Whoever had been responsible, the attack had been systematic and ruthless. And Fabian knew that it spelt disaster for Stephanie.

He raced back to the bar and told Josette to call the police, explaining what had happened.

'What's the point?' Stephanie raised her head, her question laced with defeat. 'What can they do?'

'It's criminal damage,' Fabian said. 'You have to tell them.'

She fell silent.

'They're on their way,' Josette announced as she put down the phone.

Stephanie ran a hand through her hair, her bottom lip caught between her teeth.

'It's over,' she said in a shaky voice as Fabian sat opposite her and took her hands in his.

'No it's not! We'll get this sorted.'

'How?' she asked with acerbity. 'I can't replace that stock. Or the polytunnel. There's no way I can open before the planting season which means I won't be able to pay back the bank . . .'

She gulped, fighting back tears.

'I should have got the fence up earlier,' she whispered. 'I just didn't have the money.'

Fabian felt her words pierce his heart as he thought about how he'd added to the pressure by demanding compensation for his bike. When he had an account full of money.

An account full of money!

Josette was right. There were better things to spend it on.

'I'll give you the money,' he announced, energy coursing through him as he began to see a way to help her. He held up a hand as she started to protest. 'A loan! Interest free. We'll make it formal and you can pay me back in carrots or cabbages or something. But not tomatoes. I don't like tomatoes.'

Stephanie laughed, surprising even herself and making Fabian feel invincible. He jumped up excitedly.

'And the fence! I'll get the fence done this week before you replace the polytunnel.'

'You know how to put up a fence?' asked Josette incredulously.

But Fabian couldn't be derailed.

'No, not exactly. But Christian does. And I'm sure Paul would lend a hand.'

'I'll call them,' offered Josette, immediately going to the phone.

'Are you working today at the Auberge?' Fabian asked and Stephanie nodded. He glanced at his watch. 'So that gives us about three hours. You get on the phone to suppliers and start ordering and I'll talk to the police.'

He handed her his mobile and then reached for his wallet.

'And put it all on this,' he said, placing his bank card on the table.

Stephanie was stunned. She'd been knocked sideways by the attack on the garden centre, had felt it as keenly as if she had been stabbed herself.

But this outpouring of generosity was even more of a shock.

'I don't . . . know . . . what to say,' she stuttered, looking up at the tall figure before her.

'Don't say anything!' advised Josette as she re-entered the room. 'Take the money before he spends it on a bike!'

★ ★ ★

By midday the crisis was under control. Stephanie had used the morning to call her contacts and had located enough plants to restock her business. She'd also ordered new polythene sheeting for the polytunnel and the posts and wire for the fence from St Girons before she went to work the lunch-time shift at the Auberge.

The police had turned up not long after Josette's call, eager to finally have something to do in the sleepy valley, and Fabian had gone with them to inspect the damage. They'd taken copious notes and photos and had come to the same conclusion as him.

The damage had been caused by drunken youths.

'What is the world coming to?' asked Josette as she set two plates of cassoulet down on the table. 'Do you think they have any chance of catching the hooligans?'

Fabian shook his head and reached for his fork, his stomach growling in anticipation.

'The land was too dry for footprints. Although they did find an imprint in the mud by the water butt but they discounted it. Said it was some kind of hunting boot. Le Champignon or something?'

'Le Chameau,' Josette corrected him. 'Yes, it's not likely to be the kids who left that. Those boots cost a fortune. Jacques had a pair once.'

She looked over at her husband and was surprised to see he was awake and looking very concerned. No doubt troubled for Stephanie's sake.

'I didn't know Oncle Jacques hunted,' said

Fabian through a mouthful of food as he wiped a hunk of bread around his plate.

'That was before I met him. He used to go with Serge Papon.'

Fabian grinned up at her. 'But he gave it up for you?'

'Well, it's a bit daft really. Grown men stalking defenceless creatures around the hillsides. They shot each other more often than they shot any boars.' She shrugged. 'But I didn't ask him to stop. He gave it up the first time I got pregnant. Said he didn't want to take the risk when he was going to be a father . . . '

She smiled sadly, the memories still sharp across the years and Fabian froze. He'd not heard Tante Josette talk about their attempts to have a family before. She glanced at the fireplace and then continued.

'And when I miscarried, he vowed never to hunt again. Think he thought it might be a bargaining tool with God or something. Him promising not to kill wild animals in return for a child.' She laughed softly. 'Didn't work though, daft bugger!'

She reached over and patted Fabian's hand. 'He'd be so proud of you, love. What you did today.'

Fabian resumed his meal, waving away her praise. 'It's nothing. Anyone would have done the same.'

'I don't know about that. You had your heart set on that bike.'

'I can always go down to Decathlon and get something run-of-the-mill. The money is better spent helping Stephanie out.'

'Yes, you're right. Poor thing. After all the hard work she'd put in.'

'I think she was more upset that it was senseless violence, and not the first time. She told the police about the flooding incident. Explained how she'd presumed it was me but now thought the two might be connected. And don't worry,' he said as he saw his aunt frown. 'She didn't mention the joint!'

He mopped up the last few beans with his bread and popped it in his mouth, savouring the taste. 'Good food, Tante Josette!' he exclaimed as he stood up. 'Now if you'll excuse me, I have to go and see a man about a fence!'

'Are you sure you don't want to take the bed . . .'

Fabian stopped her with a kiss on the cheek. 'I'm sure!'

Josette walked to the door with him and then waited while he pulled away.

'He's a good lad!' she said as Jacques glided alongside her.

But he didn't acknowledge her. He was staring out of the window, his face creased with worry.

'Right. I'm going to put a food parcel together for him to take tonight. At least he can eat well even if he is sleeping on the floor!'

And with that she went off, leaving Jacques to his vigil.

Le Chameau boots.

That's all he was thinking about as he surveyed the village, kicking himself for having lowered his guard.

He should have known better but he'd let a few aches and pains deter him. Allowed the comfort of the inglenook to entice him away from keeping watch. And now Stephanie was paying the price.

Because the last time Jacques had seen a pair of Le Chameau boots, they'd been right here in the bar. On the stocky legs of the stranger who'd caused him such concern.

He made a silent promise that from now on, he would do whatever it took to keep Stephanie and Chloé from the danger that he was sure was just around the corner.

14

Three weeks in Fogas could seem like an eternity. It was the length of time it took Alain Rougé to inspect the seed catalogues and make the tough decision as to which variety of haricot vert would be gracing his vegetable plot this year. It was a period which matched exactly that needed by Josephine Dupuy to finally track down the company supplying her smoke alarms, only to find her order had never been received and the salesman had never even heard of it. And it took Bernard Mirouze twenty-one days to pick up the courage to reply to the one and only response to his advertisement for love. Unfortunately, as he explained in his letter, he felt himself unworthy of the romantic outpourings it contained and so, regretfully, declined all further contact. If truth be told, the amorous words had scared him rigid and he preferred to remain in the comfortable existence he had forged with Serge the beagle.

Three weeks was also how long Fabian had been trying to find the right moment to ask Stephanie out.

'You need to grrrab the bull by the horrrns!' advised an unsympathetic Annie.

'Huh! If it hadn't been for the bloody bull, I wouldn't be in this mess,' groaned Fabian as he placed a cup of coffee in front of her on the small wooden table in the middle of his kitchen.

It was a Monday, his day off, and he'd invited Annie round for the morning. Following his removal up the hill to Picarets, Josette had insisted that they draw up a rota for running the shop, rightly pointing out that it was ludicrous for them both to be there all the time. And this was the first day he'd made the most of it.

Annie was staring at her cup suspiciously.

'Don't worry,' he laughed. 'It's the same blend as in the bar!'

She raised it to her lips and took a sip.

Amazing. And now she could get it at Fabian's house too! She eyed the compact coffee machine on the worktop next to the sink.

'Arrre they expensive, those things?'

'Not overly, why?'

'No rrreason . . . '

'Annie, I'm not sure that's a good idea,' Fabian said with the gentle tone of a counsellor.

'You'rrre prrrobably rrright,' she conceded with a mischievous grin. 'If I had my own machine I might be tempted to go back on the caffeine!'

Fabian blushed. 'How long have you known?'

'About 'Annie's Blend'? A while.'

'You never said anything.'

'It didn't taste any differrrent and I knew you werrre doing it forrr the best . . . ' She drained her drink and made a sound of appreciation.

'Would you like another cup then?'

'Thought you'd neverrr ask! And you can tell me about yourrr disastrrrous love life while you make it.'

'Not much to tell,' lamented Fabian as he

moved around the kitchen in his new home.

And it was true.

He'd spent three weeks in close proximity to the woman of his dreams and he still hadn't found the words to tell her how he felt.

The Monday after the attack on the garden centre, he'd started work on the fence. Christian had dropped down to tell him what needed doing but had been unable to help out as he was busy with calving. So Fabian had laboured alone under the April sun, hammering the fence posts into place.

A day and a half Christian had said to get the posts in the ground. It took Fabian three days thanks to an unforeseen quantity of rocks under the soil and he'd never hurt so much in his life.

Every evening as he hauled himself into the van his muscles screamed in agony, fibres knotted, tendons twisted. Then he would get a waft of incense as Stephanie changed gear or catch the soft tone of her voice as she talked about Chloé and the pain would disappear, dissipating into nothing as a warm sense of well-being filled him.

This would carry him through the evening and his solitary meal and then, not having had the time to make the trip to Paris to collect his furniture, he would collapse into his sleeping bag on the floor. He would wake the next morning eager to get back to work until finally, on the third afternoon, he lifted out the last obstinate rock and drove the sole remaining post into a hole with a sledge hammer.

Christian had arrived the next day and

together they'd fixed the wire mesh to the posts and started work on the gates and by the end of the week they were finished and Stephanie's garden centre was protected.

She'd been delighted. Enough to make Fabian's blistered hands and aching arms seem worthwhile.

But he'd been too tired to make his move and instead had gone home to his empty house, devoured a tin of second-rate cassoulet and fallen asleep in the battered armchair next to the fire.

The following week he'd worked on the polytunnel, straightening out the dents in the frame and re-covering it in plastic. When it was ready, he'd started collecting the plants and shrubs Stephanie had ordered from various places in the region, hauling heavy pots in and out of the van, his back throbbing, his shoulders on fire. He'd had some help from Paul, but not much as the beautiful spring sunshine was bringing lots of tourists to the area and the Auberge was busy. On the Friday when he'd finished, Stephanie had burst into tears at the sight of her resurrected business, and she'd invited him to have pizza with her and Chloé.

Tonight, he'd promised himself, as he walked the short distance through Picarets to her house. I'll tell her tonight. But he'd sat down on her sofa after dessert and had woken at dawn, a blanket thrown over him and a pillow under his head.

He'd let himself out and made his way home, annoyed at his own faint-heartedness.

The third week he'd hardly seen her. She'd been busy doing extra shifts in the Auberge and he'd spent time in Paris, arranging to rent out his flat and picking up his belongings. When he'd got back to Picarets, he'd found that the addition of a comfy bed didn't stop his sleepless nights. And the suffering in his heart after a week of minimal contact was more than the physical agony he'd endured in the previous fortnight.

'I think you'rrre afrrraid to tell herrr,' announced Annie. 'Afrrraid she might say no!'

'You're probably right,' Fabian agreed as he sat next to her, his knees knocking the table every time he moved. He'd been reluctant to part with the bits of furniture which had come with the house, keeping the armchair that was losing its stuffing and the old dressing table with the wonky legs in the bedroom. And this ridiculously small table which had been repaired countless times over the generations, pitted with holes from hungry woodworm and held together with brackets and screws. The idea of replacing it with his glass designer one had seemed absurd.

He shifted his legs carefully to get them out of range before continuing. 'I have a highly developed aversion to rejection. Being bullied at school will do that for you!'

'I didn't know you werrre bullied at school.'

'Véronique never said?'

Annie shook her head. 'Why would she?'

Fabian stared at the weather-beaten face of the woman who had become his friend and he felt something shift in their relationship as he realised he knew her daughter better than she did.

'Because Véronique was bullied at school too,' he said softly.

Annie slowly lowered her cup and her eyes fixed on him, bewilderment replacing her usual asperity.

'You didn't know?'

'No!' she whispered, her voice hoarse.

Fabian looked down at the table as he debated how much to tell her.

*　*　*

In the end he'd told her more than she thought she could bear.

About the kids at school and the words they used. About the way they chased Véronique, even in the holidays. And about the sanctuary she'd found in the church.

Annie had refused Fabian's offer of a lift home, wanting the cool air on her face to counteract the burning in her chest.

Shame.

She'd never felt anything like it. Coursing through her, accompanying her every step as she made her slow way down the hill.

She'd thought she knew all about humiliation. That the stigma she'd carried with her since the day of Véronique's conception was as bad as it could get. Neighbours turning away from her in the market place, conversations broken off as she approached. Her strategy had been simple. Avoid people as much as possible. She'd resigned from

254

the Conseil Municipal, stopped going to the summer fête and hadn't set foot under the plane trees on the Champ de Mars on a Saturday since Véronique was a nipper. It had alleviated some of the heartache. But still she'd lived her life in this commune, knowing she was branded with an invisible scarlet letter.

This however was far, far worse.

Her only child, the child she'd endured all of that for, had been subjected to endless abuse and all because Annie wouldn't say who the father was.

She felt sick, cold waves of nausea rising up her throat.

Poor Véronique. The things those bullies had said to her. About her own mother. No wonder she'd never come home and told.

How could she? How could she walk in the door from school and say that everyone in her class said her mother was a harlot? That the reason her Maman hadn't revealed the identity of her father was because she didn't know it.

Annie reached her front door and took a while to get the key in the lock, tremors afflicting her normally steady hands.

What else could she have done? She'd made a vow, an agreement torn from her by a cheated wife which Annie had felt was fair payment for the sordid liaison which couldn't even be called an affair. But if she had known the price would be paid not only by herself, but also by her daughter, would she have agreed?

She felt like the worst mother alive.

How lonely Véronique must have been,

shouldering all of that on her own. No wonder she'd always seemed so quiet, so pensive. How could Annie not have noticed? Not seen the distress her child was in when it was so obvious to others?

A terrible thought crossed her mind. And being Annie Estaque, she faced it honestly.

What if she'd chosen not to notice? What if she'd been subconsciously punishing the child who'd brought such disgrace to her and her family? The child she hadn't even known she'd wanted until she was forced into a corner and made to decide.

Could that be possible?

She lowered herself heavily on to a chair at the kitchen table and sat for a few moments, listening to the solid tick-tock of the long-case clock in the corner which had no doubt marked other occasions with the same sobriety over its many years in the Estaque family.

It explained so much, she thought as she turned her calmer mind to reflect on all she'd heard. Véronique's devout ways which Annie had never understood for one thing. Her reluctance to rent the flat at the school for another. And not once had she mentioned the reason for her reticence, even when Christian and Annie were pushing her into taking it. What must it be like for her living there now? Did the rooms echo with the past? Or had her trip to St Paul de Fenouillet laid some ghosts to rest?

Annie deliberately hadn't seen much of Véronique since she'd arrived back, wanting to avoid any situation where her daughter could confront her with whatever she'd discovered over there in the vineyards.

Now she was torn between anxiety and fear.

Anxiety that Véronique might never forgive her for keeping the secret that had caused so much torment. And fear that she would lose her daughter forever once that secret was revealed.

She reached across to the dresser and picked up the photo of a young Véronique, face serious as she stood before the camera, and although she knew it was futile, Annie wished she could have that time again so she could make amends.

She was tracing a broad finger over the fine features of her child when the front door opened with a bang and Chloé burst into the house, slamming it behind her.

'It's him!' she panted, eyes wild, face flushed, panic in her voice. 'He's out there!'

Annie leapt to her feet. 'Who, love?'

Chloé gestured at the window and Annie looked out just in time to see a dark green Renault van go around the bend, on its way to Picarets.

'Therrre's no one out therrre,' she said, puzzled.

'The van. The green van. It's him. I was walking down here when I saw him and I just started running.'

Annie took the girl by the hand and led her to the table, setting a glass of water in front of her.

'Now calm down and tell me this frrrom the beginning,' she said as she sat opposite, her hand resting on the girl's trembling arm.

Chloé took a few sips and then told her about

the day coming home from school with the Rogalle twins, the day they'd taken the lift with the stranger.

'Did you tell yourrr motherrr when you got home?' Annie asked as the tale concluded.

Chloé shook her head. 'She's so busy, and I thought she'd be angry at me for biting him and then . . . I just didn't.'

Annie nodded. 'Well, it might be nothing, Chloé. Afterrr all, I've seen that van arrround. Maybe he's just moved in and hearrrd yourrr name. In which case you've sunk yourrr teeth into an innocent man!'

Chloé's head dropped.

'But,' Annie continued, 'betterrr to be safe than sorrrry.'

She pulled open the drawer in the table and lifted something out.

'Vérrronique just bought me this. But I'm having trrrouble using it. Think I'm a bit past it to be trrrying to rrrememberrr a new numberrr. So why don't you hang on to it forrr now?'

She put the mobile phone in front of Chloé whose eyes lit up.

'If you see him again orrr if anything else happens, just call me. Okay? But no using it to orderrr pizzas frrrom Seix!'

Chloé picked up the phone and cradled it to her chest like an amulet.

'Thanks, Annie,' she said. 'I knew I could tell you.'

And Annie Estaque, who had no time for deities of any shape or size, wondered, just

258

briefly, if perhaps someone, or something, had heard her prayer.

★ ★ ★

Down in La Rivière, Josette was saying prayers of her own. She wished to God she knew how she could tempt Jacques away from the blasted window.

He'd resumed his position in the épicerie the day Stephanie had discovered the damage to the garden centre and he hadn't left it since. The poor man looked wretched, his unrelenting vigil now entering its third week, his hand constantly pressed into the small of his back for support. She'd seen him flexing his knees too, as though he was still plagued by aches and pains even in his afterlife. Hoping to attract him into the inglenook, she'd lit a small fire despite the beautiful late April sunshine. But still he wouldn't budge.

Stubborn. She'd known that from the first day he'd asked her out. She'd declined, thinking him too old for her, too ready for settling down with children.

It had been the end of the fifties and everything was in turmoil. The conflict in Algeria was still raging, the government was in disarray and there were even rumours that De Gaulle himself would soon be swept back into power. And then there was the music! Slowly, rock and roll had started to creep into France, bringing with it an abandon that chased away the politics and the internal wrangling, the bloody conflict across the sea. Suddenly it was good to be young and the future was as bright as the lights on a Parisian boulevard.

The flickering bulbs of a handful of streetlamps in Fogas weren't quite the same.

Who'd want to stay there when there was so much more beyond?

Josette had been seventeen, with dreams of life in a big city, maybe even in America, when Jacques had pulled up in the lay-by opposite the Auberge and offered her a lift into town. She'd not known him that well as a kid, being eight years younger, and by the time she reached her mid-teens, he was gone, off overseas on his national service, leaving his mother, Madame Servat, to run the épicerie single-handed. But now he was home, fit and tanned, the muscles on his forearm rippling as he opened the car door for her.

He asked her out half an hour later when they pulled up at the Pont Vieux. She'd politely turned him down, thanked him for the lift and had walked off over the bridge, her hips possibly sashaying slightly more than usual, her right arm out at an angle, handbag swinging from it. It was her best Audrey Hepburn impression.

She heard the patter of his feet across the cobbles and then he was in front of her. Begging. Pleading. Walking backwards as he made his case. Would she come with him to a dance that Saturday?

She stopped and leaned over the parapet, not too much so her hat was in danger of falling off, but just enough to accentuate the curve of her body.

Then she turned to him and with an expression of acute boredom, she consented.

He'd jumped, actually jumped with joy. Then he'd run back to his car and she was left on the pavement, wondering what she'd just done.

She'd been playing with him without even meaning to. She felt ashamed afterwards, betrayed by an instinct to seduce she hadn't even known she possessed. So instead of backing out as she wanted to, she'd gone to the dance as a kind of apology. Just one dance. Then she would let him down gently.

That was over fifty years ago. She hadn't expected Jacques Servat to be so persistent. And she hadn't expected him to be such a good dancer! Every night they had a date she vowed to her reflection as she got ready that it would be the last time. She wanted more than Fogas. More than the life she saw Madame Servat leading. Then, at the end of the evening, he would ask her out again, and her body, still vibrating from the music and his touch, would betray her and she would hear herself say yes.

After a few months she stopped having that conversation with herself in the mirror. And in a few more, just after her eighteenth birthday, they were married. And not once had she regretted it.

Josette gave a dry chuckle. Seemed like her body had known what it was doing all along!

She pulled back the tarpaulin covering the archway between the épicerie and the bar, and poked her head in.

He was still there, rubbing his back, eyes focused intently on the road.

261

She didn't know what he was watching for, he hadn't tried to explain. All she knew was that it was connected to the incident across the road and he was concerned enough to stand sentry all day and all night. There was no point in trying to dissuade him. She just hoped whatever it was that was bothering him was resolved soon. Otherwise this would be the death of him. If that was possible?

She cast her eyes around the épicerie which had changed so much in the last few weeks. Now instead of a building site, it was a clean, modern space. Most of the work was done, plastering finished, painting almost completed. All that was left were some shelves to go up and then Josette and Fabian would be able to start stocking it.

She couldn't wait. And in a week's time, they would be ready for opening.

She let the tarpaulin drop, catching one last glimpse of Jacques' hunched back as she did.

'Madame Servat?' A delivery man was standing in the doorway, wiping his perspiring brow. 'Christ,' he said gesturing towards the inglenook, 'it's toasty in here!'

He held out a pen and a clipboard for her to sign.

'Know what it's like though,' he continued as he placed a box on the table and took the clipboard back from her. 'My grandmother lives with us and she feels the cold something rotten. Must be an age thing. You make sure you stay warm!'

Unable to explain the real reason for the fire, Josette felt her hackles rising.

Age thing indeed! The man was barely in his van when she grabbed a jug of water off the bar and threw it on to the burning logs, clouds of steam billowing out into the room and making her choke. If he'd looked in his mirror as he pulled off, he would have seen the bar door thrown open, white smoke spiralling out and the woman he'd just delivered a parcel to standing outside, coughing and spluttering.

It took a few moments for the bar to clear but Jacques didn't move, merely glancing at his wife in surprise as she took a seat at one of the new tables Fabian had put outside. Yet another good idea from her nephew, she thought as she watched the traffic go by, barely aware that she was now claiming as a relative the man she'd wanted rid of only three months ago. The area in front of the shop had never really been utilised, a dilapidated old picnic bench the only concession to people wanting to have a drink in the sunshine. But Fabian had got the workmen to make a small terrace which was now decorated with four tables and chairs under a wooden trellis. He'd planted two young wisteria plants at either end and within a few years, they would provide shade in the height of summer.

Reluctantly, Josette got up from her warm seat and wandered back into the now fireless bar to continue with the stocktake she'd started that morning. Another of Fabian's changes. And not one as enjoyable as the outside seating! Still, she now knew that they had enough black shoelaces to last to the next century and that when sewing came back into fashion, they would be ahead of their rivals when it came to stocking coloured thread.

Glad of the chance to procrastinate, she turned her attention to the parcel, a slight tang of smoke issuing from the cardboard as she inspected it. What could it be? All the new lines they'd ordered for the shop had already arrived. Curiosity mounting, she slit the seal across the top and inside, resting on a mound of bubble wrap, was a note.

She recognised the sloping handwriting and quickly read it before peeling back the layers of protective plastic.

'Jacques!' she shouted as her hand flew to her throat. 'Come quickly!'

★ ★ ★

Jacques had lost count of the days. Lost track of the weeks. Almost lost his mind.

This vigil was the hardest thing he had ever done, standing here every second, trying not to fall asleep. He felt his head tip forward, his eyes closing despite himself and he shifted his weight from one leg to the other to counteract the fatigue.

Was he wasting his time? Should he just give up and accept that he would never lay eyes on the man in Le Chameau boots again?

Then he thought about Stephanie and how vulnerable she'd seemed, her garden centre destroyed, all her hard work for nothing. He stiffened his spine, stretched his legs and resumed his watch.

His head was just starting to nod again when Josette's strangled cry came to him from the bar.

Wide awake now, he quickly drifted through to where she was standing, her eyes fixed on a box open on the table before her.

'It's from Fabian!' she said, gesturing for him to look. 'He bought it with the proceeds of the wine auction.'

Slightly annoyed at being interrupted for something so trivial, he craned his neck to see over the edges of the cardboard and there, nestled amongst folds of bubble wrap, was a beautiful cabinet made of oak. But it was the contents of the cabinet that made his mouth drop open.

'Shall I?' Josette sought his permission with a smile.

He nodded and held his breath as she eased up the glass lid and lifted out the first thing that came to hand.

'It's real!' she whispered as she felt the weight of the Laguiole heavy in her palm. She ran her fingers over the trademark bee that decorated the handle and then carefully pulled out the blade. The patterned steel was slowly revealed, swirls running along it like oil on water.

'A Damascus blade?' she asked, staring at the most beautiful knife she had ever seen.

Jacques grinned and held out a ghostly finger, running it gently along the length of the metal. He couldn't feel the solid wood or the sharp edge of the blade but he could sense a warmth like he got when he touched Josette or sat in next to the fire.

Excited now, he motioned for Josette to show him the rest.

'Okay, okay!' she laughed as she reached into the cabinet, recognising immediately the Moor's head of the Corsican Vendetta. But this one was most definitely not made from plastic, its blade wicked and purposeful against the elegance of the Laguiole. Before she'd even finished closing it, Jacques was hurrying her up to open the next one, as eager as a child on Christmas morning.

There were ten in total, the exact ten knives that had lain in the cabinet next to the till all those years. It was like a reunion with long lost friends, only these were no replicas. Josette finally laid the last one back in its place and closed the glass lid, automatically wiping it with her sleeve to remove her fingerprints in an action that had long ago become habit.

'I'll get the builders to put them up on the wall in the épicerie,' she said as she refolded the plastic over the case. 'And they're not for sale!'

Jacques nodded in agreement and looking happier than he had in weeks, he floated back through to the window to resume his watch.

★   ★   ★

Many hours later and Josette was finding it hard to sleep. The day had been uneventful after the delivery, people traipsing in on their way home from work, a few kids drifting in to buy sweets, bored now they were into the second week of their school holidays. But she

266

had smiled through it all, a big beaming grin that just wouldn't go away.

Those knives! It had been a long time since she'd seen Jacques look like that, his face soft with wonder as she'd handled each one. It was how he'd looked on their wedding day when she walked into the town hall and took her place at his side, the mayor's words floating past him as he stared at her with an intensity she thought would melt her, as though she would disappear if he took his eyes off her for a moment. It was only the applause of their family and friends at the end of the ceremony that had broken the spell and he'd gathered her into his arms, whispering in her ear that he would never leave her.

Not sure he'd meant his promise to extend beyond death, though!

Resigned to being awake, Josette threw off the covers and put on her slippers. Might as well get up and make a drink. Maybe have a peek at the knives while she was down there.

Quietly, she made her way down the stairs, avoiding the creaks she knew from a lifetime of living there so as not to disturb Jacques from the window. She pushed open the door to the bar and in the moonlight filtering through from the épicerie, she saw the white glow that was her husband bent over the table, blowing furiously at the bubble wrap that covered the cabinet.

She flicked on the light and his head snapped up, a guilty look on his face.

'Couldn't sleep?' she asked, tongue firmly in her cheek.

He grinned bashfully and shrugged.

She laughed back at him and crossed the room to ease his torment, pulling the plastic away so he could gaze on the beautiful objects below.

'They're amazing,' she breathed. 'How on earth can we ever repay him?'

Jacques jerked upright and clapped his hands, dust silently disturbed by the motion. Then he pointed at the cupboard behind the bar.

'You want me to open it?' she asked incredulously. They hadn't used it in years as it was too high for her to reach and stupidly situated so that all the glasses had to be lifted off their shelf before it could be opened.

But he was nodding. So she dragged over a chair, stepped up on to it and started taking down the glasses one by one.

'This had better be good,' she muttered as she got another mouthful of dust and disturbed yet another spider.

Finally the shelf was clear and she pulled on the small wooden handle, the door stiff and reluctant to move. She tugged on it one more time and then it gave way, nearly toppling her on to the floor.

'Now what?' she asked curtly as she stared at a jumble of junk they hadn't missed for over a decade. But she didn't need him to answer as at the front of the cupboard, tucked carefully to one side, was a small box. She recognised it immediately and held it up to him.

'This?'

He nodded and then pointed to the whetstone which was wedged in next to it.

She knew then what he intended to do. Or rather, intended her to do.

She began the slow process of placing the glasses back on their shelf. It was going to be a long night!

15

Stephanie wasn't fooled by the blue skies that stretched across Picarets and down towards La Rivière, greeting the first day of May with the promise of an early summer.

She'd lived in the mountains long enough now to know that you couldn't tell the weather from the patch of sky above. You had to look west, to Mont Valier and whatever was amassing behind it. And today one look in that direction told her that there was rain coming. Possibly even a storm.

She checked her watch. Just enough time to nip into St Girons to pick up the sign she'd had made for the garden centre before going back to work the evening shift at the Auberge. But first, she had to do something she'd been putting off for a long while.

She leaned over the sink and rapped sharply on the window, gesturing at Chloé to come in.

'Did you see, Maman?' asked Chloé as she burst in the back door.

'See what?'

'My aerial cartwheel! Watch!' And before Stephanie could stop her, she raced back out and took up her position.

Stephanie covered her eyes with her hands, peeking out between her fingers as her daughter hurtled across the lawn and threw her legs up over her head, arms whipping across her body, upside down in mid-air for what seemed like far too long and then her feet were on the ground and she was standing triumphantly, beaming at her adoring audience. An audience that just about had the presence of mind to uncover her eyes before her daughter noticed.

'Brilliant!' Stephanie exclaimed as Chloé took her bows and then sauntered in. 'Well done, love.'

'Next up is the — '

'Stop! You know the rule. I don't want to hear about it until you've perfected it. That way I have a limited number of scenarios I can play in my head when I'm worrying about you.'

Chloé grinned and grabbed an apple from the bowl on the table, sinking her teeth into the red flesh. 'Is it time to go to Annie's?'

'Not quite. I just wanted to have a little chat, that's all.'

Chloé raised an eyebrow as she slid on to a chair, still munching.

'It's about . . . ' Her daughter waited expectantly while Stephanie faltered, the crunch of the apple distracting her. How on earth should she approach this? 'Erm . . . the thing is . . . '

'Are we in money trouble again?' asked Chloé. 'I don't mind giving up pizzas if we are.'

Stephanie ruffled the black curls that were intertwined with grass and leaves. 'No, darling. We're not in money trouble. I just wanted to tell you that I have a friend coming to stay this weekend.'

'Who?'

'His name is Pierre.' Stephanie felt her skin turning pink under Chloé's scrutiny.

'I've never heard of him.'

'No, well . . . '

'How did you meet?'

'I met him on one of the gardening forums — '

'On the Internet?' Chloé's voice got shrill. 'You're always telling me about the dangers of the Internet.'

'Yes, but — '

'So you've never met him before?'

'No, but — '

'What kind of friend is he?'

'What do you mean?'

Chloé sighed with impatience. 'Is he a good friend? A best friend? A *boy* friend?'

Stephanie paused, knowing this was the crucial question but unable to lie to her daughter. 'I'm hoping all three, in time.'

Chloé jumped to her feet, her chair scraping across the tiled floor, and grabbed her rucksack from the hook on the wall.

'Where are you going?'

'I'm going to see Fabian.'

'Now's not a good time, love. I need to — '

'It's never a good time. You're never here. And I'm always on my own. At least Fabian is a *real* friend.'

And with that the door slammed behind her and Stephanie was left to reflect on all the truths that had just issued from the mouth of her child who was no longer a babe.

★ ★ ★

'I hate her!' Chloé muttered as she swung her foot at a stone and sent it flying into the field opposite. 'How could she do this?'

She traipsed down the road, her shoulders hunched, misery written across her face, totally fed up with being nine and being ignored.

It had all been going so well. Fabian had fallen in love with Maman when she'd kissed him, all thanks to Chloé and Sarko of course. And then for the last few weeks, he'd been around all the time, working at the garden centre and even coming home with them for dinner. When she'd seen Maman placing the blanket over him on the sofa, a finger over her lips to warn Chloé to be quiet as she went upstairs to bed, she was sure that was it. Maman was falling for him in return. And now Fabian lived in Picarets, it just seemed right. It was meant to be.

Until Maman mentioned Pierre.

'Pieeerrrreee!' she mimicked her mother, kicking a few more stones for good measure. How could you love someone who was called Pierre? Chloé only knew one but it was enough. He was a kid a couple of years below her in school who never stopped crying or wiping his nose on his jumper. They all called him Snotty Sleeves as a result.

What if this Pierre was like that?

She didn't understand. How could Maman not see how lovely Fabian was? How kind he was to Chloé. He always asked about her day at school and he made the best hot chocolate. And he'd risked his life for her. Why couldn't Maman just love him so Chloé could have a dad at last?

She shrugged her rucksack further up her back, wishing she'd brought her jacket as there was a chill breeze coming over the mountains which, even with only limited years of experience, she knew meant rain.

'Chloé!'

She looked up to see Fabian in his doorway at the far side of the square, cycling kit on. She started running.

'Hello little one,' he said as she jumped into his arms and he swung her around, planting kisses on both her cheeks. 'Your mother just called. She said she'd pick you up in a minute on her way down to town.'

Chloé pulled a face as she followed him into the house, throwing herself on to his old armchair with dramatic abandon.

'What's up?' he asked as he pulled on his arm warmers.

'Maman's got a new boyfriend.'

If Chloé had been more experienced in the treacherous path that lovers tread, she would have seen that her comments had just littered the ground in front of Fabian's bare feet with huge spiky thorns.

'Has she now?' he said with what he thought sounded like nonchalance.

'Don't you care?' Chloé challenged him.

He froze. 'Why should I care?'

'Because you love her.'

'Ah. That. I suppose that would mean I should care.'

'Well, don't you?'

Fabian stopped wrestling with the tube of

274

lycra he'd been trying to pull over his arm but which suddenly seemed like the most difficult and the most trivial task in the world.

'Yes,' he said looking into the eyes of the child who was glowering at him. 'I do care. But if your mother has found someone else, there's not a lot I can do.'

Chloé let out a strangled cry of exasperation.

'You could try a bit harder!'

'How exactly?'

'I dunno! Buy her some flowers maybe. Chocolates are a good idea. Shout poetry up to her window at night. That's bound to make her fall in love with you.' She took a breath. 'Hers is the room on the front by the way.'

'Chloé, it doesn't work like that. Not in real life.'

'How does it work then?'

'You ask someone out and they say yes or no.'

'Have you asked her?'

'No.'

Chloé threw her arms up in a gesture that was so like Stephanie, normally it would have made his heart sing. Now, after this news, it simply made the pain more unbearable.

'If you haven't asked her then how can she fall in love with you?'

'It seems like I'm too late now anyway,' he said mournfully as he resumed pulling on his arm warmers. 'What's his name?'

'Pieeerrrreee!' sneered Chloé.

'Pierre?'

'He's coming this weekend.'

'Is he now?'

'For the opening of her stupid garden centre.'

'Now Chloé, that's not fair and you know it. Your mother has worked hard to get that going and you should be proud of her. I know I am.'

Chloé lowered her head to hide the shame that had suffused her as soon as the words were out of her mouth. She watched from beneath her curls as he lifted his bike off the hook in the ceiling.

'Are you going out now?' she asked sulkily after a few seconds of silence.

'Yes. Thought I'd test out my new bike. Why?'

'It's going to rain.'

'I doubt it! Have you seen the sky?' Fabian asked with a smile. But Chloé just shrugged.

A horn sounded outside and Fabian got wearily to his feet, feeling like he'd aged ten years in the last ten minutes.

'Come on, that's your mother. I'll see you out.'

'Can I come round tomorrow morning?'

'Of course you can. Why don't you come and have lunch? But make sure you ask your mother first, all right?'

She nodded and he walked with her to the door, resting against the doorjamb as he watched her climb in beside Stephanie.

'Thanks, Fabian,' Stephanie shouted out of the window and he couldn't help but notice the sunlight glinting in her hair and the soft texture of her flawless skin.

'You off on a ride?' she called out and he nodded.

'You're going to get wet then!' And with a grin she was gone.

He closed the door and refused to think about all he had just learnt. He'd get on the bike and then he would mull it over. He looked out of the window at the expanse of blue overhead and left his waterproof jacket on the hook. What did they know?

★ ★ ★

'Are you not speaking to me?' Stephanie glanced at the huddle of body that was her daughter, curled up against the van door, as far from her mother as she could get.

There was no response.

'Look, love, I'm sorry. I should have told you sooner.'

'I hate him,' came the muttered response.

'How can you hate him? You've never even met him.'

'You like him and you've never met him.'

Stephanie lapsed into silence at her daughter's unerring logic. She couldn't bear it when they argued. It was only two days until she officially opened her business but now the excitement that had been building for the last few weeks seemed hollow and pointless. She was doing all this for Chloé but if it was making Chloé miserable, was it worth it?

'Do you want me to give up the business? Because I will if you're that unhappy?'

Chloé's black curls shook in response.

'Are you sure?'

'Yes.' Her voice was almost inaudible. 'Fabian said I should be proud of you.'

'Fabian's a good man.'

'I *know*,' came the pointed reply.

'So what about Pierre? Should I call him and tell him not to come tomorrow? Tell him to stay home and look after his bees instead?'

Chloé's head jerked up. 'He has bees?'

Stephanie nodded.

'Real bees in a hive and everything?'

'Yes.'

'Does he have one of those mask things too?'

'Don't know. We'll have to ask him. If he's allowed to come.'

Chloé straightened up in her seat and laid her small hand on her mother's thigh.

'I still like Fabian,' she said with defiance.

'So do I,' replied Stephanie as she pulled up at the end of Annie's track. 'But as a friend.'

Chloé leaned over and kissed her mother and then scuttled across the road, rucksack swinging from her shoulder.

'I'll pick you up later tonight,' Stephanie called out and Chloé waved in response.

Automatically checking her watch before she pulled off, Stephanie saw she still had time to collect the sign before work. Maybe once that was in place, Chloé would feel less left out. She drove off as the first splash of rain hit the windscreen.

★ ★ ★

A bit of wet never hurt anyone! Fabian zipped up his cycling jersey, relieved to have got through Fogas without being seen. He wasn't in the

278

mood for small talk, least of all with the cabal of old men who were normally gathered under the roof of the disused *lavoir* at the start of the village and always felt the need to offer him advice on his riding technique. As though they'd once worn yellow down the Champs-Elysées or something!

Usually he'd stop and humour them, listen to their tales of races long ago with interest. Today he'd been glad the communal washhouse was deserted, no sturdy figures leaning against the stone basins, cigarette smoke hanging low as the air vibrated to the sound of laughter. Instead he only had the steady monotony of the rain falling on slates for company.

He pushed harder on the pedals as he left the last few houses behind, feeling the twinge of cramp in his right calf resurface.

Good!

Fabian was in a masochistic mood, hating himself for his lack of courage, his spineless nature.

He'd deliberately chosen the route from La Rivière, taking the back road past the burnt-out post office and round the church to begin the difficult climb up to Fogas which clung to the edge of a mountain. He'd wanted to punish himself. Had hoped that the physical agony would relieve his mental torment.

But even the sudden incline which twisted up to the town hall and seemed designed to discourage all but the determined from visiting the mayor, had merely raised his heart rate and caused his thigh muscles to burn.

It hadn't stopped him thinking about her.

He cast a glance to his right as he hit the plateau that stretched beyond the village, the normally stunning view of the mountains obscured by the billowing black clouds that were tumbling over them as though replicating his mood.

He couldn't even predict the weather! Lured by the promise of a small patch of blue, he'd landed himself in the middle of a storm. Even though they'd warned him.

Everyone had warned him. Told him she'd break his heart. And she had.

She'd found someone else. While he was dithering and losing his nerve, someone else had made Stephanie theirs.

Pierre. What kind of man was he?

Probably rippling with muscles with perfect white teeth and a full mane of blond hair. The sort of bloke who was able to drive home ten fence posts before breakfast and not even get out of breath.

Fabian grimaced and accelerated again, trying to clear his head. But it was useless. It was the only thing he could think about. And it was making him miserable.

His previously beige existence had exploded into vivid colour the moment her lips had touched his and for the last four weeks his life had been full of potential, the possibility of Stephanie draping every mundane moment with bright hope.

Chloé's words had torn through that optimism like blunt scissors through tissue and he was left to acknowledge that his dreams had never had substance.

René had been right. Stephanie was out of his league.

But as he pounded along, legs pumping and heart thundering, that was scant consolation for the way he felt. He didn't even know if he could stomach staying in Fogas after this. How could he bear to live there and see her every day, knowing there was no chance of him winning her and no chance of him ever forgetting her.

His life was meaningless.

The rain was falling more heavily now, slanting in from his right as it gusted over the high peaks, soaking through the thin lycra that clung to his body and running down his face in rivulets. He should really turn round. Know when to call it quits.

But he simply lowered his head and drove on, some small part of him rejoicing in the tangible manifestation of his misery that the elements had so kindly provided.

It was his sunglasses that saved him.

Caught between the warmth generated by his exertion and the cooler air temperatures rushing past them, the glasses started to mist up. He lifted his head to wipe a glove over the lenses and that's when he saw it, coming at him out of nowhere.

A green Renault van.

It had veered over to his side of the road and was so close that he could make out the dark head of the driver above a camouflage jacket.

And it didn't look like he was about to stop.

Fabian had few options. He pulled on the brakes and swerved to the right, taking the bike off the tarmac and on to the sodden grass and as the tyres skidded on the slick surface, he heard the crunch of impact as the van clipped the back wheel, spinning him around so that he fell in a tangle of metal.

He lay there for a few seconds, part on the road, part off, aware of pain but not sure where it originated from. The sour smell of wet asphalt assailed his nostrils and he could feel a warm trickle of blood on his leg.

What had just happened?

He opened an eye and saw the Renault bouncing across the pasture and back onto the tarmac, deep, muddy tracks left in its wake. It stopped, some distance away now owing to the slight curve in the road, and Fabian heard the crunch of gears and then a high-pitched whine as it started to reverse.

Thank God. They were coming back to check up on him. Just as well as he didn't think he was able to make it home in this state.

He watched the van approach through the driving rain and then it halted, not more than twenty metres from him. He waited for the door to open, for footsteps.

Nothing but the sound of the engine idling.

He lifted his head and immediately felt dizzy, the edges of his vision a blur. What was taking so long?

Then the van started moving again. Backing towards him. At speed.

Hadn't the driver seen? Didn't he know there

was someone lying in the road behind him?

Fabian panicked, adrenaline focusing him as he tried to free his gangly frame from the bike. But his left shoe refused to unclip from the pedal and no matter how much he twisted his foot, he was held fast. Frantic now as the van got closer, he pulled and pushed the bike, his breath tearing in his lungs, hands clawing uselessly at the metal. And then he knew with sharp clarity.

He was going to die.

He closed his eyes, fragments of prayers he'd long forgotten on his lips and a hazy memory of Jacques teaching him how to ride rising unbidden before him, the square hand planted firmly in the centre of his young back, both pushing him forward and holding him upright.

He'd inhaled his first lungful of exhaust fumes when he heard the blast of the horn. He didn't know where it came from. Somewhere behind him. But it was loud and prolonged and he saw the brake lights flash on the Renault far too close to his eyes for comfort and then it was moving again, this time racing away from him down the hill. His last thought before the darkness descended was that he was glad he'd taken Josette's advice and not spent much on his new bike.

★ ★ ★

'Careful, be gentle.'

'We are being gentle! How can someone so thin weigh so much?'

'We shall taking him upstairs?'

283

'Yes, his bed's ready.'

Fabian heard the voices, muffled and faint as though he was submerged in water. He tried to respond, to thank them, whoever they were, but only a groan emerged.

'Watch it! You're hurting him!'

'God, my arms are killing me! Can't we just leave him on the bar?'

'Not far now.'

Stairs. His body being jerked from side to side as he was carried upwards, hot garlicky breath on his face and the sound of someone panting with exertion close to his ear.

'You should be giving up cigarettes sooner!'

A man's voice eliciting a woman's laugh.

And then he was being laid on a soft bed, pillow cool beneath his face. Blankets were placed over him and a familiar hand smoothed his hair off his forehead.

'I'll let him rest. The doctor said he'd drop by and check on him later.'

Then the voices faded and he heard the sound of shoes on the stairs and then nothing. Just blessed sleep.

★　★　★

'I can't believe the driver drove off!' declared Josette as she handed Paul and René a beer each, still shaking her head in disgust.

'It looked like he'd stopped. We thought he was going to get out and help. But then we saw him reversing as though he didn't know Fabian was there.'

'So I sounds my horn!'

'And a good job you did too!' said René as he slapped the Englishman on the back making him splutter.

'And was it the Renault that hit him?'

René and Paul both shrugged.

'We are not seeing it.'

'I don't know whether I should call the police,' said Josette.

'I'd leave it until you've spoken to Fabian,' advised René. 'For all we know, he came off his bike in the rain and the Renault driver was simply going to help.'

'I suppose that's possible.' Josette wiped a cloth over the bar, her face worried. 'At least he doesn't look too bad. Just that nasty graze on his hip.'

'He's not going to be riding that bike for a while though! Not without new wheels and a derailleur.'

'I can't thank you enough,' said Josette and her voice trembled as the shock of seeing Fabian carried unconscious into the bar caught up with her.

'Lucky we are not finding mushrooms so we come home early.'

'You were looking for mushrooms?' Josette asked sharply.

Paul nodded but René said nothing.

'Where?'

'Up by . . . ow!' Paul rubbed his ankle and shot a bemused glance at René who was glowering at him.

'You know the rules!' he hissed at the English man.

285

'Not even Josette?'

'Not even Josette!'

Paul turned back to Josette with an apologetic smile. 'Sorry. I can't telling. Or René kicks me again!'

'That's fine. I understand. Pity though,' Josette said archly.

'What is a pity?' asked Paul.

'Well, if you let me know where it was then I could tell you if it's the best spot in Fogas for finding mushrooms.'

'Don't listen to her,' warned René. 'She's just trying to trick you into revealing my secret place. Been in the Piquemal family for generations and her lot have been trying to find out for years. Well, he's not going to tell you, Josette!'

Paul laughed and downed the last of his beer.

'You French. You are crazy about your mushrooms! Now I must going back to work.'

He sauntered out of the bar with René in tow and Josette smiled at her husband who was standing at the window, having abandoned the épicerie for the day due to the noise from the workmen who were putting up the last lot of shelving, working late in an effort to get finished.

'Nearly got him to tell me,' she said with a grin as she moved alongside Jacques. 'Next time!'

He smiled back and then his frown reappeared and he pointed up at the ceiling.

'I'll go and check on him now,' said Josette and then she saw him gesturing at the cupboard behind the glasses. 'It's all right, I haven't forgotten!'

She reached behind the bar for the small box

she'd taken from the cupboard four nights ago. At least this might make him smile when he comes round, she thought as she started up the stairs.

★　★　★

Fabian didn't know where he was when he woke up.

His legs were hanging over the end of the bed which was a single, not his kingsize. And he could hear the soft sound of snoring coming from a room nearby.

It took a few seconds, lying there in the dark, for it all to come back to him.

He was at the épicerie. They'd brought him here after the accident.

The accident!

He shuddered as the details surfaced vividly. The whine of the van. The smell of the tarmac. The taste of fear on the back of his tongue.

And the relief when the Renault finally drove off.

He vaguely remembered being lifted into a car and then being carried up the stairs, he was pretty sure by Paul and René. But he hadn't been able to stay awake, drifting in and out of a hazy world of sleep and silence. He thought he could recall the deep voice of the doctor from Massat but not a word of what he'd said. Although, judging by the bandaging he could feel through his pyjamas, someone had taken care of the graze on his right hip.

His pyjamas?

He didn't own any pyjamas.

He reached out and switched on the bedside lamp and in the soft pool of yellow light it cast over the bed he inspected his attire.

Jersey cotton, button up, blue-striped pyjamas with a pocket. And bottoms that reached to mid-calf.

They must belong to Oncle Jacques!

He lowered himself gingerly back on to the pillow, aware of the throbbing in his head that had started as soon as he lifted it. And his hip felt like it had been rubbed up and down a cheese grater.

Still, at least he was alive.

Would he have been if Paul and René hadn't turned up? Had the driver of the Renault really meant to kill him or had he been merely reversing to help, albeit a bit fast? And then got scared about what he'd done so took off?

Fabian couldn't say for sure. All he knew was that it had felt bloody frightening at the time. And very deliberate.

He turned over to switch off the lamp and his eye was caught by a small, oblong box lying next to it, the lettering on the battered cardboard faded with age.

'It can't be . . . ' he whispered as he reached for it.

He slid off the cover and there it was. His Opinel knife which he had presumed long gone, the weight an ancient memory.

Expecting spots of rust and a blunt edge after so many years, he opened it. But it was like new. Someone had clearly spent a lot of time on the knife, the metal shining in the lamplight, and as he gently ran his finger along the length of it, he could feel the sharpness of a recently honed blade.

He closed it firmly in his fist and laid it back in the box. Then he tucked it into the pocket of his pyjamas and lay down. He was asleep within seconds of the light going out.

16

The storm that had been so accurately forecast by the more knowledgeable residents of Fogas petered out during the night. The clouds dispersed and by dawn, the sharp peaks that divided France and Spain were etched against clear skies, the last vestiges of snow on their steep sides dazzling in the early sunlight. But although the temperature had dropped dramatically, when keen gardeners like Alain Rougé threw open their shutters with trepidation, fearing the worst for the tender plants they'd brought on earlier than usual thanks to the warm weather, there wasn't even the merest hint of white on the ground. And for that, Stephanie was profoundly grateful as she made her way down to La Rivière.

Still a week away from the three saints' days which traditionally marked the end of overnight frosts and the start of the gardening calendar, she too was taking a chance and holding an opening ceremony for her new business on Sunday, hoping to catch the early worms.

Tomorrow! Less than twenty-four hours to go.

She couldn't help smiling.

And what a twenty-four hours it would be! She'd wangled the weekend off from the Auberge, Lorna declaring that she wasn't one to stand in the path of true love, and for the first time in months, Stephanie had time to herself.

Chloé was spending the morning with the Rogalle twins, no doubt teaching them how to throw themselves up in the air, and was calling in on Fabian later. She'd informed her mother that she wouldn't be home for lunch as she was going to dine with her friend, her emphasis on the final word the only indication that their argument yesterday hadn't been fully resolved. But Stephanie hoped that by the afternoon Chloé would be more resigned to the fact that a friend was all Fabian was ever going to be.

Because in the afternoon, Chloé would be meeting Pierre.

He was due to arrive in a couple of hours and rather than have him face her daughter's hostility immediately, Stephanie thought it best if she took him up into the mountains for a picnic. Give them a chance to get to know each other better before Chloé came on the scene.

She was so nervous, it was bordering on fear.

In the seven years since she'd fled Finistère she hadn't had so much as a date. It had taken longer for the bruises on her heart to heal than those her husband had left on her face and she'd shunned all male attention.

But this felt different.

It was almost as if Pierre knew her. Really knew her in a way only an old friend could.

He'd read books that she loved, been to places that were special to her and shared her passion for the outdoors. But more than that, he never failed to ask about Chloé and his interest in her was what had won Stephanie over.

So as she drove down to the épicerie to get

291

supplies for their lunch, she ignored the voice in the back of her head that was warning her to be careful. Her fear, she decided, was nothing more than anxiety. Anxiety that he wouldn't like her.

★　★　★

Fabian was still in bed, aware of the sunshine creeping around the closed shutters, stealing into the room and cajoling him out of his slumbers. He turned over and groaned.

The whole of his right side had stiffened up during the night and now he could barely move. Gingerly he pushed back the covers and pulled down his pyjama bottoms.

Bruises. Purple welts spreading down his thigh and disappearing behind the white bandages only to reappear again below. Then a few scrapes, small patches of red to just above his knee which was swollen, the skin puffy and dark like a bad spot on an apple. His right arm was aching too, the elbow twice its normal size and a long graze adorning his forearm.

As if woken by his attentions, everything suddenly started to hurt.

He swung his legs out of the bed and sat there for a few moments, getting used to the pain.

He'd been lucky. If you could call deliberately being knocked off your bike lucky!

Deliberately.

Was he sure of that now, after a night's sleep? It had been raining. Visibility was poor. And he hadn't had his lights on. Maybe the Renault driver simply hadn't seen him. But why had he been on Fabian's side of the road?

Drunk possibly. That would explain why he shot off the minute someone else came along.

That was it. Fabian had been the victim of a drink-driving accident.

Didn't make him feel any better.

Although, he had to admit, he didn't feel as filled with self-pity as he had in the minutes leading up to the incident!

He touched his pocket and felt the knife box within it. To think he'd actually been contemplating leaving Fogas! Turning his back on Tante Josette and his new friends when he'd just started to make a life for himself here.

He eased himself up on to his feet, the pyjama bottoms flapping loosely below his knees.

It had taken that blow to the head for him to get things in perspective. He was going to stay, of that he was decided. In time his heart would heal and Stephanie would become no more than a friend, his ridiculous love for her a fond memory.

Voices filtered up to him from the bar followed by the gorgeous aroma of fresh coffee and he moved slowly towards the stairs.

It was time for him to get on with life.

★　★　★

'How is he?'

'A few cuts and bruises. The doctor reckons he'll be all right in a day or two. Just have to keep an eye on him for concussion.'

'Talk of the devil!' Annie gestured behind Josette where a very pale Fabian had appeared.

293

'Are you sure you should be up?' Josette asked with concern as he swayed slightly and put a hand on the bar to steady himself.

'I'm fine.' He smiled, enveloping her in his thin arms and she felt him flinch as she hugged him back.

'Sorry! Forgot about the bruises!' She pulled away and studied his face, a dark shadow on his jawline, his eyes bright despite the pallor. 'You seem cheerful, considering.'

'Found this when I woke up.' He produced his Opinel box from his pocket. 'Thanks.'

'It's nothing. We . . . I . . . can't thank you enough for the knife cabinet. You really shouldn't have.'

'You liked them then?' Fabian beamed.

'Love them.'

'Think I prrreferrrrrred it when you two werrre at each otherrr's thrrroats!' cackled Annie.

The door opened and even before he looked, Fabian knew who it was by the trace of incense that accompanied her.

'Bonjour, Stephanie!' Josette called out and Fabian steeled himself as the willowy figure kissed first Annie and then Josette and then she was before him, her cheek brushing his, the scent of flowers on her soft hair.

She turned to talk to the two women at the bar and he watched her like a thirsty man watches another down a beer, eyes following her every movement. She was gorgeous. Her graceful hands were constantly in motion, a jingle of bracelets accompanying her gestures and when

294

she tipped back her head to laugh, exposing the full length of her white throat, Fabian's mouth went dry.

'Put yourrr tongue away,' muttered Annie and Fabian snapped to attention, realising that Stephanie was laughing at him.

'Stephanie was just asking why you're in pyjamas,' said Josette.

'Especially ones that don't fit!' Stephanie chuckled again at the sight of the tall Parisian with his arms and legs sticking out of the old fashioned nightclothes.

'I had an accident,' he spluttered. 'On my bike. Josette gave me these.'

'Another accident?' Stephanie raised her eyebrows. 'And the bike?'

Fabian shook his head.

'At least it wasn't my fault this time! Are you okay?'

'I am now,' he said and Annie snorted.

'That's good.' She gave him a warm smile and he felt his knees buckle. 'Chloé would be devastated if you didn't make your lunch date. I can give you a lift back up there when I'm done if you want?'

Fabian wanted. Very much so. He nodded mutely.

'So, Josette,' Stephanie continued. 'Do you have any of Philippe Galy's honey left? I'm taking someone special on a picnic!'

'I thought I did. It should be by the window.' Josette came round from behind the counter and Stephanie followed her to the shelving at the far end of the room.

'I hearrrd you left it too late, young man,' said Annie, when they were out of earshot. 'Could have been you going on that picnic!'

'I'm an idiot.'

Annie nodded. 'I'll grrrant you that. But at least you'rrre not a dead idiot.'

She reached across and laid a sturdy hand on his arm.

'That incident yesterrrday sounded serrrious. Had me worrrrried, you did.'

'Had us all worried,' Josette added as she rejoined them. She regarded Fabian closely, the distress in his eyes alarming her. 'You look like you're suffering. Do you want me to fetch the tablets the doctor left?'

'I don't think they'd help,' he groaned, watching the pleasure on Stephanie's face as she inhaled the smell of the vine-ripe tomatoes she'd chosen before putting them in her bag.

'What he needs is something to take his mind off herrr!'

'Like what?'

'Worrrk! I always find that helps.'

'Well, there's plenty of that needs doing today.' Josette gestured at the table where Stephanie was mulling over the handmade local biscuits, her long fingers trailing over the packets as she tried to decide which ones to take with her, each touch burning Fabian like a naked flame on his skin. 'Once next door has had a final clean, all that stock needs to go through in time for tomorrow and the extra stuff we've ordered needs to be brought up from the cellar.'

She groaned at the magnitude of the task and slumped against the bar. It had seemed like a good idea to have a joint opening ceremony with Stephanie. But that had been decided when the renovation work had been progressing at a decent rate. Now, with the builders only having vacated the épicerie the night before and with the new counter in the bar still to be fitted, it seemed like the stupidest thing she'd ever agreed to. Especially with Fabian in no condition to help with most of it.

'Don't worry, Tante Josette,' Fabian said, having finally managed to tear his gaze away from Stephanie. 'We'll get it done today. I'll be fine once I get going.'

'So did you see the drrriverrr?' asked Annie, returning to the news of the day.

'No, just the car.'

'You saw the car?' Josette queried with surprise. 'Paul and René couldn't tell me anything more than that it was a dark van.'

'I saw it all right. Very close it was too! A Renault 4 Fourgonnette. Could probably tell you how much wear he had left on his tyres if I thought about it!'

Josette laughed but Annie had gone silent, her face serious as something Fabian had said brought to mind another conversation on a different day.

'What colourr was it?' she asked.

'Dark green.'

'Arrre you surrre?'

'Positive.'

'How bizarrrrrre . . .'

* ★ ★ ★

Stephanie was miles away. While her hands chose cheese and honey and a bottle of wine, a few pieces of fruit and some of the gorgeous bread that Josette now stocked, her mind was focused on Pierre.

What would he look like? Not that it mattered, she hastily told herself. But then, she didn't want him to be really short. Or have bad breath. Or right-wing views. Actually, she might learn to live with the first two. She could always wear flat shoes and buy him some mints. But the thought of dating a capitalist made her shudder.

Of course, she was worrying over nothing. There'd been no indication in his emails to suggest they weren't suited politically. Just the opposite. In fact . . .

How odd.

Stephanie's train of thought was distracted by an eddy of fine white powder which was drifting across the floor towards her in fits and starts, the unnatural staccato of its progress catching her eye. Something about it didn't seem right. She glanced up at the blue tarpaulin that was still hanging between the épicerie and the bar.

That must be it. A draught coming through from the shop, blowing the detritus with it.

Strange that the tarpaulin wasn't fluttering though.

She looked down again and saw that the dust was gathering at her feet like iron filings drawn to a magnet, a fair quantity now amassed. There

298

was a slight pause as it settled and she was about to step over it and continue her shopping when the dust started to shift again, this time like an invisible finger was drawing in it.

Fascinated, she watched as the straight back and curved front of a capital *B* materialised, closely followed by the letter e.

Someone or something was trying to write a message.

She spun round to the group of people at the bar to see if they were aware of the phenomenon but they were busy talking, oblivious to what was happening. And when she turned back, the first word had been written.

'Beware . . . ' she whispered, reading it out loud and she shivered, wishing she hadn't left her jumper in the van.

But it hadn't finished, whatever it was. Slowly, painstakingly, the next letters were already appearing.

' . . . of . . . '

'Stephanie?' Annie's voice startled her and she jumped.

'Sorry?'

'I said, that sounds like the van Chloé was on about.'

'What van?'

'Hasn't she told you yet?' Annie's voice had taken on a sharpness that worried Stephanie.

'Told me what?'

'She got a lift home one night with the Rrro-galle twins. She got scarrred by the drrriverrr. Darrrk swarrrthy type with grrreasy hairrr and pierrrcing blue eyes. When she went to get out, she thought he trrried to make a grrrab for herrr.'

'What did she do?' asked Fabian.

'She bit him.'

'She didn't tell me that,' said Stephanie, her attention now fully on Annie.

Annie shrugged. 'She thought you'd be angrrry. It's just strrrange that Fabian was rrrun overrr by what sounds like the same van.'

Alarm bells. Ringing loudly. But she didn't know why. As she tried to make sense of the messages her subconscious was sending her, Stephanie was vaguely aware of the continuing conversation.

'Don't suppose you saw if yourrr hit and rrrun man had a tattoo of the Brrrittany flag on his rrright arrrm did you? With bite marrrks in it?' Annie was asking Fabian.

Fabian laughed and shook his head. 'No. Didn't get that close. But the van did have a Brittany number plate. Probably just a coincidence though.'

'WHAT did you say?' Stephanie's shrill voice cut across him.

'I said probably just — '

'No, not you. Annie, what did you say about a tattoo?'

Everyone was staring at Stephanie now, her face white and her eyes huge with horror.

'The man who drrrove the van. He had a tattoo on his arrrm. Of the Brrrittany flag.'

Stephanie felt the shopping bag slip from her numb fingers and as her eyes followed its descent, she saw that the magic writing in the dust was complete.

Beware of imitations

'Oh my God,' she whispered as she stared at the familiar words which had been hanging on Chloé's wall for months and the final piece of the puzzle tumbled into place.

He was here. He'd found them. And their lives were in danger.

MOVE!

Her body screamed at her and she took heed, stumbling out of the bar and racing towards the van. She might still have time. If she was quick she could get them out of this before it was all too late.

★ ★ ★

'What on earth . . . ?' Fabian watched — open mouthed as Stephanie flew out of the door, her shopping discarded on the floor, tomatoes rolling under the table and the bottle of wine smashed, a pool of red liquid seeping into some dust that had collected under the tarpaulin.

'What caused that?'

'I've no idea!' Annie answered with concern. 'Do you, Josette?'

Josette didn't reply. She'd been observing Jacques for the last half an hour as he laboriously blew dust from every corner of the room into a neat pile right in front of Stephanie. And then he'd written a message in it, each letter carefully formed on an exhalation. It had nearly killed him. Now he sat slumped against the wall, breathing heavily, his cheeks puce and his face

301

smeared with debris.

But it had worked, whatever it meant, scaring Stephanie witless and sending her running. Josette had just managed to read it before the wine blurred the letters but she had no idea what it meant. Or why it had frightened Stephanie so much.

'Why would mentioning a tattoo make her panic?' she mused, desperately trying to see the connections.

'I don't think it was the tattoo so much, Tante Josette, as the fact it was of the Brittany flag.'

Annie and Josette both gasped.

'You don't think . . . ' Annie's face had gone pale. 'He couldn't have . . . '

'It would make sense!' Josette exclaimed.

'But how? She's been so carrreful.'

'I don't know but I can't think of any other explanation that would have terrified her like that. Can you?'

Fabian was lost, excluded from the conversation by his relative newness to the commune. 'What's going on?' he demanded.

'The man driving the Renault is from Brittany, right? What department?'

'The last two numbers of the registration were 29. So, Finistère. But what has this — '

'Finistèrrre! That's wherrre she's frrrom.'

'I'm sorry, but I don't — '

'We think he might be Stephanie's ex-husband,' Josette explained.

'And that's a problem because . . . ?'

'Because he's violent and Stephanie has spent the last seven years trying to hide from him.'

'And now, God knows how, he's found herrr!'

'Christ!' A tidal wave of anxiety crashed over Fabian as his memory brought forth the stranger, all those weeks ago, who'd asked so many questions about Stephanie and her daughter. 'I think he was here.'

'Here? In the bar?'

Fabian nodded weakly.

'When?'

'The night you went up to the council meeting. He came in dressed in hunting gear. Asked loads of questions about Stephanie. I didn't think much of it at the time. Except that he didn't look like an organic gardener. And then I saw him again . . . '

Fabian trailed off, a hollow feeling in his gut as he realised how much he could be to blame for the predicament Stephanie now faced.

'Where did you see him?' Josette prompted.

'Up at her house.'

Annie sucked air in through her teeth, a sharp sound of alarm.

'And you never thought to say anything?' his aunt asked with incredulity.

Fabian shook his head despondently.

'Neverrr mind looking so forrrlorrrn! She's in dangerrr and we need to do something,' barked Annie.

'You're right. I need to get up there.'

'How? Yourrr carrr is up at yourrr house and yourrr bike is buggerrred. Best if we call Chrrristian.'

Annie grabbed the phone and started dialling but the ringing went unanswered. She replaced the receiver with a shaking hand and a grim expression.

'Try Paul,' urged Josette and Annie did as she said, getting Lorna on the second ring.

'Is Paul therrre? No, oh I see.' Annie shook her head at Josette. 'No, no need to worrrrrry him. I'll catch him laterrr.'

She hung up.

'He's down in St Girrrons. He'll be back in an hourrr.'

'This is ridiculous!' Fabian thumped the bar in frustration, making the ladies jump. 'I could be up there in twenty minutes. I just need a bloody bike!'

Josette's hand shot to her mouth. 'Oh! I'm an idiot! I've got a bike. In the shed. Go and get changed, love and — '

But she was talking to thin air. Fabian had already gone, taking the stairs two at a time, the aches and pains he'd woken up with negated by the fear that was driving him.

★　★　★

Jacques watched from the window as everyone bustled into action.

He'd done all he could. Just about exhausted himself in the process. Who'd have thought moving dust could be such hard work.

He'd been concerned about Fabian when he'd been carried into the bar the night before, convinced that the van had been driven by the hunter in Le Chameau boots. And after hearing René and Paul talk about it, he'd been sure

304

that it was no accident.

So when he'd heard Annie describe what had happened to Chloé, he'd known it was time to warn Stephanie.

She'd seemed to understand. There was nothing more he could do now.

He sighed heavily and sat on the window ledge as Josette wheeled his Peugeot bike around from the shed and propped it against a table, brushing off the spiders' webs and giving the saddle a quick wipe while Annie pumped up the tyres.

'Wow!' exclaimed Fabian as he emerged from the bar pulling on his shoes, his shorts torn on the hip and his jersey streaked with mud. 'Where did you get this?'

He ran his hand down the thin tube and marvelled at the weight, so much heavier than the carbon bikes he was used to.

'It was your Oncle Jacques' racing bike.'

'I didn't know he raced!'

Josette smiled proudly. 'He was good. Almost good enough to be a professional.'

'What stopped him?'

'Work. We were so busy in those days. He couldn't find the time to train. And the money was no good.' She shrugged.

'I'll take good care of it. I promise!' Fabian gave her a kiss on the cheek and then swung his leg over the frame.

'Call us when you get therrre,' urged Annie. 'Let us know she's okay.'

'Will do. And see if you can get hold of Christian in the meantime. And Chloé. Tell her to stay at the Rogalles. She's probably safer there

305

for now until we know what's happening.'

He pushed off, the saddle a little too low, the frame a little too short, the bike heavy under him and when he hit the start of the climb to Picarets, his hip started to protest and his knee was already in agony. He knew this wasn't going to be easy. But it was an emergency. Stephanie needed him. And for that he was prepared to put up with anything.

He grimaced and picked up the pace, hoping desperately that it wouldn't be in vain.

* * *

'We could be worrying over nothing,' said Josette as they watched the rangy figure of Fabian cycle off into the distance.

'That's as maybe. But betterrr safe than sorrrrrry.'

'I'll try the Rogalles. See if we can catch Chloé.' She picked up the phone while Annie started tidying up the mess left behind by Stephanie's dramatic exit. She'd retrieved the tomatoes and picked up the cheese when she noticed the pile of dust, partially saturated by the wine. She was puzzling over the remaining letters when Josette's worried voice distracted her.

'Chloé's not there! The call diverted to Madame Rogalle's mobile. She's on her way to St Girons with the boys and said Chloé left some time ago.'

'Bloody hell!' Annie felt the tension grip her chest. 'We need to warrrn herrr not to go home but therrre's no one left up in Picarrrets to call!

Why did this have to happen on marrrket day?'

'What about a mobile? Does Chloé have one?'

'Yes! I gave herrr the one Vérrronique gave me.'

'What's the number?' Josette asked, fingers poised over the phone.

Annie's face crumpled. 'I've no idea,' she whispered, hating herself.

'We'll call Véronique then! She'll know it.'

'No good. She's at a funerrral in Massat. Someone she worrrked with at the post office up therrre. She'll have herrr phone off.'

'So there's nothing we can do. We'll just have to sit and wait.'

'I feel like a useless old lady!'

'Not as useless as I am. I've just remembered that we have a brand new car sitting in the garage and I sent Fabian up the hill on a museum-piece of a bike!'

Annie raised a half-smile and Josette patted her arm.

'That's better. I'll try Stephanie. She should be home by now.'

Josette dialled the number but as the phone rang and rang in her ear, a sense of dread built up inside her. And she made the decision, there and then. She was damn well going to learn how to drive.

★   ★   ★

He was ready. He'd waited so long for this. But finally the time had come.

He felt cramp inch into his legs where he was

307

hunched down but he ignored it the way he'd learnt to when he was hunting.

And today he was hunting.

It had been the most difficult prey of his life so he'd done everything by the book. Spent ages learning the terrain. Observed and listened until he knew everything there was to know about her habits, her routines, her probable route of flight.

He was confident he had everything covered.

All he had to do now was wait. She would come to him. Of that he was sure.

17

Stephanie drove up the hill at a speed she'd never thought the van capable of, throwing it around the bends, foot to the floor on the few straight sections as the forest blurred outside the window.

She'd grab what they needed, pick Chloé up from the Rogalles and then . . .

Then they would be on the run again.

There was no alternative. He'd warned her not to leave, as though he could read her mind and see the plans she was forming. Told her what he would do when he caught up with them and she'd believed him.

So when she'd finally found the courage to flee, her face a swollen mess, she'd come here, thinking the mountains would give her and Chloé some anonymity, that the small commune would mean she'd always know if a stranger was around.

But it hadn't worked like that. Somehow he'd found them and from what Annie had said, he'd been here a while. Watching them. Stalking them.

Seemed like the whole community had noticed his presence. But not her. So much for her famed sixth sense. She'd been too caught up in her own concerns.

To think he'd had Chloé in his van!

A sob rose in her throat and she let out a

strangled cry of anger at herself.

Why hadn't Chloé told her? Had Stephanie been so busy that her daughter hadn't felt she could reach out to her?

She took a deep breath in an effort to calm the swelling panic.

At least she had a head start. She knew he would be coming.

Bruno Madec.

Her husband.

She'd told everyone she was divorced but she'd never filed the papers. Never dared to. That would have meant revealing her location. Better to live with the legal contract still binding her to him than to have him find her and terminate it in the only way he knew how. With his fists.

It hadn't started like that. Stephanie had been the wild one, her fiery temper often getting her into trouble. He'd been considerate. Gentle even. The day he'd got the tattoo done he'd wanted to entwine her name through it so that his two passions, Brittany and Stephanie, would be with him forever. But she'd persuaded him not to, perhaps sensing even then that their future wasn't certain. He'd turned to her outside the tattoo parlour and shown her his arm, emblazoned with the black and white horizontal stripes of the flag, eleven black arrows in the top left corner.

'I'll always be your Brittany Boy!' he'd said with fervour.

But once they'd got married, things had changed.

The first time he hit her, she'd made excuses for him. It was her fault. She'd goaded him into it. Who could blame him? Afterwards, he'd sobbed in her arms and she'd held him while her cheek throbbed and blood dripped from her split lip.

The second time she'd found it harder to justify. He'd come home drunk, out of work again. She'd said something. Or maybe just looked at him. She couldn't remember. All she recalled was the speed of his arm as it lashed out and then she'd come round with him pressing a cold towel to her forehead. She'd asked him to get help. He'd promised he would but he hadn't.

Months passed and she'd been in turmoil. She'd known their relationship was toxic and when she'd made the mistake of getting pregnant, she'd known she had to leave. He'd come home to find her packing and had begged her to stay. Begged her to help him change. As she slowly put her clothes back in the drawers and the case on top of the wardrobe, she kept telling herself she was doing the right thing.

From the moment she was born, he adored Chloé. Doted on her. And at first Chloé's laughter or a gurgling smile had been a shield for Stephanie. But then, not long before Chloé's second birthday, he'd lost his temper again. They'd been sitting down for dinner, the three of them, and he'd made a comment about her cooking. She'd retorted with something smart and wham! That time he'd broken Stephanie's arm but the pain had been nothing compared to the anguish of hearing Chloé screaming in her

311

highchair as Bruno stormed out and her mother tried to pick herself up off the floor.

When he'd found her packing, one arm in a sling, this time he hadn't begged or pleaded. He'd calmly told her what he would do to her when he tracked her down. She'd quietly emptied the case and put it back on top of the wardrobe.

And she'd started to make plans.

He must have known. He watched her all the time. Never left the keys to the car lying around. The suitcase disappeared. But she waited. And finally she'd made her move.

It was his birthday and he'd come home drunk, shouting at her before he even had the door closed, his fists flailing the minute he was within range. She took a blow in the face, tried to roll with it as it landed, his knuckles glancing off her cheekbone and then as he moved in to deliver the next one, she'd taken a sudden step back and he'd lost his balance, crashing to the tiles with a thump.

He'd knocked himself out.

She grabbed a ball of gardening twine off the table, roped his hands together and then raided his pockets for his keys. And his wallet.

Chloé was on the landing, crying at all the commotion. Stephanie had raced up the stairs and swung the child into her arms, grabbed the clothes she'd had stashed in a small suitcase behind the bath panel, jumped into the car and fled. The only other items she'd had with her had been a cheque book for a bank account in her name that she'd opened after her mother died and a car boot full of Bruno's gardening tools. And with those, she'd learnt to make her living.

Seven years ago. For the first year she'd lived in terror, startled by every loud noise, nervous around strangers. But gradually things had settled down and this new life in the mountains had become normal. She'd stopped being afraid of shadows and learnt to relax. Finally Fogas had become home.

Now everything was going to change.

How had he managed to find them?

She'd been so careful. She never used her married name, never gave out her address to people she didn't know. The only thing she could think of was the registration for the business which was on public record and the paperwork for the bank loan. She'd been wary about filling them in but had decided it was worth the small risk. And anyway, from what Annie had said, he'd been in the area before she'd even sent the forms off.

So how had he done it?

She parked the van on the verge and hurried inside the house, checking her watch. Chloé would still be at the Rogalles.

She'd pack for her. It would be quicker. She was halfway up the stairs when the phone started ringing but she didn't stop. Whoever it was could wait.

Ignoring the persistent trilling, she pulled open her wardrobe and dragged out the same suitcase that she'd used all those years ago, threw it on the bed and began filling it with the bare essentials.

313

Where would they go this time? Abroad maybe? How far would they have to go to be safe?

Mid-ring the phone stopped, making Stephanie jump, the silence of the cottage unsettling now that she appreciated the danger they were in. But she forced herself to keep moving, aware that every second was a bonus and she might not be able to bank on many more of them before he arrived.

Because he would arrive. Now that he was this close. He would find their house. He would find them. And then . . .

How many seconds? How many had she just wasted? This was how he would catch them. Through the fear that froze Stephanie to the floor and turned her limbs to stone.

She rushed into Chloé's room and grabbed an armful of clothes, catching sight of the gymnastics manual lying open on the bed. It was such a big book and so heavy, it was a wonder the child wasn't permanently deformed from carrying it around with her all the time.

And as Stephanie stared at it, the enormity of what was happening hit home.

Chloé was about to leave the only place she had ever really known. She would be devastated. How was Stephanie ever going to explain it to her?

She seized the book and thrust it into the suitcase with everything else. At least Chloé would have that continuity.

She was wrestling with the zip on the case, pushing down on the lid to make it close, when she suddenly remembered Pierre.

Christ! He'd be on his way, expecting her to be at the Auberge when he turned up in twenty minutes. But she'd be long gone.

She fished her mobile out of her back pocket and searched for the number he'd given her the day before. She'd give him a quick call and apologise for cancelling their weekend at short notice. Tell him she'd be in touch again soon.

Not that she would be. What was the point?

Suitcase in hand, Stephanie started down the stairs with the phone pressed to her ear. Almost there. All she had to do now was get Chloé . . .

Funny. She stopped halfway down and moved the receiver away so she could hear better.

There! A ringing sound. Close by, like it was in the house.

She automatically checked the phone in the hallway. But it wasn't that. Couldn't be that because it had been pulled out of the wall. Disconnected. Which didn't make sense.

The ring tone continued, faint but clear. Another mobile maybe?

'Pierre?' she called out in confusion, wondering if he'd somehow made his way to the cottage. But how? She hadn't told him where she lived.

It was only when the ringing subsided that she realised she was trembling. She glanced at her mobile and saw her call had been answered.

'Hello, Pierre,' she said into the phone. 'Sorry, didn't realise you'd picked up. I'm just — '

'Hello, Stephanie,' a voice interrupted, simultaneously in her ear and beside her. 'It's been a while.'

315

She didn't have time to scream as he reached out and grabbed a handful of her hair and yanked her down the last few stairs.

'Pleased to see me?'

Stephanie stared into the face of the man she'd hoped never to set eyes on again and as his arm drew back, she just had time to whisper one word before his fist made contact with her face.

'Pierre?'

He laughed as she crumpled to the floor. 'There is no Pierre, *ma chérie*. Never was. There's only me and you.'

★ ★ ★

Chloé was bored. She'd been with Max and Nicolas most of the morning but when they'd descended into the usual sibling rivalry, she'd decided it was time to go. As she'd left their garden, Max was kneeling on Nicolas and ordering him to submit which Chloé knew was never going to happen.

So she'd taken the path down to Fabian's house, knowing she was early for lunch but when she'd knocked on the front door, there'd been no response. She'd moved over to the window and pressed her face against the glass, peering into the gloom inside.

Nothing. No movement.

The back door hadn't yielded a result either. Except that she'd been able to see the interior better and she'd noticed that his bike wasn't hanging from the bracket he'd fixed into the ceiling.

Presuming he was out on a ride, she'd sat on the step to wait. And she'd waited a long time. The clock on the mobile phone Annie gave her told her that she'd wasted thirty minutes of her life sitting in the sun, watching the bees dip in and out of the few flowers in Fabian's garden. And now she was bored.

Might as well go and do some acrobatics on the lawn at home.

She gave one last rap on Fabian's door but it was pointless. He wasn't there despite what he'd said yesterday. Despairing at the way adults seemed to be constantly letting her down, she slouched round the corner of the house and made for home. She'd only gone a few steps when she saw Maman's blue van parked outside their cottage. If she hurried, she might be able to persuade Maman to take her on the picnic too. And maybe this Pierre might have his bee mask with him.

She started running, forgetting her antipathy of the day before towards this stranger that Maman had introduced into their lives. Whatever he was like, spending time with him had to be better than sitting on a doorstep waiting for Fabian.

It was only as she reached the front door that she noticed something odd.

The shutters were closed, the big moons that Maman had painted all over the reverse of them shining out in the bright midday sunlight.

But it wasn't enough to stop Chloé turning the handle.

'Maman, I'm — '

317

She choked on the last words as a strong arm grabbed her around the neck and pulled her inside. She just had time to see the familiar black and white markings on the inside of his wrist when the door slammed closed behind her.

★   ★   ★

Down the valley, on the road to Picarets, Fabian didn't know if he could take any more.

The sun was high overhead, the air humid and heavy and the sweat was dripping off him. His eyes were dust-filled and irritated, unprotected by sunglasses as his hadn't survived the crash the day before. And the flies were unbearable. Circling around him, landing on his face, on his arms, in his ears. No matter how many he swatted, there were always more, attracted to him as though he was carrion.

Which wasn't far off the mark.

He bent his head and dug deeper, trying to ignore whatever was grinding in his right knee which was on fire and his hip which was aching, blood seeping though the bandages where he'd reopened the cuts. He was more concerned by the throbbing in his head, black edges starting to creep around his vision.

Hoping to ease his burden, he moved his hand to change gear and realised there were no more. He was in the lowest one available. Ten-speed instead of his twenty.

How did Jacques ever manage to race on this beast, he wondered?

But it was all Fabian had.

He had no idea how long he'd been riding. There was no cycle computer to tell him. No heart rate monitor to gauge how much effort he was putting in. No power meter to measure his efficiency. None of that mattered though. Getting to Stephanie was what counted.

What if he was too late? What if this ex-husband of hers had already found her?

It was enough to make Fabian grit his teeth and demand more from a body already at its limits and more from a bike that was long past its prime. As he felt his legs protest and his head start to swim, the bike creaking under him, he made a promise to whatever God was watching down on him.

If he made it to Stephanie's in time, he would restore this machine and he'd ride it in the Ariégeoise Cyclosportive at the end of June in homage to Jacques. He rounded the corner into Picarets, the familiar blue van visible at the far end, and he hoped it was a promise he would live to regret.

★　★　★

'Still no answer?'

'Not on the mobile orrr the landline.' Annie put the phone back down. It was the third time they'd tried Stephanie with no success. 'She should have been therrre by now.'

'There could be any number of explanations,' Josette said, trying to calm her friend.

'I'd still feel a lot happierrr if we werrre up therrre and knew what was going on.'

319

'Bonjour!' Véronique entered the bar and was amazed to see both Josette and Maman leap to their feet with a cry of delight. She'd never had a welcome like that before.

'I thought you werrre going to a funerrral?'

Véronique blushed. 'I was supposed to. But the weather is so nice . . . I didn't know him that well anyway. And I was getting a lift off Bernard Mirouze which is always a good reason not to go! If I'd had my own car . . . '

But the two women weren't bothered by her excuses. They were staring at each other and nodding excitedly.

'Do you know wherrre the key is?'

'Not exactly but it won't take me long to find.' Josette scampered out of the bar leaving a perplexed Véronique with her mother.

'What's going on?'

'We think Stephanie might be in dangerrr.'

'In *danger*?' Véronique's voice was filled with disbelief as she checked the bar to see if there were any signs of midday drinking. But there were no empty glasses or bottles of beer. 'This is Fogas. What kind of danger could she be in?'

'Frrrom herrr ex-husband. We think he's herrre. That he's been herrre a while.'

And Annie explained. When she got to the description of the van that had run Fabian over, Véronique gasped.

'Oh my goodness. That's the van I saw up at the house.'

'When?'

'Valentine's Day. You and Chloé had just got in and he went past really slowly outside. Then he reversed and I remember wondering what he'd seen because there was nothing there but Chloé's bike . . . '

She faltered and Annie gripped her arm.

'He followed us. I rrrememberrr it now. Followed us all the way home.'

'But why would he be following you if he's after Stephanie . . . '

They looked at each other in horror.

'Got it!' Josette came back into the bar with a shiny key in her hand. 'Shall we go?'

She paused as she saw the expressions of terror on the two Estaque women.

'What's the matter?' she asked.

'I think we've worrrked it out,' said Annie grimly. 'He's not herrre for Stephanie.'

'But if he's not here for Stephanie then why . . . ' Josette's hands flew to her mouth. 'Chloé!'

Annie nodded. 'He's come to take Chloé.'

And for the first time in all the years Josette had known her friend, she saw a tear trickle down her weathered cheek.

'If anything happens to that child I will neverrr forrrgive myself,' she declared.

Josette grabbed a key from behind the counter and threw it at Véronique. 'Here! Get the garage open and the car out while I lock up.'

The three of them hustled out of the bar leaving Jacques to watch from the window as Véronique flung open the garage doors and then backed out his beautiful cherry red Peugeot on to the road. Under any other circumstances he would have been enraged. A woman driving his car!

But Chloé was in danger. And if it meant the Peugeot came back with no wing mirrors and a huge dent in the bumper, then that was fine by him. As long as that little girl was unharmed.

He gripped the windowsill and prayed with all his might that the women would be in time. Because there was nothing else he could do.

18

Chloé couldn't breathe. The solid slab of hand that was wrapped around her face was blocking her mouth and nose, filling her senses with the rank smell of sour beer and cigarettes, the hairs on his arm rough against her cheek.

She'd entered the house and he'd grabbed her, pulled her into the dark room where her eyes struggled to adjust to the sudden gloom and she'd heard the key being turned in the lock behind her. The glimpse of his black and white tattoo in the sunlight before the door slammed shut was the only thing giving any meaning to the nightmare that her world had become.

The stranger had come back for her.

She'd wriggled and writhed, tried to bite him, kicked him. But he'd been prepared and had simply lifted her off the ground with one arm, pulling her against him so that the air was pushed out of her lungs, her ribs protesting at the force upon them.

'For God's sake! You're suffocating her!'

Maman!

Chloé froze. Maman was in the house too, back to the stairs, the flesh under her left eye mottled and swollen, stark against the extreme pallor of her skin. At her feet was a suitcase, lid open, the contents strewn across the floor. T-shirts, jeans, some of Maman's underwear, Chloé's best coat.

Were they going somewhere? With Pierre maybe? But wouldn't Maman have told her?

She saw her book, discarded on the floor, thick cover bent back, spine buckled and next to it was Maman's phone. Smashed.

And if Chloé hadn't known the trouble they were in, one look at the terror in Maman's eyes would have told her.

All of Jacques' warnings had come true.

She felt the pressure on her face relax and took a gulp of air.

'Don't even think of screaming!' a low voice hissed in her ear and the tattoo flashed as his wrist twisted to show her a knife, blade out, the point so close she could see what looked like dried blood on the tip, black hairs stuck to it.

A sour taste filled her mouth and she fought the urge to vomit.

'Chloé. It's okay.' Maman sounded calm, icy, her eyes willing Chloé to look at her but Chloé didn't understand. How could it be okay? This man, this stranger, was going to kill them.

She heard a whimpering sound and realised with disgust that it came from her. She was about to cry. She never cried. A warm tear trickled down her cheek.

'Aren't you going to introduce us, then?' His breath was hot in Chloé's ear.

Introduce him? Did that mean Maman knew him?

Chloé's brain worked frantically trying to make sense of it. She knew everyone Maman did, knew them all by sight. But maybe he was someone Maman had met recently. Someone she hadn't told Chloé about. And finally she understood.

'Stephanie? Do you want to do the honours?' the man asked again, the sound of her name on his lips like glass scratching across silk.

But Maman didn't reply. Just curled her lip in distaste.

He gave a sarcastic laugh.

'Apparently not! Well, Chloé, I bet you can't guess who I am?'

'I know who you are,' Chloé spat with all the derision she could muster. 'You're Pierre, off the Internet.'

This time the man threw back his head to laugh while Maman winced as though Chloé had pinched her. Was she wrong? But who else . . .

'Not bad, Chloé. Not bad at all. Seems you're less gullible than your Maman. But it's not quite right.' He leaned in even closer until his voice dominated Chloé's awareness. 'I'm your Papa. Remember me?'

The words dropped casually into the tension-filled space and Chloé, who'd spent hours of idle fancy imagining this very moment, the joy of meeting her father for the very first time, suddenly wanted to die. A horrified scream rose inside her but as the first burst of air left her lungs, the hand slapped across her mouth again. Somebody was banging on the door.

'Quiet!' The knife dug into the soft skin below her chin and she flinched. 'No tricks, Stephanie! Whoever it is, get rid of them. Or you know what I'll do.'

Chloé watched Maman slowly cross the floor,

her eyes never leaving her child's face, and then her fingers were stretching out towards the key he was holding.

★ ★ ★

Fabian was exhausted. Barely able to get off the bike. Legs wobbling as he made the short walk down Stephanie's path. Hand shaking as he lifted up the brass knocker and let it fall.

He stood back as he heard footsteps approach on the inside and then the door opened the merest sliver.

'Yes?' Stephanie's voice was clipped, her face barely visible through the narrow opening.

'Hi . . . er . . . is everything all right?' Fabian stuttered, unnerved by the frost in her tone.

'Fine.' She was already shutting the door.

'But we were worried about you,' he gabbled, trying to get the words out before the gap closed. 'You left the shop so quickly — '

Slam! He was left talking to wood, his nose a few centimetres from the roaring lion's mouth of the knocker as he heard the door being locked.

Bizarre. But then this was Stephanie and her behaviour was never predictable. Still, it seemed excessive even by her standards.

Perplexed, he stood there, hand half-raised to knock again. But he didn't have the courage. The last thing he wanted was to annoy her.

So instead, he turned to leave. And that was when he noticed the shutters were closed on the downstairs windows.

Curious, he walked to the edge of the house

and peered around the side.

Shut there too.

Was that normal? Stephanie normal? He tried to remember if he'd ever seen the house shuttered up during the day but he couldn't recall.

He stood there for a few moments, listening. But all he heard was the shrill call of the kites in the sky above and the far distant buzzing of a chainsaw.

Wearily he made his way back out to the road and the waiting bike. He'd drop down to his house and call the épicerie. Let them know he'd tried. If she wouldn't let him in, then there wasn't much he could do.

He swung his leg over the saddle, fresh blood seeping into the bandages as he did so, and then he took one last look at the cottage.

It was odd. Closed up like that.

Odd enough to make him turn the bike in the opposite direction to home. Up the hill. He'd go to the Dupuys and see if Christian was back. And if he was still worried after talking it over with the farmer, then they could use Christian's spare key to enter the cottage.

He started pedalling, each rotation an exercise in agony but nothing compared to the anxiety in his chest.

★ ★ ★

'He's gone,' Maman whispered as the click of Fabian's cleats on the path faded, followed by the creak of a bicycle on the road.

The man snatched the key back off her and slipped it in his pocket.

Chloé was aghast.

Fabian had been outside. Standing there. She'd heard him ask Maman if everything was all right. And Maman had snapped at him and closed the door.

Why?

She should have shouted. She should have run. Fabian would have saved her.

Instead, she'd turned away their one chance of being rescued from this stranger. This man.

Chloé's Papa.

She felt her eyes fill again.

Her father.

It couldn't be true. She didn't want a father like this. She wanted someone who loved her. Who loved Maman. She wanted Fabian.

She sniffed angrily as another tear rolled down her face and dripped off her chin on to the blade of the knife that was still digging into her skin.

'You're scaring her, Bruno,' Maman said softly. 'Put her down. You're not here for her.'

'Oh, but that's where you're wrong, Stephanie darling,' the man said as he lowered the knife fractionally. 'I am here for Chloé. Very much so!'

It was as though someone had slapped Maman. She recoiled against the door and her jaw dropped.

'Didn't figure it out, my dear? Thought I was here to settle scores with you?' he scorned, voice sharp like stones under winter-soft feet. 'Do you think I would spend seven years hunting you just for that? You would be dead by now if that was the case.'

'But how . . .'

'Easy. I tracked you. Knew your strengths. Knew your weaknesses. And then I targeted areas where you would go. Where you could find work.'

Maman gasped. 'The yoga centre!'

The man shook his head mockingly. 'Should have thought about that, shouldn't you? They were all very helpful when I called, even the ones that didn't have a Stephanie teaching there. Took a while, I'll admit. Had a few false alarms. But finally last December, I caught your trail. And I waited. Then I followed you home. In the snow. Remember, Stephanie? That day when you drove back through the storm and there were trees falling everywhere?'

Maman nodded, her face grey as that awful journey back from Toulouse to a commune cut off by a blizzard took on a horrifying significance, now that she knew it had led this man to their door.

'You've been here all this time,' Maman murmured, appalled. Then her eyes widened. 'It was you! You attacked the garden centre!'

'But of course. Almost had you believing it was your pretty Parisian boyfriend who'd done it.'

'Fabian? He's not my . . .' she stopped and her hand flew to her mouth. 'That's why you knocked him off his bike!'

'Don't play the innocent,' he snapped, the knife jerking back up as his temper flared, making Chloé squirm in his arms. 'I saw the pair of you. Kissing. In front of my child.'

The point of the blade now sharp against her throat, Chloé went still, primeval senses alerting her to the simmering rage that was building inside the man who held her. And the danger it posed for them. As though realising it too, Maman tried to change the subject.

'And the Internet? Pierre . . . ' She faltered, the name choking her.

'A distraction. Kept you busy. Gave me time to plan. And I have planned, Stephanie. Planned it so well that I'm even going to spare you. Let you live out your days alone, always wondering where Chloé is.'

The last vestiges of energy drained from Maman and her whole body seemed to deflate like the badly tied balloons Chloé had put up for her birthday last year.

'You can't . . . '

'BUT I CAN.' He was really angry now, Chloé knew from the way his arm had tightened around her, locking her against his chest, hand still fast over her mouth. But she remained frozen, afraid that one small movement would topple him into violence. 'And I will. She's my daughter and she's meant to be with me. And when we leave, you will never find us. Never!'

It was the final straw for the young girl and she couldn't have stopped the tears if she tried. They were welling out of her eyes, rolling down her face, soaking into her T-shirt. She felt his grip ease on her as they fell on to his arm and she squeezed one word through the stout fingers that covered her lips.

'Maman!'

It was all it took.

Mother and daughter stared at each other and an unspoken message flashed between them.

Then Maman struck.

She pushed herself off the door and with both arms outstretched, lunged for the knife. As she did so, Chloé threw back her head and caught the man with the full force of her momentum. She had the satisfaction of feeling his nose take the brunt of the blow and then he howled, his knife jerked from his grasp and spun across the room to land on the kitchen tiles as his hands flew up to his face.

Suddenly free from his stranglehold, Chloé fell to the floor and instinctively rolled away, getting to her feet at the base of the stairs.

'RUN CHLOÉ!' Maman shouted, as she tried to wrestle the man to the ground.

But he was too strong for her. He flung her aside, Maman landing heavily against the coffee table, and then he started moving towards Chloé, blood streaming down his face.

'CHLOÉ! RUN!' Maman was struggling to her feet, gesturing frantically at her daughter to flee.

Where?

Chloé was trapped. They were locked in and he had the keys. The stairs were her only option.

With a last desperate glance at Maman, she fled, taking the steps two at a time as she heard his lumbering tread coming after her. She rounded the bottom of the dog-leg and she could hear his breathing. Two more steps. Another two.

Two more and then she would be on the landing.

Her right foot. One moment it was in mid-air. The next it was caught, fingers digging into her heel. She started to lose her balance, hands flailing for the banister rails. Then, out of the corner of her eye, she saw Maman throw herself at the man's legs, whipping them out from under him and he crashed to the ground, his chin hitting the stairs.

But his fall pulled Chloé down with him.

They landed several steps apart and for a split second they surveyed each other, the way a deer and a hunter will before the trigger is pulled, and then Chloé was scrabbling to get back on her feet, legs pushing her upright, propelling her away from the danger.

He was too close. His arm was moving in slow motion. Stretching. Closing the distance between them. Reaching for her back foot as Chloé gained the top of the stairs.

'*She's not your daughter!*'

It wasn't a scream. Maman hadn't even really raised her voice.

But it was enough.

The man paused. Turned to Maman who was still holding on to his legs. And in the silence she said it again.

'She's not your daughter, Bruno. Leave her alone.'

Chloé didn't stop. She ran to her bedroom and as she turned in the doorway, she saw the man lash his hand across Maman's face, making her head snap back against the wall.

'YOU LYING BITCH!'

Chloé slammed the door shut and immediately realised her mistake.

No lock.

She should have chosen the bathroom.

Too late. He was moving.

She grabbed her chair and shoved it under the door handle and then backed away, sobs tearing at her throat as she heard him roaring, telling Maman he was going to kill her.

Then she heard him rattle the door.

★   ★   ★

'Can't you go any faster?' Josette asked from the rear as Véronique took a corner in third, tyres squealing, engine screaming.

Véronique didn't respond. She was concentrating fully on her driving. And the gorge which dropped beneath them to the right. She'd come a bit too close to it on several of the bends.

Realising she wasn't going to get a reply, Josette turned her attention to the co-pilot.

'Have you managed to work out that phone yet?'

Annie muttered something back and then held Véronique's mobile to her ear as she was jostled in her seat by the twisting road.

'It's rrringing!' she announced.

It rang a few times, the sound faint and crackly, like she was calling India or somewhere exotic rather than just up the hill. Then the ringing stopped and what she heard next would stay with her for the rest of her life.

Panting. Fear. A child in danger.

'Chloé! Is that you, love?'

'Annie! Help. Please. Help.'

A scream. High-pitched. Lonely. And behind it, the sound of wood splintering and a man's voice.

'Chloé!' Annie yelled into the receiver. 'Chloé, we'rrre coming.'

But there was no answer. Only background noise. Panicked breathing. Sobbing. And then the heavier sound of a man grunting and shouting.

Then the line went dead.

'What is it?' Josette demanded as Annie lowered the phone, her face ashen.

'Vérrronique,' she said, her speech measured and all the more emphatic for it. 'You rrreally do need to go fasterrr. That little girrrl needs ourrr help.'

Véronique glanced at her mother and seeing the drawn features and the worrying greyness of her skin, she pressed harder on the accelerator.

'Hang on, Chloé,' Annie muttered to the passing trees. 'We'rrre coming.'

★   ★   ★

Chloé had forgotten all about the phone. When it rang she'd not known what to do. The door handle was rattling and she could hear the soft murmur of his voice as he tried to persuade her to come out.

She wanted to come out.

She was worried what would happen to

334

Maman if she didn't.

Then the phone trilled loudly and he'd started shouting. And smashing the door with his fists.

Annie. Lovely Annie on the end of the line. Chloé had wanted to slip into the mouthpiece and transport herself out of here.

But what about Maman?

She couldn't leave her.

She'd blurted out a few words to Annie and then there'd been a crash as he hit the door with force, the wood starting to crack.

She'd dropped the phone in fright. Terrified. There was no way out.

Another crash. This time the frame started to split.

Panicked, Chloé turned to her poster of Jules Léotard, her normal source of inspiration. But he didn't even look at her. Just stared out at the big oak tree.

The big oak tree.

She ran to the window and flung it open.

How far was the branch?

Close enough?

'Chloé! You can't escape!'

She glanced back and saw that he'd ripped a hole in the door, his arm thrust through it, trying to move the chair. And she stepped up on to the windowsill.

Heart thumping. Palms damp.

She wiped them on her jeans. Needed them dry if this was to work.

Then she looked down. Fatal mistake.

It was a long way.

Behind her she could hear him tussling with

the chair and then she heard it scrape along the floor and knew her time was up. She wasn't cut out for this. Not ready to be an acrobat. All her training amounted to nothing if she couldn't take this plunge.

'You will obey me!' he roared as he stepped into the room and stamped on the mobile phone. 'You are my daughter!'

Her fear dissolved. Her mind cleared. And as she leapt out of the window, short arms stretched across the expanse of air between the house and the tree, she felt freedom and belonging and the security of a love that had always been enough.

Plus she knew that Maman never lied.

19

Fabian hadn't made good time. It had taken all his strength just to turn the pedals. All he wanted to do was lie in a hot bath and then go to bed. For a week.

He'd just turned the corner that lay beyond the village and was about to start the steeper section that rose up to Christian's, running parallel to the field that housed Sarko the bull, when something caught his eye.

Something to his left. In the direction of Stephanie's house.

He stopped and looked across but his view was obscured by the beginnings of the copse which now lay between him and the cottage.

He waited a few moments, trying to peer between the trees, but he saw nothing.

Still, he was glad of the rest.

Promising his legs that it wouldn't be much longer, he started off once more.

★　★　★

She'd done it!

After what had seemed like an eternity in the air, Chloé had grabbed the gnarled branch of the oak tree, the sudden drop of her weight nearly pulling her arms out of her sockets. She'd held on long enough to absorb some of the impact of her leap and then her hands had given way and

337

she'd dropped to the ground, rolling as she landed.

Her palms were ripped to shreds and she'd twisted her ankle, but she'd done it. Even better than that, as she picked herself up off the ground, unsure of what to do next, she'd seen the unmistakable figure of Fabian toiling up the road on his bike.

Fabian. From what Maman had said in the house, he'd already faced this man. Been knocked off his bike by him. And he'd survived. He would know what to do.

Instinct had warned her not to shout at him. If the man knew she was going for help he might hurt Maman.

Instead she'd dashed for the cover of the woods at the back of the house, disregarding the burning sensation in her ankle that flared with every step. She reached the trees and hurtled along the path, leaping over rocks and tree roots, scrambling up the incline as she pushed herself.

If she was quick, she would catch him on the other side of the bend.

If she wasn't, then . . .

Then Maman might die.

★ ★ ★

He heard her before he saw her. The crack of twigs, the panting, the sounds of an animal in flight.

He'd been prepared for another boar to drop out of the woods before him.

But not Chloé!

338

She landed right in front of his wheel, twigs in her hair, mud smeared all over her face, her hands bleeding.

'What the hell?' He jumped off the bike and rushed to her side, lifting her gently to her feet. 'What's happened, Chloé?'

'Maman's in danger!' she wheezed, still holding her ribs and out of breath. 'The man who ran you over. He's in the house and he's threatening to kill her.'

Fabian's blood turned to ice.

'The man from Brittany? Is he armed?'

Chloé nodded. 'A knife.'

Tears welled in her eyes and he pretended not to notice as she brushed them angrily aside.

'Right,' he said in a tone that was braver than he felt. 'Can you run to Christian's and get help? Call the police?'

She nodded again and he picked up his bike, turning it back in the direction he had just come from.

'Are you going there alone?' she asked, her voice small.

'Yes. Your mother's in trouble.'

She nodded a final time, as if she understood the force that was driving him to behave with reckless abandon.

'How did you get out?' he asked as an afterthought.

'I jumped out of my bedroom window,' she said and then she was off, running up the hill, the sound of her breathing fading as he started racing towards the cottage.

And as he neared the house and his fears

began to surface, knowing for certain now that the man he was about to face had already tried to kill him, it was that single comment, delivered with such understatement, that gave him the courage to continue.

★ ★ ★

'Nearly there,' said Véronique, wrenching the car round the bend. She put her foot to the floor as they reached the plateau in front of the Estaque farm and Annie and Josette were shot back in their seats by the sudden acceleration.

But neither of them complained.

Annie sat rigid, jaw clenched, fingers gripping the mobile phone, her only tangible connection to Chloé. In her head she could hear the last frantic seconds of the call, the child's desperate pleading replaying in her mind. When the conversation had been abruptly, and possibly violently, terminated, Annie had tried Christian again but had got an engaged signal. So she'd dialled the police.

Whatever good that would do.

They'd immediately dispatched two officers but they all knew the geography. The police were based in Massat at the top of the valley. It would take them fifteen minutes to get to Picarets. And judging by the shouting Annie had heard in the background during her brief contact with Chloé, fifteen minutes would probably be too long.

So it seemed that Fabian might be Stephanie and Chloé's only hope. An unarmed, injured man against a violent thug with a history of abuse. Annie really didn't rate the Parisian's chances.

A low murmuring came from the back seat, fragments of prayer audible over the roar of the car engine. Annie twisted round to see Josette counting off Hail Marys on her fingers as she quietly recited the rosary.

'Sorry,' she said, breaking off as she caught Annie looking. 'Can't think of anything else useful to do.'

Annie understood. She turned back to stare out of the window and as the car sped forwards, she found herself joining in.

' . . . blessed art thou amongst women, and blessed is the fruit of thy womb, Jesus . . . '

The two women's voices intertwined, the softer intonation of Josette complementing the more strident sounds of Annie, until the car was filled with mesmeric chanting.

Véronique didn't participate. She was concentrating totally on her driving. But in a part of her mind she was trying to decide which was the more astounding: that Maman, who despised the Church, actually knew the words of the Hail Mary or that a Peugeot 308 could take a tight turn at sixty kilometres an hour and still have all four wheels on the ground.

' . . . pray for us sinners, now and at the hour of our death . . . '

'AMEN!' chorused all three women as the small sign that signified the start of Picarets finally came into view.

★ ★ ★

Stephanie knew she was going to die.

In all her experience of Bruno's rages, she'd never seen him so angry. So violent.

It had to be what she'd said, telling him that he wasn't Chloé's father. But she hadn't had much choice. She'd revealed the secret she'd kept for nine years, knowing it might be her death warrant, simply to save Chloé's life.

It hadn't worked though. He'd still smashed his way into the bedroom, Chloé's screams as he tore the door apart piercing Stephanie's heart. She'd just about managed to drag herself up the last few remaining stairs in time to see Chloé jump head-first out of the window, Bruno throwing himself across the room in an attempt to grab her as her shoes dropped out of sight.

Stephanie couldn't see if Chloé had landed safely. If the oak bough that she'd failed to cut off had in fact saved her daughter's life.

But she trusted her. Trusted those inherited acrobatic skills.

Chloé was away. She was safe.

That was all that mattered.

Bruno had torn apart Chloé's room in frustration, ripping posters off the wall, buckling the enamel plaque with a punch and turning the wardrobes over. Using his display of temper as cover, Stephanie had crawled back down the stairs, her breath coming in jagged gasps through the sharp edge of pain in her ribs. She must have broken them when he threw her against the coffee table.

But she kept going.

Escape. It was possible now that Chloé had

gone. She knew her choices were limited if she made it beyond these walls as he'd taken the keys to the van from her handbag before Chloé had got home and in her present condition, Stephanie wouldn't be able to outrun him.

Still, she'd rather take her chances in the outside world.

If she was quick, she could grab the spare key to the back door from under the plant pot on the kitchen windowsill and be out of here before he finished wrecking Chloé's room.

Holding her side carefully, she started moving across the room. She was just past the sofa when she felt something strike the back of her head and she stumbled to the floor.

'You bitch!' he roared from the top of the stairs. 'That's for teaching my daughter to deceive me!'

She stared at the mobile phone he'd thrown at her nonplussed, the screen mangled and the back hanging off. Where had it come from? Had Chloé had it? Had she managed to call for help?

Hope surged through Stephanie even as her hands came away from her head, sticky and warm with blood. And then he started down towards her, his face contorted with fury, steps heavy with violent intent.

Now. She had to move now.

She struggled to her knees but everything went hazy, the room tipping to one side as she started to faint.

Best to crawl, one hand in front of the other, first across one tile and then the next. Past the dining table, towards the kitchen area.

'What have you done to her?' he screamed, closer now.

She tried to move faster, hands damp on the cold tiles, knees banging against the ridges between them, her eyes stinging where the blood had trickled down her face and breathing so painful, she was afraid she was going to be sick.

The back door. It was within touching distance. But the key!

'Telling her all those lies!'

He was beside her now and she felt the tip of his boot land on her hip, the force propelling her over, flat on to her back.

Totally defenceless. Arms out. Him standing over her.

How? After all the years. After all her efforts to escape. How had she landed back here in the same position? In the same violence. Facing him on her own again. Just in a different kitchen.

Still she refused to give up, her palms flat against the floor as she crawled backwards, her heels slipping on the smooth surface, legs sliding along beneath him.

Then he reached down, the thick fingers of his right hand grabbing her hair, pulling her face close to his until she could see the bristles on his cheeks, smell the alcohol on his breath.

'I'll find her,' he whispered. 'Once I've finished with you, I'll track her down and take her home.'

He threw her back down, her head smacking on to the tiles and her arms shooting out sideways. And her fingers struck the edge of something metal that sliced through her skin.

His knife.

Like a flash she twisted to the side to reach the handle. But he was too quick and as his boot crunched down on to her left elbow, she heard the bones snap beneath his weight and she screamed, a last defiant sound of terror and of defeat.

★ ★ ★

'HURRY!' Chloé yelled again, scampering across the farmyard as the big farmer ran after her.

'The key!' Christian came to a halt and slapped himself on the forehead. 'I need the key to the cottage.'

He'd arrived home from a Farmers' Union demonstration in Foix, filled with pessimism about the future having spent the day with fellow farmers also faced with the prospect of selling their businesses, and had been met by sheer pandemonium. Maman and Papa had been trying to calm down a distraught Chloé who was frantic to get back to her house, adamant that Stephanie was in danger.

In gulping breaths she'd explained that some man, who'd tried to kidnap her a couple of months ago, was in the house with Stephanie and had a knife. Somehow Chloé had managed to race up the stairs and jump out of her bedroom window to escape. She'd alerted Fabian who'd gone off to rescue Stephanie, armed with nothing more than a bicycle pump.

It all seemed so ludicrous.

If it had been any other child, they might have

dismissed her claims as pure fancy. But this was Chloé. She didn't lie. Plus there was the physical evidence, the state of her clothes, the cuts on her hands, her badly swollen ankle.

And she'd been crying and Christian knew that it took an awful lot to make this little girl cry.

'Who is he?' Christian had asked. 'Do you know him?'

Chloé shook her head. 'Maman called him Bruno.'

'Stephanie knows him?' Josephine Dupuy's voice took on a worried tone as she glanced at her son. 'Could it be her ex-husband?'

'Chloé's father?'

'He's NOT my father! Now please HURRY! He'll kill her!' shouted Chloé, and she'd taken off.

So Christian had found himself running for the car in her wake. Now she was giving him a baleful look as he turned back to the farmhouse.

'Two seconds, Chloé. Just wait there.'

Maman was already on the phone to the police when he reached round the kitchen door to the hook where the big silver key normally hung.

It was empty.

'The police are on their way,' said Maman as she hung up. 'Annie Estaque has already called them.'

But Christian's attention was elsewhere. He was searching through all the keys that had gathered on the rack over the years. Keys for the barn, the tractor, spares for the postbox and the back door. Not one of them was the right one.

'Where is it, Maman?' he asked, Chloé now in the doorway, left foot tapping out her impatience on the floor.

'The key to the cottage? It should be there.' Josephine Dupuy pointed at the empty hook while Christian let out an exasperated sigh. 'How strange.'

'When did you last have it?'

'Now let me think.' She tried to ignore the young girl who'd started making high-pitched noises of anxiety. 'I was over there a while back. I offered to do a bit of ironing for Stephanie seeing as she was so busy. When was that . . .'

She tapped a finger on her forehead and then it came to her.

'Of course! It was March. The day the salesman called about the smoke alarms. He met me at the door when I returned and we came in together and I put the key on the hook . . .'

Her voice trailed off.

'What is it, Maman?'

'Chloé, what does the man with the knife look like?'

'Dark, bad, mean,' came the reply. 'And he has a tattoo.'

'What kind of tattoo?' asked Christian.

'Black and white stripes — '

'The flag of Brittany!' Josephine Dupuy interrupted, her face grey. 'Oh my God. What have I done?'

'You know him?' Christian demanded, confused.

'It's the salesman. The man who took my order for the smoke alarms which never came. I remember seeing his tattoo when he was filling out the form. A tattoo of the Brittany flag. And I remember thinking he was a long way from home.'

'Jesus! You think this is the same man? And he's had the key all this time?' Realising that Stephanie's life really was in danger, Christian spun on his heel and raced back outside, the hens sent flapping as he thundered across the yard with Chloé and Maman at his heels.

They'd just reached the car when André Dupuy emerged from the back of the house and scurried over to them with his antiquated rifle in his arms, a box of ammunition in his pocket. He opened the passenger door and got in.

'Where do you think you're going, Papa?' demanded Christian as he held back the driver's seat to let Chloé in.

'To save Stephanie of course!' came the curt reply and the old man defiantly fastened his seat belt.

'Me too!' said Josephine Dupuy and she was in the back beside Chloé before Christian could protest.

'Christ!' he muttered as he got into the car and slammed the door. 'Just promise me you won't use that thing, okay?'

André simply pursed his lips and stared out of the windscreen.

Christian pulled off at speed, bits of gravel flying out from under the wheels.

'It's all my fault,' he heard Maman murmur from the back, her voice quavering as she reached over to take Chloé's hand. 'I'm so sorry.'

Christian didn't say anything. Bad enough that his bull had nearly killed Chloé but now his family were directly responsible for letting Stephanie's violent ex-husband back into her life. He applied more pressure to the accelerator.

Might as well see what the old girl was really capable of. They had nothing to lose.

★　★　★

Fabian landed on the bedroom floor with a thump, wincing as the impact jarred his injured thigh. He remained crouched, listening to see if his arrival had been noticed and taking in his surroundings.

Chloé's room. The ground floor of the cottage had proven impossible to access, doors locked, shutters latched. But in one of the bedrooms, the one next to the oak tree, the windows were thrown open, cheerful yellow curtains flapping in the breeze. He'd dismissed the idea of climbing the tree and instead had broken into Stephanie's shed in his first ever criminal act, and had taken the ladder. Aware that he could be better dressed, perhaps in something that offered more protection than lycra shorts and cycling jersey, he'd climbed upwards, the cleats on his shoes slipping on the metal rungs. He'd tumbled over the windowsill in time to hear the man roaring at Stephanie downstairs.

It was a vicious sound. A primitive sound. Something Fabian had never encountered before.

And as he looked around, Chloé's room told

the tale of the tornado of violence that had ripped through the house. Strips of paper from torn posters all over the place, the wardrobe overturned, a mirror smashed, the doorframe splintered and the enamel plaque Chloé had taken from the épicerie all buckled and bent.

Fabian tensed his jaw and crept across the room, inching along the wall and onto the landing. Below was the unnatural dark of a shuttered space. He would be totally visible to anyone beneath him as he descended, the sunshine from Chloé's room acting like a spotlight. He would have to be careful.

'Telling her all those lies!' The man was shouting again, the words clear now that Fabian was at the top of the stairs.

He could hear Stephanie too. A low whimpering sound that chilled him.

He tiptoed forwards, taking the stairs carefully, palms and body flat against the wall, hoping that he wouldn't be seen. It seemed an age before anything came into view but at last, in the gloom, he made out a suitcase lying open by the sofa, clothes heaped around it as if someone had emptied it from a height. And Chloé's treasured gymnastics book, discarded with the spine bent back on itself.

It wasn't until he was nearly at the bottom that he saw Stephanie. She was on her back, slithering towards the kitchen door, her assailant standing over her like a hunter moving in for the kill, his broad body blocking her view of Fabian.

He took the last few stairs, freezing when one of them creaked under his weight.

But the man was oblivious. His fist was entwined in Stephanie's beautiful red hair, her head wrenched upwards by his grasp, and Fabian could see the terracotta tiles stained scarlet underneath her.

She was bleeding. Badly.

The man whispered something in her ear and threw her back to the floor, the sound of her skull hitting the hard surface making Fabian want to retch. And then she was twisting, scrabbling for something and her attacker raised his foot and brought the full weight of his body down on her outstretched, vulnerable arm. Her scream tore through the air and Fabian saw the man pick up the knife she'd been groping for and he knew he had to act.

In one swift movement, he flipped on the light, grabbed Chloé's book and thrust himself across the floor, cleats sliding on the tiles as he lunged at Stephanie's ex-husband with a cry that came from the depths of his heart. Book held in both hands, he swung with all his might and felt the reverberations in his arms as the thick tome caught the man on the side of the head, sending him sprawling. But the momentum was too much for the cycling shoes and Fabian's feet flew out from underneath him. He landed heavily, air pushed out of his lungs as his back smacked on to the floor.

'Fabian!' Stephanie was gasping, panting in distress, her left arm lying useless beside her. 'Be careful!'

But Fabian wasn't quick enough. His adversary was already on his feet and was roaring, a man possessed, storming towards them, knife held ready to strike.

'You!' he bellowed at the prostrate Parisian. 'Should've killed you when I had the chance!'

'Fabian!' Stephanie cried again, this time her eyes locking on to his as if she knew that he was about to die with her.

Time slowed. Fabian could see the man approaching, the blade glinting, but he couldn't move. He was aware of Stephanie's mouth shaped in a scream but he couldn't hear a sound.

All he was conscious of was an uncomfortable lump in the small of his back. Irritating him. As if he was on a beach somewhere and had lain his towel on a stone.

Without thinking about it, his hand was reaching towards his back pocket as though his body had worked out what the irritant was before his brain had. And as the hunter bent in over him, his eyes dark with fury, the tip of the knife inches from Fabian's throat, Fabian saw his own hand emerge with a small silver canister held tight.

He pressed the button and watched a jet of liquid stream out, straight into the man's face.

The effect was immediate.

The man reeled away with a howl, the pepper spray beginning to sting, and as he staggered backwards, blinded, Stephanie used the last of her energy to hold out a leg, tripping him to the floor.

'The top drawer,' she shouted while the man thrashed around in agony, fingers clawing at his burning eyes. 'Quickly.'

And Fabian was on his feet in seconds.

'Stay in the car. All of you!' Christian ordered as he leapt out of the Panda and raced towards the cottage.

He might as well have been talking to Sarko the bull.

'Chloé, hold my hand,' Josephine insisted, emerging from the rear with the young girl and taking cover behind Stephanie's van.

'Try the door!' André shouted, already out with his rifle raised to his shoulder. 'I'll cover you.'

'Good Lord! You lot watch too much TV.' Christian shook his head in despair. 'What do you think this is? *CSI*?'

He rattled the door handle to no avail and was just stepping back to consider his options when a scream ripped through the silence making all of them jump. It sounded like a man's voice. But Christian couldn't be sure.

'Maman,' cried Chloé, struggling to escape the tight grip Josephine had on her. 'Christian, you have to save Maman!'

Christian knew she was right.

He took a deep breath, summoned all of his strength, and then he ran as fast as he could at the front door, shoulder first, the weight of his bulk behind it. The wood groaned in protest but the door didn't budge.

'Do you want me to shoot the lock?' asked André, trigger finger twitching.

'No, I do not! Just stand back and let me have a proper run at it.'

Christian walked as far as the road, rotated his neck a few times in preparation and then started moving, concentrating on the barrier in front of him. He hit it straight on and at speed and heard the satisfying screech of the hinges being ripped from their holdings. And with an almighty crash, the walnut door so lovingly chosen by his grandmother over half a century ago fell to the ground, the huge farmer lying on top of it like a surfer heading out to the waves.

He was vaguely aware of André scampering over him into the cottage, rifle at the ready.

'Don't shoot!' came a voice he recognised and he looked up to see Fabian sitting on the floor, propped against the kitchen cabinets at the far end of the room cradling Stephanie in his arms. Her face was swollen, the dark promise of bruises visible below the white skin, her hair was matted with blood and her left arm was hanging at an unnatural angle. She was barely conscious.

'Call an ambulance,' Christian shouted to Josephine while Chloé had already torn her hand free and was running towards her mother.

'Maman,' she wailed as she dropped to her knees and threw her arms around the battered figure, not even trying to stop the tears.

Stephanie was sufficiently aware to bury her head in the mass of dark curls, ignoring the pain that was trying to drag her into oblivion as the familiar small body nestled into hers.

'You're a brave girl,' she mumbled as the child sobbed against her. 'You saved us both.'

'Where is he?' asked Christian, picking himself up.

Fabian gestured towards the far end of the kitchen and Christian walked over to see.

'You did that?' he asked, not even trying to hide the incredulity in his voice.

Fabian nodded.

'Mon Dieu!' He looked at the skinny Parisian, his cycling kit torn, blood seeping through his shorts, and then at the robust lump of man who lay trussed up on the floor like a hog about to be slaughtered, eyes raw and streaming, nose twisted and broken.

'What did you use?' asked Christian as André took up guard, rifle pointed at the writhing figure.

'Chloé's book, some dog-repellent and garden twine,' replied Fabian with pride while Christian nodded, impressed.

'Thank God you'rrre all safe!' came a familiar voice from the doorway and the three women, still high on adrenaline from the fastest ascent of the Picarets road in living memory, bustled into the small cottage.

'Fetch me some water,' ordered Véronique as she started tending to Stephanie using a tea towel, while Annie gently removed Chloé from her mother's arms.

'You had us so worrrrried,' she said fiercely as she embraced the child, relief coursing through her with a feeling that was better than caffeine. 'That phone call ... ' She shuddered and hugged Chloé even tighter. 'How on earrrth did you escape?'

'I jumped out of the window,' Chloé explained, leaning back to look into Annie's wrinkled face. 'I did it, Annie. I'm a real acrobat now!'

And Annie just pulled her closer and cleared her throat, rubbing her eyes with the back of her hand.

'Think the pepper spray is getting to Annie,' chortled Christian as he helped Fabian up off the floor, the cyclist wincing as Josette fussed over the wounds on his thigh. 'So if Chloé jumped out of the window,' continued the farmer, 'how on earth did you get in?'

'I used a ladder.'

'Oh!' Christian looked at the mess that was the front door and scratched his head ruefully while his mother regarded him with mock annoyance.

'Good job you know the landlady,' muttered Stephanie with a weak grin as the sound of approaching sirens filled the room. She rested her head against the cupboard and as she felt herself slipping into the greyness of a faint, her last conscious thought was how crowded her kitchen was.

She really wasn't on her own any more.

20

Serge Papon, mayor of Fogas, had never been more pleased to see the roundabout at Kerkabanac. As he crossed the Salat river and took the turning for the valley up to Fogas, he felt like he was already home.

Three months he'd been gone. Closeted away with well-meaning family who'd fussed around him, trying to make up for the fact that he'd just lost his wife. Still couldn't get used to that expression. Losing his wife. As if it was his fault cancer had come between them. As if he'd been somehow careless and let her drift from his grasp.

Which was exactly how it felt most days when he woke up, the traffic in the road below tearing him from dreams filled with Thérèse. He had a sense of guilt he couldn't shift, that maybe his philandering had brought about the illness, that Thérèse's death was a punishment inflicted on him at a terrible cost to her.

He opened the window and inhaled, letting the already warm air into the car. He'd forgotten how stunning the valley was in early May. The trees that lined the road were in full leaf, a multitude of greens against the blue sky, and the river was sparkling in the morning sunshine as it raced down from the hills above Massat to meet the much larger waters of the Salat below.

How different from the suburb of Toulouse

357

where he'd been sequestered, the view from his bedroom window of other houses, all identical, featureless new-builds stretching out on the horizon. Instead of the serrated edges of the mountains, he'd looked out upon an endless vista of red roofs, not a Pyrenean slate in sight.

He'd missed the greenery, the dramatic glimpse of the peaks as you turned a corner, the ramshackle barns and the pastures filled with animals. And the smells. Grass and blossom and the earthy scent of cattle. So much more preferable to the cloying perfumes of the Toulousaine women, the fug of exhaust fumes that lingered in the streets and the stink of cigarettes outside every café, all of it exacerbated by the heat which was already building on the flat lands around the city.

How did they stick the summers, he wondered. There'd be no cooling breeze off Mont Valier. No lush landscape to lessen the impact of the intense temperatures. It must be like being a rotisserie chicken, slowly grilled by the sun.

He lifted a hand off the steering wheel in greeting at a passing car. Louis Claustre from the neighbouring commune of Sarrat. Going down to the village of Oust to see his elderly cousin like he did every Sunday. The man gave an automatic response and then did a double take and Serge could see him in the rear-view mirror, checking that he really had just seen the mayor of Fogas after all this time, his car swerving dangerously towards the river in response to his diverted attention. He'd be on his mobile before he got to the roundabout.

Serge chuckled. That was what he'd really missed. The local politics. The interest in the neighbours around you. A pace of life where people had time to say hello and weren't walking around the shops with a phone glued to one ear, lacking the courtesy to acknowledge the people serving them.

Tradition. It had a lot going for it. And that was what had finally made Serge decide to come home. He'd contemplated giving up his life in Fogas, not brave enough to face living there now Thérèse had gone. But after three months in Toulouse all he'd wanted was to return to the commune he knew so well, where nothing changed, where the old ways were still revered and where there was no such thing as a stranger.

He turned the final corner and the gorge widened into a welcoming sunlit idyll, the Auberge standing sentry at the start of the village and there, just in the distance he could see the épicerie.

He was home.

But as his car approached the familiar bridge over the small stream and he prepared to park in his usual space, right outside the shop window, he began to get confused.

What the hell had happened?

There were people everywhere, milling around and sitting at tables outside the bar. Which was unrecognisable. New signage, a terrace with wooden lattice work over it and plants climbing up the side. The mouldy old bench that had been the only seating now nowhere to be seen. And

359

standing in the doorway giving out leaflets like he owned the place was a tall, skinny man Serge had never set eyes on before.

★ ★ ★

Fabian couldn't believe it. There were hordes of people, all of them waiting for the grand opening of the garden centre which was due to take place in thirty minutes. And in the meantime, they were bringing great business to the épicerie, buying drinks and ice creams and local produce.

'Get your loyalty cards!' he shouted again, thrusting a couple of cards into the hands of two tourists who were heading into the bar. 'Buy ten coffees and get your next one free. Here you are, Monsieur.'

He placed a card in front of the stocky old man who'd just parked right in front of the shop window, as if he owned the place! The man growled, his arthritic fingers grasping the paper and scrunching it into a small ball which he threw into the bin.

'Loyalty my arse!' Fabian heard him exclaim as he marched inside.

It was enough to make Fabian abandon his post and follow him.

And he was glad he had. For the minute the man stepped across the threshold, tension filled the room. Josette snapped to attention behind the counter and Christian jerked upright over at the bar where he'd been lounging with Véronique. And Annie Estaque, who'd been sitting at the table with Stephanie and Chloé, went very pale.

'Serge!' Josette finally managed and she rushed forward to kiss him. 'You're back. We weren't expecting you.'

'Huh!' he barked as his eyes scanned the new-look épicerie.

It was so different.

The dark space that he'd known all his life had been opened up and extended, the long rows of wood replaced with more modern shelving, the light bouncing off the shiny surfaces. The vegetables were now displayed in tiered baskets, no more cardboard boxes cluttering the floor, and the cheese cabinet was twice the size of the old one, beautiful fat rounds just begging to be sliced. Down the middle of the shop was a new set of shelving, one side devoted to daily essentials and the other to local items, including some of Philippe Galy's honey and jam from St Girons. And instead of loitering at the back, Josette now had a seat by the door, a till and a set of electronic scales in front of her, strings of saucisson hanging to her right, and on the wall behind, Jacques' knife cabinet looking as good as new.

'What do you think?' Josette asked him and he was aware of the tremor in her voice.

He didn't answer. Too overcome.

He took a few more steps, passing the stand filled with newspapers, maps and guide books to look through the new archway into the bar and take in the changes that had been wrought there. He was pleased to see the long table still in place but other smaller tables had been added and the counter had been reshaped so that it fitted more snugly in the back corner, a complicated looking coffee machine dominating its surface. The glasses now hung from bespoke racks above it and the bottles of drinks had proper optics. No more guessing the measures. And around the walls were framed black and white photos of the Fogas he remembered from his childhood.

'Whose idea was all this?' he said at last.

'Mine.' The tall, young man who'd been at the door stepped forward.

'And you are?' Serge fixed him with a glare.

'My nephew, Fabian,' explained Josette. 'Fabian, do you remember Serge Papon, the mayor of Fogas?'

'Oh, of course!'

Fabian held out his hand and Serge took it with a grunt.

'Fabian, eh? Should have left you at the bottom of that quarry when you were a nipper!'

'Do you like what we've done?' Fabian asked unabashed.

Serge took one last glance around, disturbed by the unwanted changes and so preparing to be rude. But then he spotted something down at the far end of the shop. A set of wicker baskets displayed one above the other containing what looked like . . .

It couldn't be.

'Are they fresh croissants?' he demanded, his steps quickening as he approached them.

'Yes,' said Fabian, his longer stride easily keeping him abreast of the smaller man. 'We have them delivered from the bakery on the Col de Port every morning. You can place an order if you like. Fresh bread too. Pain au chocolat. Chausson pomme. All made in the old fashioned way.'

Serge stretched out a hand and took hold of the nearest baguette, his fingers caressing the crusty resistance of a perfect loaf. Excited now, he reached for a croissant, the layers flaking off deliciously as he raised it to his mouth and bit down.

Amazing.

'Perhaps you would like a coffee to go with that, Monsieur Papon,' said Fabian with a smile. 'And I'll get you a loyalty card too.'

But Serge wasn't listening. He was deafened by the singing in his heart. At last, proper bread and pastries. And in his commune!

'So,' he said as he swallowed the last morsel and licked his fingers in appreciation. 'What other surprises have you lot got lined up for me?'

★　★　★

Stephanie had been adamant that she was well enough to attend the opening of her garden centre. Determined that it shouldn't be postponed. But now, as Fabian helped her across the road, he wasn't so sure she was right.

The ambulance hadn't been far behind the police yesterday and the doctors in St Girons had insisted that Stephanie stay in hospital overnight for observation. She in turn had insisted that Chloé be allowed to stay with her.

But this morning when Fabian had arrived to visit, she'd been dressed in clothes brought down by Josephine Dupuy and had declared herself up to the task of opening her business. Despite the bruise which encircled her eye, the broken ribs, the stitches she'd had in the back of her head and her fractured left arm, the cast already signed by Chloé.

When Fabian had tried to protest, she'd simply stuck out her chin and with a look he now knew all too well, she'd walked past him and out the door, Chloé acting as a walking stick.

She was amazing. He'd known that all along, from his very first minute in Fogas when he'd come to and seen her towering over him in the bar, hair wild, eyes flashing, weapon ready to strike. It scared him to think how close he'd come to losing her.

His world had undergone a cataclysmic shift in the last forty-eight hours. Plunged into abject misery by Chloé's revelation that someone else had stolen Stephanie's heart, he'd survived what turned out to be an attempt on his life; an attempt motivated, ironically, by a presumption that he was dating the very woman whose love he couldn't win.

No sooner had he recovered than he had found himself on a mission to save her.

And he'd done it. Him of all people. The nerd. The geek. The outsider.

As he'd cradled her in his arms, waiting for the ambulance, he'd known then that he would never love anyone else like this. Love someone so much that he was willing to die. And when she'd come round in the hospital and reached for his hand, he'd thought his heart would explode.

Then Christian had told him how Bruno Madec had tracked her down. How he'd tricked her, toying with her through the Internet while he watched her daily from the hills around the village. It had taken a moment or two for the implication to sink in. There was no Pierre. Never had been.

Granted a second chance, Fabian had vowed he wasn't going to make the same mistake twice.

'What are you smiling at?' she asked, her weight a comfort as she leant against him.

'Nothing!' He replied, guiding her through the throng of people waiting for the grand opening. 'Are you sure you don't want to sit down?'

She smiled and squeezed his arm which was supporting her.

'Honestly, I'm fine.'

And she was.

The day before, when she'd seen Bruno being bundled into the back of the police van, she'd felt as though invisible shackles had finally been removed from around her ankles. She was free now. She could stop looking over her shoulder all the time. Stop worrying about the future and the possibility of him tracking them down. He had found them. It was over. And he wouldn't be coming back.

'How arrre you feeling, Stephanie?' Annie Estaque had come alongside her, face still carrying remnants of worry from the events up in Picarets.

'I'm good, Annie. Thanks to you and the others, I'm good.'

Annie waved a brusque hand of dismissal at Stephanie's gratitude.

'Didn't do nothing you wouldn't do forrr us. Not that long since you took on an intrrruderrr with a stale baguette I seem to rrrememberrr!'

Everyone laughed.

'She might have to fight him off again soon,' retorted René and Fabian blushed.

'Speech!' called Christian who was standing to one side with Serge Papon and Véronique. 'It's time for you to make a speech, Stephanie.'

She cleared her throat and stepped forward to the front of the sizeable crowd that had assembled on the patch of land which had lain unused for so long. The land she had turned into her own organic garden centre.

Pride flowed through her.

The gates which formed the entrance had been draped with a ribbon which in turn was attached to a large sheet covering a placard on the side of the fence. And beyond the fence were the plants and shrubs, herbs, bushes, and colourful pots which would help determine her and Chloé's future.

'I'd like to thank you all for coming today,' she began. 'And especially Serge Papon, our mayor. It's lovely to have you home, Serge.'

Warm applause broke out amongst those gathered and Serge nodded his head in acknowledgement.

'She'll go far,' he muttered to Christian. 'So, did I vote for this little business?'

'But of course,' came the murmured response. 'You're all for sustainable development. Or didn't you know that?'

The mayor gave a dry laugh and turned his attention back to the speech.

' . . . and so with no more ado, I'd like to call on Chloé to perform the final honours.'

Chloé looked surprised as Maman beckoned her forward, brandishing a large pair of scissors.

'Just cut the ribbon, love,' whispered Maman as she stepped back, leaving Chloé in the limelight.

Chloé did as she was told. She took hold of the beautiful red ribbon with one hand, and with the other, she closed the blade of the scissors on it, feeling a twinge of remorse as the ribbon fell in two.

'Oh!' marvelled the crowd and Chloé looked up at the fence where a sign was now visible, the sheet having fallen to the ground, ornate green writing against a cream background showing the name of the business Maman had worked so hard to create.

Le Jardin de Chloé

'Maman!' breathed Chloé with pleasure. 'It's beautiful.'

Stephanie ruffled her hand through her daughter's hair and then helped her to open the gates.

'Champagne for all customers,' Christian called out as he popped open the first bottle and took up his place behind a table laden with glasses while Lorna and Josette started bringing out platters of food from the bar.

'And the best of Bordeaux for our friends!' muttered René as he discreetly whipped a bottle of 1959 Château Latour from under the table.

'Where did you get that?' demanded Christian as René poured a glass for the mayor. 'I thought Fabian sent it all to auction?'

'He could only find eleven bottles.' René winked at him and tapped the side of his nose. 'Shame to waste it all on some prats up in Paris.'

'Hear, hear,' agreed Serge Papon, raising a glass to the others and then taking a sip, the velvety texture of cherries dipped in spices bursting over his taste buds.

'Got something to steady my nerves?' asked Fabian, who'd strolled up to the table and was holding out a glass.

'The very thing,' René declared and magnanimously poured Fabian his own wine. 'A 1959 Bordeaux.'

Fabian spluttered, nearly choking on his drink. Then he checked the bottle that René was cheekily handing on to Paul.

'How did you . . . But that's worth . . . ' He stopped. What was it worth, sitting in a bottle in someone's cellar? Surely better to share it around with his new friends?

'So, what is it worth?' Christian asked, as he savoured the rich taste.

'It's worth opening to celebrate a special occasion!' Fabian declared and René thumped him on the back in appreciation.

'You can tell he's in love!' Véronique observed as she joined the small group and took the proffered wine. 'Always makes a man generous.'

'What, like Bernard with his beagle?' quipped René and tipped his head in the direction of the chubby *cantonnier* who was pulling the meat off his canapés and feeding it to the small hound at his feet while Pascal Souquet and his wife, Fatima, regarded him with disdain.

Serge gave a throaty chuckle. 'Bernard's found true love at last, I see.'

'And guess what he called him!' René said while everyone else started laughing in anticipation.

Annie didn't hear the mayor's reaction over the noise. She was standing a small way apart, watching it all from the sidelines. She'd been tense all morning, from the moment he'd arrived back. Walking into the épicerie like that unannounced. It had been enough to give her a heart attack.

But it had answered her questions about Véronique and her visit to St Paul de Fenouillet two months ago. Her daughter had learnt nothing from her cousins. Annie knew that now as she watched her chatting to him, making him laugh at some anecdote or other, totally unaware of their connection.

Could anyone tell, she wondered as she watched them together, Serge Papon's bulbous head tipped forward to catch what Véronique was saying.

'I'll tell them soon, Thérrrèse,' Annie muttered quietly.

'Tell them what?' asked Chloé at her elbow. The child had stolen up on her like a ninja.

'Tell yourrr Maman and Fabian that I think

369

they make a lovely couple!' Annie replied quickly.

Chloé pulled a face. 'He still hasn't asked her!'

'I harrrdly think yesterrrday was the rrright time. Do you?'

'I don't think he'll ever find the right time,' Chloé moaned and continued circulating with her tray of asparagus tarts.

But Chloé was wrong.

After thinking he had lost Stephanie forever and having survived the trauma of facing death head on, Fabian had decided the moment was right. Fuelled by desire and the best of French wine, he wandered over to where she was talking with Josette and some of the customers.

'You know,' he said as he manipulated Stephanie away from the crowds, a blossoming camellia providing them with some privacy. 'I wonder if you've noticed the effect you've had on me?'

He kept his tone light despite the pace his heart was beating at.

'What do you mean?' asked Stephanie, not sure why her nerves were jangling.

'Well, every time I get anywhere near you, I seem to fall at your feet!' he explained with a shaky laugh. He took her right hand in his and held up one of her fingers. 'The day I met you was the first time.'

She lowered her gaze, still embarrassed by the temper that had guided her arm that day.

'Then there was the time on the bike.' He lifted a second finger and she giggled at the memory.

'And then, yesterday, it happened again. I

come in to help you out and bang! Somehow I end up on the ground in front of you.'

He shifted slightly on his feet and she sensed the atmosphere change as though what he was about to say next was momentous.

'Thing is, Stephanie, I seem to have fallen for you in a big way. And I wonder if you feel the same?'

He was watching her. Waiting for a response while his heart rate soared as though he was climbing the road to Picarets on his bike.

But Stephanie was staring at her own hand. At the three fingers he was holding gently.

'Three times,' she murmured, her head filled with a prophecy from long ago. How could she not have noticed? Not have made the connection with what Maman had told her? She looked up at him, slightly stooped as he leaned in towards her, hair in his eyes, face full of concern.

Sweet Fabian. Gentle Fabian. *Her* Fabian.

'You've fallen for me three times.'

'You could put it like that — '

Fabian broke off as Stephanie slipped her one good arm around him and pulled his lips down to hers.

'Thank you,' she said, bringing the kiss to an end as she felt his knees starting to tremble. 'Thank you for saving our lives. And if you were about to ask me out, then the answer is yes!'

But Fabian was oblivious. He was aware only of the birds singing, the bees buzzing and the overpowering scent of flowers. And of a small voice exclaiming 'Yes!' from the other side of the camellia bush.

Chloé had seen and heard enough and she walked away with a grin etched from ear to ear.

She still didn't know who her father was. It didn't matter. That was a question for another day. For now, it was enough knowing that Fabian was going out with Maman.

She thrust her tray at Véronique and raced after Josette who was walking back towards the bar.

'Had enough of the party, love?' Josette enquired as Chloé overtook her.

Chloé shook her head. 'No. Just going to tell Jacques the latest.'

And as she burst into the bar, Jacques looked up from his seat in the inglenook with a smile. There was only one thing that could make Chloé grin like that. And he couldn't have been happier at the news.

We do hope that you have enjoyed reading this large print book.

Did you know that all of our titles are available for purchase?

We publish a wide range of high quality large print books including:
Romances, Mysteries, Classics
General Fiction
Non Fiction and Westerns

Special interest titles available in large print are:
The Little Oxford Dictionary
Music Book
Song Book
Hymn Book
Service Book

Also available from us courtesy of Oxford University Press:
Young Readers' Dictionary
(large print edition)
Young Readers' Thesaurus
(large print edition)

For further information or a free brochure, please contact us at:
Ulverscroft Large Print Books Ltd.,
The Green, Bradgate Road, Anstey,
Leicester, LE7 7FU, England.
Tel: (00 44) 0116 236 4325
Fax: (00 44) 0116 234 0205

Other titles published by
The House of Ulverscroft:

L'AUBERGE

Julia Stagg

The Auberge des Deux Vallées has fallen into the hands of an English couple — the end of gastronomic civilisation for the commune of Fogas in the French Pyrenees. The incensed mayor, who had intended his brother-in-law to take over, determines to eject *les rosbifs* by any means possible, and soon Paul and Lorna are up to their eyes in French bureaucracy. But the mayor hasn't reckoned on the locals. With their own reasons for wanting *l'Auberge* to succeed, they take the young incomers to their hearts. If they pull together, can they outwit the mayor, or will *l'Auberge* end up in the *merde*?